W9-BGR-317

THE LABORATORY OF THE LIVING DEAD

I awoke in a strange room where a musty odor permeated the air . . . lining the walls were jars which held a menagerie of human anatomical specimens.

A door slid open and a familiar, sinister shadow crossed before me. I looked up, into the intolerable gaze of Dr. Fu Manchu, and watched as he described the gruesome fragments from his mad experiments. . . . I reached for my automatic and fired. To make doubly sure of ridding the world of this monster, I fired twice!

"They were live bullets," said the ominous voice from the figure still before me. I had to turn away. I had witnessed a miracle, and I was shaken to my soul. . . .

Thus does Nayland Smith come face-to-face with an extraordinary scheme for world control engineered by the resourceful arch-fiend, Dr. Fu Manchu! And thus continues another of the awesome adventures of Sax Rohmer— thrillers that have been read by millions throughout the "known" world.

THE ADVENTURES OF
NAYLAND SMITH

•

THE ISLAND OF
FU MANCHU

SAX ROHMER

PYRAMID BOOKS ▲ NEW YORK

THE ISLAND OF FU MANCHU

A PYRAMID BOOK
Published by arrangement with Doubleday and Company, Inc.

Pyramid edition published May 1963
  Second printing, February 1966
  Third printing, May 1971

Copyright, 1940, 1941 by Doubleday, Doran & Company, Inc.

All Rights Reserved

Printed in the United States of America

PYRAMID BOOKS are published by Pyramid Publications
444 Madison Avenue, New York, New York 10022, U.S.A.
A Division of The Walter Reade Organization, Inc.

Contents

1 / Something in a Bag

"THEN YOU HAVE no idea where Nayland Smith is?" said my guest.

I carried his empty glass to the buffet and refilled it.

"Two cables from him found me at Helsinki," I replied: "the first from Kingston, Jamaica, the second from New York."

"Ah! Jamaica and New York. Off his usual stamping ground. Nothing since?"

"Nothing."

"Sure he isn't back home?"

"Quite. His flat in Whitehall is closed."

I set the whiskey and soda before Sir Lionel Barton and passed my pouch, for he was scraping out his briar. My dining room seemed altogether too small to hold this huge, overbearing man with a lion's mane of tawny hair streaked with white, piercing blue eyes shadowed by craggy brows. He had the proper personality for one of his turbulent, brilliant reputation; the greatest Orientalist in Europe is expected to be unusual.

"Do you know, Kerrigan"—he stuffed Rhodesian tobacco into his pipe as though he had been charging a howitzer— "I have known Smith longer than you, and although I missed the last brush with Fu Manchu——"

"Well?"

"Old Smith and I have been out against him together in the past. To tell you the truth"—he stood up and began to walk about, lighting his pipe as he did so—"I have an idea that we have not seen the last of that Chinese devil."

"Why?" I asked and tried to speak casually.

"Suppose he's here again—in England?"

Sir Lionel's voice was rising to those trumpet tones which betrayed his army training; I was conscious of growing excitement.

"Suppose, just for argument's sake, that I have certain reasons to believe that he is. Well—would you sleep soundly tonight? What would it mean? It would mean that, apart from Germany, we had another enemy to deal with—an enemy whose insects, bacteria, stranglers, strange poisons, could do more harm in a week than Hitler's army could do in a year!"

He took a long drink. I did not speak.

"You"—he lowered his voice—"have a personal interest in

the matter. You accepted the assignment to cover the Finnish campaign because——"

I nodded.

"Check me when I go wrong and stop me if I'm treading on a corn; there was a girl—wasn't Ardatha the name? She belonged to the nearly extinct white race (I was the first man to describe them, by the way) which still survives in Abyssinia."

"Yes—she vanished after Smith and I left Paris, at the end of Fu Manchu's battle to put an end to dictators. Nearly two years ago——"

"You—searched?"

"Smith was wonderful. I had all the resources of the secret service at my command. But from that hour, Barton, not one word of information reached us, either about Doctor Fu Manchu or about—Ardatha."

"I am told"—he pulled up, his back to me, and spoke over his shoulder—"that Ardatha was——"

"She was lovely and lovable," I said and stood up.

The agony of Finland, the wound I had received there, the verdict of Harley Street which debarred me from active service, all these tragedies had failed to efface my private sorrow—the loss of Ardatha.

Sir Lionel turned and gave me one penetrating glance which I construed as sympathy. I had known him for many years and had learned his true worth, but he was by no means every man's man. Ardatha had brought romance into my life such as no one was entitled to expect; she was gone. Barton understood.

He began to pace up and down, smoking furiously, and something in his bearing reminded me of Nayland Smith. Barton was altogether heavier than Smith but he had the same sun-baked skin, the same nervous vitality; he, also, was a pipe addict. His words had set my brain on fire.

I wondered if an image was before his mental vision—the same image which was before mine: a tall, lean, catlike figure; a close-shaven head, a mathematical brow; emerald-green eyes which sometimes became filmed strangely; a voice in its guttural intensity so masterful that Caesar, Alexander, Napoleon might have animated it: Dr Fu Manchu, embodiment of the finest intellect in the modern world.

Now I was wild for news, but deliberately I controlled myself. I refilled Barton's glass. He belonged to a hard-drinking generation and I never attempted to keep pace with him. I sat down again, and:

"You must realise," I said, "that you have stirred up——"

"I know, I know! I am the last man to raise hopes which may never materialise. But the fact that Nayland Smith has been in the West Indies practically clinches the matter. I threw myself on your hospitality, Kerrigan, because, to be quite frank, I was afraid to go to a hotel——"

"What!"

"Yes—and my town house, as you know, went to the auctioneers on the day war started. Very well. In the small suitcase—all the baggage I carry—is something for which I know Doctor Fu Manchu has been searching for many years. Since I got hold of it there have been some uncommonly queer happenings up at my place in Norfolk. In fact, things got so hot that I bolted!"

I stood up and walked across to the window; excitement grew in my brain by leaps and bounds. There was no man whom I feared as I feared the brilliant Chinese doctor—but if Ardatha lived, Fu Manchu was the one and only link by means of which I might find her.

"Go on," I said, "I am all attention."

Grey, wintry dusk was settling over Kensington Gardens. Few figures moved on the path which led, from the gate nearly opposite, to the Round Pond. At any moment now would come the mournful call of the parkkeeper: "All out!" And with the locking of the gates began the long night of black-out.

"I know why Smith has been to the Caribbean," Barton went on. "There's something in that bag which would have saved him the journey. The United States government—— Hello! What's wrong?"

A figure was standing at the park gate looking up at my window, a girl who wore a hooded cape. I suppose I uttered an exclamation as I clutched the ledge and stared across the road.

"What is it, Kerrigan?" cried Barton. "What is it?"

"It's Ardatha!" I whispered.

2 / A Second Visitor

I DOUBT IF ANY MAN ever descended a long flight of dark stairs faster than I did. A pulse was throbbing in my head as I dashed along the glass-roofed portico which divided the house from the front door. Yet as I threw the door open and ran out already the hooded figure had vanished.

Then, as I raced across to the gate, I saw her. She had turned back into the park and was just passing out of the shadow of a big tree near the corner where a path at right angles crossed that leading to the Round Pond. Normally, Bayswater Road at this hour would have been a race track, but war had muted the song of London and few vehicles were on the road.

In the park a grey mist swam among the trees whose leafless branches reached out like lean and clutching arms menacing the traveller. But there, ahead, was the receding, elusive figure.

I continued to run. My condition was by no means all that it might have been, but I found breath enough to call.

"Ardatha!" I cried. "Ardatha!"

Step by step I was overhauling her. Not another pedestrian was in sight.

"Ardatha!"

I was no more than twenty yards behind as she paused and looked back. In spirit she was already in my arms, her kiss on my lips—when she turned swiftly and began to run!

For one incalculable moment I stood stock-still.

Astonishment, mortification, anger, fought for precedence in my mind. What, in sanity's name, could be the meaning of her behaviour? I was about to cry out again, but I decided to conserve my resources. Fists clenched and head up, I set out in pursuit.

She had reached the path which surrounds the pond before I really got into my stride. In Rugby days I had been counted one of the fastest men in the pack, but even allowing for loss of form due to my recent illness, an amazing fact demanded recognition. Ardatha was outrunning me easily: she ran with the speed of a young antelope!

Then, from near by, came the expected mournful cry:

"All out!"

I saw the parkkeeper at about the same moment that I accepted defeat in the race. Ardatha had passed him like a flash. He had assumed that she was running to reach a Kensington gate before it closed and had no more than glanced at her speeding figure. For my part I was determined to keep her in sight, but as I bore down on the man some suspicion seemed to cross his mind—a suspicion which linked my appearance with that of the flying girl. He glanced back at her for a moment and then stood squarely in my path, arms outstretched.

"Not this way!" he cried. "Too late. Porchester Gate is the only way out!"

Porchester Gate was the gate by which I had come in, and for one mad moment I weighed my chances of bowling the man over and following Ardatha. I think, disastrous though such an assault must have been, that I should have risked it had I not sighted a constable heading in our direction.

I pulled up, breathing heavily, and shrugged my shoulders. That lithe figure was already a phantom in the misty distance. Such a cloud of despair succeeded to the wild joy I had known at sight of Ardatha, such a madness of frustration, that frankly I think I was on the verge of tears. I clenched my teeth and turned back.

"One moment, sir."

The parkkeeper was following me. Struggling as I was for self-control, I prompted myself: "Don't hit him. He is only doing his duty. She ran away. You have no case. Be tactful or you will spend the night in a lockup."

I slowed my pace.

"Yes—what is it?"

He ranged up alongside. Out of the corner of my eye I could see the nearing figure of the constable.

"I was just wondering why you was in such a hurry, like."

We were walking along together now, and I forced a smile, looking at the man's lined, ingenuous face; I decided that he was an old gamekeeper.

"I wanted to catch somebody," I said. "I had had a quarrel with my girl friend and she ran away from me."

"Oh, is that so?" He continued to regard me doubtfully. "Run away, had she? Young lady with a cape?"

"Yes. She was wearing a cape. I have no idea where she has gone."

"Oh, I see. Neither of you lives over on Kensington side, like?"

"No—neither of us."

"Oh. I see." He had accepted me now. "That's hard luck, sir. She's a bit high mettled, like, no doubt."

"She is."

"Well, them's sometimes the best, sir, when it comes to a pinch. I reckon when the paddy's worn out she'll come back as sweet as honey."

"I hope so."

And indeed the man's simple philosophy had helped to restore me. I was glad that I had not quarrelled with him— and glad that I had told him the truth.

We walked along together through growing dusk. In the shadows about us nothing stirred. Moisture dripped mournfully from the trees. Already London grew silent at the touch

11

of night. Of Ardatha I dared not think; only I knew that the mystery of her reappearance and of her flight belonged to the greater and darker mystery which was Dr Fu Manchu.

A sense of evil impending, of some unwelcome truth fighting for admission, oppressed me. When I left Kensington Gardens and heard the gate locked behind me I stood for a while looking across at my windows.

There was a light in the writing room and the blinds were not drawn. Except for a big Packard just turning the corner into Craven Terrace there was no near-by traffic. As I ran across, fumbling for my keys, subconsciously I noted the number plate of the car: BXH77. It was rememberable, and I was in that troubled mood when one notes trivialities.

Opening the door, I hurried upstairs. I had much to tell Barton—and much to learn from him. The whole current of my life had changed. I remember that I banged my front door and dashed into the lighted workroom.

Standing by the desk was a tall, thin man, his face tropically brown, his hair nearly white at the temples and his keen eyes fixed upon me. I pulled up suddenly; I could not accept the fact.

It was Nayland Smith!

"Smith—Smith! I was never so glad to see any man in my life!"

He wrung my hand hard, watching me with those questing eyes; but his expression was stern to grimness.

"What has become of Barton?" I asked.

Smith seemed to grow rigid. He positively glared at me. "Barton!" he exclaimed. *"Barton!* Was Barton here?"

"I left him here."

He dashed his right fist into the palm of his left hand.

"My God, Kerrigan!" he said. "And you left your front door open—for so I found it. I have been searching London for Barton, and now——"

My fears, sorrows, forebodings, in that instant became crystallised in a dreadful certainty.

"Smith, do you mean——"

"I do, Kerrigan!" He spoke in a low voice. "Fu Manchu is in London . . . and he has got Barton!"

SMITH WENT RACING into the spare bedroom; in broken syllables I had told my tale. At the threshold, as I switched on the lights, we both pulled up.

The room was in wild disorder!

"You see, Kerrigan—you see!" cried Smith. "It was a ruse

to get you out of the house. Poor Barton put up a fight, by heaven! Look at that smashed chair!"

"His bag has gone!"

Smith nodded and began ferreting about among the wreckage. A heavy cloisonné vase lay beside the bed, although its proper place was on the mantel. He examined it carefully, although I could not imagine what evidence he hoped it might afford. Then I saw something else.

The room was equipped with an old-fashioned open grate, beside which rested tongs and poker. The fire was not laid, for I had not anticipated receiving a guest, but the iron poker lay half under an armchhair! Taking it up, I uttered an exclamation.

"Smith—look!"

The poker was bent in an unmistakable, significant manner. Smith grabbed it, held it under the bedside lamp—for darkness had fallen—and touched it at several points with the tip of his forefinger. He tossed it on the bed and began to stare around, tugging at the lobe of his left ear, a mannerism which I knew well.

"Barton is a powerful man," he said. "Something snapped when that poker was bent! Amazing that no one heard the row."

"Not at all. The rest of the house is empty, and my daily woman was gone before Barton arrived."

My voice sounded dull in my ears. Ardatha had lured me away, and my poor friend had been left alone to fight for his life. . . . Ardatha——

"There are other curious features, Kerrigan."

Smith dropped to his knees and began to examine the disordered carpet with close attention. He crawled as far as the door.

"Assuming, as we must, that Fu Manchu's agents entered shortly after you ran out, they had come on very urgent business——"

"Barton's bag! He told me that it contained something which would have saved you a journey to the Caribbean."

"Ah!" He stood up. "As I expected. They came for the chart. Barton put up a fight. Now—if they killed him, why carry a heavy body down all those stairs and run the risk of meeting a policeman outside? If he survived, where is he?"

"You say the street door was open?"

"Yes. Quick, Kerrigan! Let us examine the stairs. But wait—first all the cupboards and other possible hiding places."

Outside, in Bayswater Road, I heard a bus go by. I imagined it to be laden with homebound City workers anxious to reach their firesides. The black tragedy of war oppressed them; yet no one, in passing, would suspect that within sight from the bus window two of their fellows faced a terror deeper than that of the known enemy.

My flat was become a theatre of sinister drama. As Smith and I ran from room to room, sharing a common dread, the possibility that we should come upon Barton's body checked me more than once. It was Smith who opened the big store cupboard, Smith who explored an old oak wardrobe.

We found no trace.

"Now the stairs," he snapped. "We are wasting precious time, but we cannot act without a clue."

"What do you expect to find?"

"No body was *dragged* from the bedroom. I have satisfied myself on that point. But it may have been carried. The stair carpet should show traces if any load had been dragged downstairs—— Hullo! What's this?"

A bell had begun to ring.

"Street door!"

"Down you go, Kerrigan. Have you got a gun?"

"No—but I'll get one."

I hurried to my desk, slipped a friendly old Colt into my pocket and went down. Smith, using a pocket torch, was already crawling about on the landing peering at the carpet.

When I reached the front door and threw it open I don't quite know what I expected to find there. I found a constable.

"Is this your house, sir?" he asked gruffly.

"No—but I occupy a flat on the second floor."

"Well, then it's you I want to see. It's ten minutes after black-out time and you have lights blazing from all your windows!"

As I stared into the darkness beyond—there was no traffic passing at the moment and the night was profoundly still—I realised anew the strange power of Dr Fu Manchu. So completely had the handiwork of that satanic genius disturbed us that Smith and I (he an ex-commissioner of Scotland Yard) had utterly forgotten regulations and had offended against the law!

"Good heavens! You're right," I exclaimed. "We must be mad. The fact is, Constable, there have been queer happenings here and——"

"None of my business, sir. If you will go up and draw all the blinds in the first place, I shall then have to take your name and——"

From behind me came a sound of running footsteps.

"He was not carried out, Kerrigan!" came Smith's voice. "But there's blood on the third stair from the bottom and there are spots on the paving—— What the devil's this?"

"A serious business, sir," the constable began, but he stared in a bewildered way. "All the lights——"

Smith muttered something and then produced a card which he thrust into the constable's hand.

"Possibly before your time," he said rapidly. "But you'll still remember the name."

The constable directed his light onto the card, stared at Smith and then saluted.

"Sorry, sir," he said, "if I've butted in on something more important, but I was just obeying orders."

"Good enough," snapped Smith. "I switched off everything before I came down." He paused, staring at the stupefied man, and then: "What time did you come on duty?" he asked.

"Half an hour ago, sir."

"And you have been in sight of this door how long?"

The constable stared as if Smith's question had been a reprimand. I sympathised with the man, a freckled young fellow with straightforward blue eyes, keen on his job and one to whom the name of Sir Denis Nayland Smith was a name to conjure with. It occurred to me that he had been held up on his patrol and that he believed Smith to be aware of the fact.

"I know what you're thinking, sir, but I can explain my delay," he said.

Smith snapped his fingers irritably, and I saw that a hope had died.

"It was the car running onto the pavement in Craven Terrace," the man went on. "There was something funny about the business, and I took full particulars before I let 'em go." He delved in a back pocket and produced a notebook. "Here are my notes. It was a Packard——"

Odd are the workings of the human brain. My thoughts as the constable had been speaking, and, it seemed, speaking of matters beside the vital point, had drifted wretchedly to Ardatha. I had been striving to find some explanation of her behaviour which did not mean the shattering of a dream. Now, as he spoke of a Packard, I muttered mechanically:

"BXH77."

"That's it, sir!" the constable cried. "That's the car!"

"One moment," rapped Smith. "Tell me, Kerrigan, how you happen to know the number of this car."

I told him that a Packard bearing that number had turned

from the main road into Craven Terrace as I had crossed to the door.

"Quick, Constable!" He was suddenly on fire. "Your notes. What was suspicious about BXH77?"

"Well, sir, I have the particulars here." The man studied his notebook. "The car barged right onto the pavement and pulled up with a jerk about ten yards in front of me. Several people from neighbouring shops ran out. When I arrived I saw that the driver, a foreign-looking man, had fainted at the wheel. In some way which I couldn't make out—because it wasn't a serious crash—he had broken his arm——"

"Left or right?"

"Left, sir. It was hanging down limp. He was also bleeding from a cut on the head."

"Good. Go on."

"In the back I found a doctor and a patient he was removing to hospital. The patient seemed in a bad way—a big powerful man he was, with reddish hair streaked with white; he was only half conscious and the doctor was trying to soothe him. A mental case——"

"Do you understand, Kerrigan?" cried Smith, his eyes alight. "Do you understand?"

"Good God, Smith—I understand too well!"

"Describe the doctor," Smith said crisply.

The constable cleared his throat, and then:

"He had a very yellow face," he replied, "as yellow as a lemon. He wore spectacles with black rims and was a short-ish, heavily built man. He was not English."

"His name?"

"Here's his card, sir."

As Smith took the card:

"H'm!" he muttered: "Doctor Rudolph Oster, 101 Wimpole Street, W.I. Is there such a practitioner?"

"I was on my way to a call box when I saw all the lights blazing upstairs, sir. I was going to ask this gentleman to allow me to use his phone."

"Have you got the doctor's number?"

"Yes sir: Langham 09365."

"Efficient work, Constable," said Smith. "I'll see that it is recognised."

The man's freckled face flushed.

"Thank you, sir. It's very kind of you."

"How did the matter end?" I asked excitedly.

"We got the car back onto the road, and I helped to lift the chauffeur from the driving seat and put him in the back.

That was when I noticed his arm—when he began to come to."

"How did the patient behave?" Smith asked.

"He just lay back muttering. Doctor Oster explained that it was important to get him to a safe place before he recovered from the effects of an injection he had had to administer."

Smith uttered a sound like a groan and beat his fist into the palm of his hand.

"A suitcase marked L.B. was beside the driver. It was covered in foreign labels. The doctor took the wheel and drove off——"

"At what time?" snapped Smith.

"According to my watch, sir, at 7.13—that is, exactly five minutes ago."

3 / BXH77

"STOP FOR NOTHING," Smith cried to the driver, "short of murder! Use your horn. No regulations apply. Move!"

I had had a glimpse of the efficiency of the metropolitan police which had been a revelation. Within the last six minutes we had learned that Dr Oster was a naturalised British subject, a dermatologist and was not at home; that BXH77 had been held up for using an improperly masked headlight by a constable on duty in Baker Street; that Dr Oster, who was driving, said that he was taking a patient to a private clinic at North Gate, Regent's Park. Five motorcyclists were out, and every police officer and warden in that area had been advised.

Smith was too tensed up for ordinary conversation, but he jerked out a staccato summary as we sped through the blackout; for this London was a place of mystery, a city hushed; the heart of the world beating slowly, darkly.

"The United States have realised that the Panama Canal has two ends. Strange incidents in the Caribbean. Disappearances. Officers sent to West Indies to investigate. Never returned. Secret submarine base. I followed Fu Manchu to Jamaica. Lost him in Cuba. Barton has picked up some clue to the site of this base. Suspected before I left. Certain now. Got the facts in Norfolk only this morning. Fu Manchu has returned to England to silence Barton—and, my God, he has succeeded!"

We seemed to be speeding madly into darkness black as the pit. I could form no idea of where we were: we might have been in the Grand Avenue of Karnak. Vague, elfin lights I saw in the shadows, to take the place of illuminated windows, blazing sky signs. Sometimes a car would materialise like a form at a spiritualistic séance, only to disappear again immediately. The traffic signals, green, amber and red crosses, appeared and disappeared also like manifestations from another world. . . .

Our car was braked so suddenly that I was nearly pitched out of my seat.

I saw the driver leap to the road and sprint forward to where a torch was flashing—in and out, in and out. Smith was on the running board when the man came racing back.

"Jump in, sir!" he shouted. "Jump in! They passed here only three minutes ago—I have the direction!"

And we were off again into impenetrable darkness. Angry cries I heard as we flashed past crawling traffic, in contravention of law, issuing blasts of warning. Smith had commandeered Scotland Yard's ace driver. I was wild with the spirit of the chase. Barton's life was at stake—and more. . . .

Our brakes shrieked again, and the speeding car skidded to a perilous halt. We were all out in a trice.

In the light of torches carried by Smith and the driver I saw a police cyclist lying beside a wrecked motor bike almost under our front wheels!

"Are you badly hurt?" cried Smith.

The man raised a pale face to the light. Blood was trickling down from his brow; his black steel helmet had fallen off.

"Broken ankle, I think. This"—he touched his head—"is nothing. Just get me onto the pavement. It wasn't your car that hit me, sir."

We lifted him out of the traffic way, seating him against the railings of a house veiled in darkness. Our driver bent over him.

"If you can bear it, mate," he said, "give us the news. Have you sighted the Packard? We're Scotland Yard. This is Sir Denis Nayland Smith."

The man looked up at Smith. Obviously he was in great pain, but he spoke calmly.

"I followed BXH77 to this spot, sir. Having identified the number, I passed the car and signalled to the driver to pull up——"

"What happened?" snapped Smith.

"He ran me down!"

"Where did he go?"

"First left, sir—two houses beyond."

"How long ago?"

"Less than two minutes."

We were in one of those residential backwaters which are to be found north of Regent's Park. Reduction and slowing of traffic had so dimmed the voice of London that when the man ceased speaking an almost complete silence fell. Black night cloaked us, and in it I could hear no sound of human activity.

"You have done a good job, Constable," said Smith rapidly, "and you won't lose by it." He thrust a torch into my hand. "There's a house behind there, somewhere. Find it, Kerrigan, and phone for an ambulance. Just call 'police' and mention my name. Sorry. No other way. Understand how you feel. But I must push on."

"Turning to the left is a dead end, sir," the Yard driver cried back over his shoulder as he sprang to the wheel. "You can't go wrong, Mr Kerrigan, in following on foot."

"Ah!" cried Smith. "Good! We've got 'em!"

He jumped in, and the Yard car was off again, leaving me standing beside the injured man.

"So that's Nayland Smith," he muttered. "I wish we had a few more like him." He looked up. "Sorry to be a nuisance, sir. I'm fairly new to this district, but I think the gate of the house is just along to your right. The Regent Canal runs behind; that's why the next turning leads nowhere."

"I suppose there's no call box near?"

"No sir. But I must stick it till you find a phone."

4 / The House in Regent's Park

UP TO THE MOMENT that I discovered the gate not one pedestrian passed that way.

I groped along a neglected gravel drive bordered by dripping shrubberies and presently found myself before the porch of a house to which it led. There I pulled up. An estate agent's bill, announcing that "this desirable residence" was for sale, occupied the centre panel of the door. I had found an empty house.

Muttering savagely, I turned away. I suppose I had gone a dozen paces before it occurred to me that there might be a caretaker. I swung about to retrace my steps. As I did so I faced that wing of the ugly Victorian building which lay to the right of the entrance—and I saw a chink of light shining from a long french window.

Wondering why I had not seen it before, I pressed through wet bushes, crossed a patch of lawn and reached the lighted window. It proved to be one of three which opened onto a verandah, and I stepped up with the intention of rapping on the glass. Just in time I checked my hand.

I stood there, suddenly dizzy, my heart leaping furiously.

Heavy velvet curtains were draped inside the windows, one of which was slightly ajar, and the disarranged draperies had created that chink through which light shone. I could see right into the room and beyond an open door into a furnished lobby. It was from this lobby that the light came.

Standing there, looking back, so that I suspected it to have been she who had opened the window, was a girl wearing a hooded cape. The hood, thrown free, revealed a mass of gleaming, bewilderingly disordered curls, a pale lovely face; great eyes, blue in the dusk with the dark blue of lapis lazuli, were turned in my direction.

Ardatha . . . Ardatha whom I adored, who once had loved me, whom I had torn from the clutches of the Chinese doctor; Ardatha, for whom I had searched, desperately, during many weary months—who, when I had found her, had tricked me, used me, played upon my love so that I had betrayed my friend: Ardatha!

Yet, throwing discretion to the winds and forgetful of the injured man who depended upon me, I was about to spring into the room when—a second time I checked.

Slow, dragging footsteps and a sound resembling that of a rubber-shot stick became audible from somewhere beyond the corner of the verandah.

I grew suddenly cool, master of myself; my brain ceased to buzz like a nest of wasps: I could think clearly and quickly. A swift calculation told me that I had just time to leap into cover behind a holly bush before the one who walked so laboriously reached the angle of the house. I achieved my objective and threw myself flat on sodden turf.

Holding my breath, I watched. Water dripped from the leaves onto my head. I lay not three paces from the verandah. Quite distinctly I saw Ardatha draw the curtain and look out. Those dragging footsteps passed an unseen corner, and I knew that someone was approaching the window.

At that moment, in my new clarity of mind, I grasped a fact hitherto unsuspected:

The turning into which BXH77 had been driven communicated with the back premises of this house, probably with a garage. I had blundered into the enemy's headquarters!

A figure walked slowly along the verandah—that of a very tall, gaunt man wrapped in a heavy overcoat and wearing some kind of cap. He leaned upon a stick as one uncertain of his steps. The french window was thrown open. I saw Ardatha outlined against the light beyond. The gaunt figure went in, passed Ardatha and then half turned.

"Lock the window," I heard, spoken sibilantly.

It was Dr Fu Manchu!

As the window was fastened the curtain dropped and I rose to my knees.

"Ss!" came a hiss from close behind me. "Don't move, Kerrigan!"

My heart seemed to miss a throb. Nayland Smith was lying less than two yards away!

"You saw her?" he whispered.

"Of course!"

"I quite understand, old man. . . . No wonder we failed to find her. But even now don't despair——"

"Why?" I groaned. "What hope is left?"

Smith's reply was curious:

"Doctor Fu Manchu once had a daughter."

He had drawn nearer, and now he touched my shoulder. At that moment I had no idea what his words meant, but I was to learn later.

"Come on—this way."

In darkness I stumbled along behind him until I found myself under a clump of trees in what I divined to be a neglected garden. Beyond loomed the bulk of the mystery house—the house which harboured the most dangerous man in the world . . . and Ardatha.

"The lane into which the Packard turned," he said rapidly, "simply leads to the garage of this house and the one beyond. The latter also is apparently vacant. I grasped the position in time, backed out and came to look for you. Sims, the Yard driver, has gone for a raiding party. He will take the injured man with him."

"But—Barton?"

"We can only do our best until reinforcements arrive. But one duty we owe to the world—that we do not allow Doctor Fu Manchu to slip through our fingers!"

"Why didn't you shoot him where he stood, Smith?"

"For two reasons. The first concerns yourself; the second is that I know this place to be occupied by agents of the doctor —and Barton is in their hands . . . Good God! What's that?"

I think I began to reply, but the words perished on my tongue.

It was one of those sounds which it is good to forget, a sound which otherwise might haunt one's dreams. It was a strangled cry, the cry of a strong man in the grip of mortal terror. It died away. From leafless limbs of trees stretching over us came the drip-drip-drip of falling water.

Smith grasped my arm so hard that I winced.

"That was Barton!" he said hoarsely. "God forgive me if they——"

His voice broke. Shining torchlight on the path, he set out headlong for the house.

I have often wondered since what he had planned to do—what would have happened if that Fate which bound two destinies together had not intervened. I can only record what occurred.

We were scrambling across a thorny patch which I judged to be a rose bed when Smith pulled up, turned and threw me flat on the ground! His nervous strength in moments of excitement was astounding; I was down before I realised that it was he who had thrown me!

"Quiet!" he hissed in my ear; he lay prone beside me. "Look!"

A door had been opened; I saw a silhouette—I should have known it a mile away—that of a girl who seemed to be in wild distress. She raised her arms as if in a gesture of supplication, then pressed her hands over her ears and ran out, turned swiftly right and vanished.

Smith was breathing as rapidly as I, but:

"Ardatha has opened the door for us," he said quietly. "Come on, Kerrigan."

As we ran across and stepped into a lighted lobby Smith was self-possessed as though we were paying a formal call; I, knowing that we challenged the greatest genius who ever worked for Satan, admired him.

"Gun ready," he whispered. "Don't hesitate to shoot."

Something vaguely familiar about the place in which we stood was explained when I saw an open door beyond which was an empty room, its french windows draped with sombre velvet. This was the lobby I had seen from the other side of the house. It was well furnished, the floor strewn with rugs, and oppressively hot. The air was heavy with the perfume of hyacinths, several bowls of which decorated the place. A grandfather clock ticked solemnly before the newel post of a carpeted staircase. I found myself watching the swing of the pendulum as we stood there listening. The illumination was scanty, and from beside a partly opened door in a recess left of the stairs light shone out.

In the room beyond a voice was speaking. Smith exchanged a swift glance with me and advanced, tiptoe. The speaker was Dr Fu Manchu!

"I warned you as long as six months ago," came that singular voice—who, hearing, could ever forget it? "But my warning was not heeded. I have several times attempted, and as often failed, to recover Christophe's chart from your house in Norfolk. Tonight my agents did not fail——"

A bearskin rug had deadened the sound of our approach; now Smith was opening the door by decimals of an inch per move.

"You fought for its possession. I do not blame you. I must respect a man of spirit. You might even have succeeded if Doctor Oster had not managed to introduce an intramuscular injection of *crataegusin* which produced immediate crataegus katatonia—or shall I say stupor——"

Smith had the door open nearly six inches. I obtained a glimpse of the room beyond. It looked like a study, and on a long narrow writing table a struggling man lay bound; I could not see his face.

"Since this occurred in the street it necessitated your removal. And now, Sir Lionel, I have decided that your undoubted talents, plus the dangers attendant upon a premature discovery of your body, entitle you to live—and to serve the Si-Fan. My plans for departure are complete. Doctor Oster will operate again, and your perspective be adjusted. Proceed."

Smith now had the door half open. I saw that the bound man was Barton. They had gagged him. His eyes, wild with horror, were turned to the door. . . . He had seen it opening!

A man who wore black-rimmed spectacles was bending over him, a man whose outstanding peculiarity was a bright yellow complexion. From the constable's description I recognised Dr Oster. Barton's coat had been removed, his shirt sleeves rolled up. The yellow Dr Oster grasped a muscular arm near the biceps and pinched up a pucker of flesh. The agony in those staring eyes turned me cold—nurderously cold. The fang of a hypodermic syringe touched Barton's skin——

Smith threw the door open; Dr Oster looked up.

To this hour I cannot recall actually pressing the trigger, but I heard the report.

I saw a tiny bluish mark appear in the middle of that yellow forehead. Dr Oster glared straight at me through his spectacles, dropped the syringe and, still glaring, voiceless, fell forward across Barton's writhing body.

"DON'T MOVE, FU MANCHU! The game's up this time!"

Smith leapt into the room, and I was close beside him. The dead man slipped slowly to his knees, still staring glassily straight ahead as if into some black hell suddenly revealed, and soundlessly crumpled up on the floor. One swift glance I gave to Barton, strapped on the long table, then spun about to face Dr Fu Manchu.

But Dr Fu Manchu was not there!

"Good God!"

Smith, for once, was wholly taken aback; he glared around him, one amazed beyond belief. The room, as I supposed, was a study. The wall right of the door through which we had burst in was covered by bookcases flanking an old oak cabinet having glazed windows behind which I saw specimens of porcelain on shelves. No other door was visible. But, although we had heard Fu Manchu speaking, Fu Manchu was not in the room. . . .

At the moment that Barton began to utter inarticulate sounds Smith raised his automatic and fired a shot into the china cabinet.

A crash of glass followed; then, as he ran forward:

"Release Barton!" he cried. "Quick!"

I slipped my Colt into my pocket and bent over the table. Smith had wrenched open the glazed door; I heard a further crashing of glass. I tore the bandage from Barton's mouth; he stared up at me, his florid face purple.

"Behind the cabinet!" he gasped. "Get him, Smith—the yellow rat is behind the cabinet!"

As I pulled out a pocket knife to cut the lashings came a second shot; more crashing.

"He's gone this way!" Smith shouted. "Cut Barton loose and follow!"

As Sir Lionel rose unsteadily and swung his feet clear of the table something fell to the carpet. It was the hypodermic syringe, the point of which had just touched his skin at the moment that I had fired. Barton rested against the table for a moment, breathing heavily and looking down at the dead man.

"Good shot, Kerrigan. Thank you," he said.

The sound of a third report, more distant, echoed through

the house; and, turning, I saw that the china cabinet was a camouflaged door. A gap now yawned beyond.

"I'll follow, Kerrigan. Find Smith."

Good old Barton! I had no choice.

Stumbling over shattered china, I entered the hidden doorway. A flash of my torch showed me that I stood in a large unfurnished room. A second door was open, although no glimmer shone beyond. I ran across and out. I found myself back in the lobby, but the lights were all off!

"Smith!" I cried. "Smith! Where are you?"

From far behind a sound of crunching footsteps reached me. Barton was coming through. Near by, in the shadows, the grandfather clock ticked solemnly. I stepped to the newel post and moved all the switches which I found there.

Nothing happened. The current had been cut off from some main control.

Knowing that the house, only a matter of minutes before, had been occupied by members of the most dangerous criminal group in the world, I stood quite still for a moment, glancing up carpeted stairs. The scent of hyacinths grew overpowering; a foreboding—almost, it seemed, a pre-knowledge of disaster —bore down upon me.

"Kerrigan!" came Barton's voice, "the damned lights have gone out!"

"This way!" I cried and was about to step back to guide him when I saw something.

One of the flower bowls lay smashed on the floor. A draft of cold, damp air bore the exotic scent of the blooms to my nostrils. The door by which we had entered, the door to the garden, was wide open; and now from out of the blackness beyond came the wail of a police whistle.

"Make your way through to the garden!" I shouted. "Smith is out there—and he needs help!"

Something in the scent of the hyacinths, in the atmosphere of the house, spoke to me of that Eastern mist out of which Dr Fu Manchu had materialised. It was a commonplace London house, but it had sheltered the Chinese master of evil, and his aura lay heavy upon it. I ran out into the garden as one escaping. Dimly the words reached my ears:

"Go ahead! I can take care of myself. . . ."

The skirl of the whistle had died away, but it had seemed to come from a point far to the right of the route which Smith and I had followed when we had approached the house. Now, using my torch freely, I saw that a gravelled path led from the door in that direction; a short distance ahead there were glasshouses.

I grasped a probable explanation: the garage . . . Fu Manchu was making for the car. Smith had followed!

As I ran down the path—it sloped sharply—I was mentally calculating the time that had elapsed since Sims, the Yard driver, had gone for a raid squad and asking myself, over and over again, if Smith had been ambushed. I was by no means blind of my danger; the friendly Colt was ready in my hand as I passed the glasshouses. Beyond them I pulled up.

Except for a dismal dripping of moisture from the trees the night was uneasily still. I could hear no sound from Barton, but I had heard another sound, and this it was which had pulled me up sharply—a low whistle on three minor notes.

Switching off my light, I stood there waiting. The whistle was repeated, from somewhere nearer; I heard footsteps. And now came a soft call: I could not catch the words. Then a faint glimmer of light showed in the darkness.

A high red brick wall surrounded the garden; the forcing houses were built against it. There was an arched opening, in which perhaps at some time there had been a gate.

There, where reflected rays from the lamp she held struck witch fires from her disordered hair, stood Ardatha!

Certainly I had never known, nor have known since, any wild conflict of emotions such as that which shook me. The expression in those wonderful eyes, their deep blue seeming lustrous black in the darkness, was so compounded of terror and of appeal that I knew I must act quickly. I had given my heart to a soulless wanton—and she held it still.

She had seen me, and at the moment that she extinguished the lamp I saw that she carried what looked like a shawl. She turned to run, but I was too swift for her. A vigour not wholly of heaven drove me tonight; things witnessed in that hyacinth-scented house, the ghastly fate from which we had saved Barton, the leering yellow face of Dr Oster (for whose end I experienced not one jot of remorse)—these had taught me the meaning of "seeing red."

I leapt through the archway and seized the hooded cape, streaming out behind as she ran. She slipped free of it—I stumbled—sprang again—and had her!

As I locked my arms around her she quivered and panted like a wild creature trapped; her heart was drumming against mine.

"Let me go!" she cried: "Let me go!" and beat at me with clenched fists, nor were the blows light ones.

But I held her remorselessly, perhaps harshly, for her struggles ceased and her words ended on a sound like a sob. She lay, lithe, slender and helpless, in my grip. My heart-throbs matched her own as I crushed her to me so that my face touched her hair—and its fragrance intoxicated me.

"Ardatha—Ardatha!" I groaned. "My God, how I love you! How could you do it!"

That beating heart drummed hard as ever, but I detected a relaxation of tensed muscles. No effort of acting could have simulated the agony in my voice. Ardatha knew, but she did not speak.

"I searched the world for you, Ardatha, after you left me in Paris. For weeks I rarely slept. I couldn't believe, even if you had changed, why you should torture me. And so I thought you must be dead. I came very near to madness. I went to Finland—hoping to die."

She looked up at me. To this hour I have no idea what lay beyond the brick arch, what surrounded us as we stood there. But either I saw her psychically or some faint light reached the spot, for I knew that there were tears on her lashes.

"I am so sorry," she whispered. "Because you must mean —some other Ardatha."

Every quaint inflection of that elusive accent, the sympathy in her musical voice, tortured me. I turned my head aside; I could no longer trust myself. She spoke as the Ardatha I adored, the Ardatha I had lost; her pretence, her actions, spoke another language.

"There is only one Ardatha. I was the fool, to believe in her. Where is Fu Manchu? Where is Nayland Smith?"

"Please don't hurt me." I had tightened my hold automatically. "I would, indeed, help you if I could. Nayland Smith is my enemy, but you are not my enemy, and I wish you no harm. Only I tell you that if you stay here you will die."

"Where is Nayland Smith? He has never been your enemy. Why do you say such a thing? And don't mock me because I love you."

She was silent for a moment. Those slim curves enclosed by my arms taunted me. One nervous slender hand stole up and rested on my shoulder.

"I am not mocking you. You frighten me. I don't understand. I am very very sorry for you. I want to save you from danger. But there is some great mistake. You ran after me across Hyde Park tonight, and now you are here. You tell me"—her voice faltered—"that you love me. How can that be?"

Her fingers were clutching my shoulder, and I knew, although I kept my head averted, that she was looking up; I knew, too, and wondered if war had driven the whole world mad, that there were tears in her eyes.

"It has always been, since the first moment I saw you. It will always be—always, Ardatha. Now lead me to Smith—I shall not let you go until we find him."

But she clung to me, resisting.

"No, no! Wait—let me try to understand. You say since the first moment you saw me . . . The first moment I saw *you* was tonight, when you cried out to me—cried my name—in the park!"

"Ardatha!"

"Yes—you cried out 'Ardatha.' I looked back and I saw you. Perhaps I liked you and wished that I knew you. But I did not know you, and your eyes were glaring madly. So I ran. Now——"

I suppose, for the whole situation was illusory, dreamlike, that my grasp had changed to a caress; I had stooped to kiss her, liar, hypocrite though she might be. I know that her voice, as she trembled in my arms, had thrust out everything else in the world except my blind, hopeless love of Ardatha.

"No! You dare not!" She dashed her hand against my lips; I kissed her palm, her fingers. "Do you think I am a courtesan? I don't even know your name!"

I stood suddenly still but I did not release her.

"Ardatha," I said, "has Doctor Fu Manchu ordered you to torture me?" At those words I felt a quiver pass through her body. She inhaled a sobbing breath and was silent. "I loved you—I shall love you always—and you ran away. You sent me no message, no word, even to tell me that you were alive. Now, when I find you, you say that you don't know my name. . . . Ardatha!"

She crushed her head against me and burst into passionate tears.

"I want to believe!" she sobbed. "I want to believe! I cannot understand, but I have no one in all the world to turn to! If it were true, if in some way I had forgotten, if you were really——"

And as I held her, tenderly now, certain words of Nayland Smith's were singing in my brain: "Don't despair . . . Doctor Fu Manchu once had a daughter." The significance of the words was not yet clear to me, but I found in them, gladly, something to reconcile the seemingly irreconcilable.

"Ardatha, my dearest, you *must* believe. How could I know your name—or worship you as I do—if we had never been lovers? You *have* forgotten—God knows why or how—and it *is* true."

28

She made a perceptible effort to control herself, and when she spoke, although her voice was unsteady it had regained its natural timbre.

"I am trying to believe you—although to do so means that I must have had a mental breakdown and forgotten that too. You asked me where Nayland Smith had gone. He ran to the garage: it is straight along this path. I cannot tell you where Doctor Fu Manchu is: I do not know. But unless you let me go, I shall die."

"Die! Why should you die?"

"Next time we meet I will try to tell you." She pressed her face against my shoulder. "But if I am to believe *you,* then you must believe *me.* See—I trust you. I took it a long time ago from your pocket."

And she handed me my Colt!

I released Ardatha and stood there, the automatic in my hand, trying to adjust my ideas to a new scheme of things, when from far away up near the house came Barton's great voice:

"Kerrigan! Where are you? Give me a hail."

I turned and shouted:

"This way, Barton."

But as I swung about again—Ardatha had vanished! Her cloak I held over my arm, the Colt was still grasped in my hand. I dropped it back in my pocket, snatched out the torch and flashed a ray ahead.

Nothing moved, and I could hear no footsteps. Water was dripping mournfully from the roof of a glasshouse, and a long way off I detected insistent hooting of a motor horn.

The raid squad was coming.

Why was Nayland Smith silent? There was something ominous about it. I have said, and I confess it again, that at first sight of Ardatha every other idea in my mind had been swept out; and whilst I had stood there (my heart was still pounding madly) it was quite possible——

"Have you found Smith?" Barton cried. "Show a light. I've caught something, and——"

I turned back and threw a moving fan of light on the path which led to the house. As I did so an overpowering smell of hawthorn swept down upon me as if borne on a sudden breeze. Too late, a decimal of a second too late, I ducked and half turned.

My head was enveloped in what felt like a moist rubber bag . . . I experienced a sensation of sinking, not swiftly but as if floating gently downward, into deep clouds of hawthorn blossom.

6 / *Dr Fu Manchu's Experiments*

I SEEMED TO BREAK THROUGH some brittle surface into a plane of violet light—and silence. There was a rapidly receding background, a memory of wild action, of the drip of moisture, of a noisome tunnel and moving water. Here all was still; nothing was visible in that luminous expanse. Then, a long way off, I heard the voice of Dr Fu Manchu. . . .

"A member of my family, a mandarin of my rank, is bound by codes stronger than bands of steel. For myself I ask nothing. I hold the key which unlocks the heart of the secret East; holding that key, I command the obedience of an army greater than any ever controlled by one man. . . ."

This must be delirium, for no living thing was in sight: I was alone in a violet void.

"My power rests in the East, but my hand is stretched out to the West. I shall restore the lost grandeur of China. When your civilisation, as you are pleased to term it, has exterminated itself, when you have reduced to ashes your palaces and your temples, when in your blindness you have set back the clock which so laboriously you fashioned, I shall stir. Out of the fire I shall rise. The red dusk of the West will have fallen, the golden dawn of the East will come. . . ."

The voice faded, and at the same time that mysterious radiance also grew dim, as though it had been a mirage created by the voice or the aura of the speaker. . . .

I was lying, in a constrained position, upon a cushioned settee which had a metal base, in a long, narrow, low-ceilinged room which possessed no visible windows. It was lighted by hanging lamps and permeated by a carnal smell: I thought of the morgue. That half of the room which contained the settee or couch was unfurnished except for a tall glass-fronted cabinet. In this cabinet, preserved in jars, were all kinds of anatomical specimens: a collection so gruesome that I doubted the verity of this phase too.

There were several human hands, black, yellow and white; there was a brown forearm; there were internal organs which I need not describe; and, half covered by a sheet of gauze, a decapitated Negro head grinned from the largest jar.

The lower half of the room was a small but well-equipped laboratory where some experiment was actually in progress. An apparatus resembling a Bunsen burner, but dissimilar in some way which my indifferent knowledge of chemistry did not enable me to define, hissed below a retort fitted with a condenser.

One glance I took at the object in process of distillation and looked elsewhere. I grew nauseated and closed my eyes for a moment. But I had seen something which might have accounted for the violet mirage:

On a smaller bench there stood a low, squat lamp, resting on what I took to be a block of crystal. It produced a strange amethystine radiance—and instantly I thought of the eyes of Ardatha.

With that thought came complete consciousness. . . . Ardatha!

Had she betrayed me? Had she tricked me again and left me to the mercies of Fu Manchu's thugs? I remembered that she had stolen my Colt and then returned it. Was this evidence of her innocence or merely of a moment's remorse prompted by knowledge of those who covered me, who at that instant she had seen behind me?

A door hidden in the wall near the large bench slid soundlessly open. I became aware of a sensation in my skull which resembled that experienced on quickly climbing to a high altitude. A man entered with slow, curiously feline steps and closed the door behind him. He wore a long coat of what appeared to be varnished green silk. Turning, he stared in my direction.

It was Dr Fu Manchu.

He was more emaciated than I remembered him to have been, and as he seated himself at the bench I noted the weariness of his movements. To one who had not met Dr Fu Manchu it would be impossible, I suppose, to convey any idea of the peculiar *force* which he seemed to project.

With the exception of Nayland Smith I had never known one who could stand up to it. And now, alone with him in that long, narrow, sinister room, silent save for the hiss of the burner, I recognised the fact that this power emanated entirely from his eyes.

His imposing figure, tall, angular, high shouldered, lent him a sort of grotesque majesty; and as he sat there before me, a vitalised skeleton clothed in wrinkled silk, his shrunken skin exposing all the contours of that wonderful skull, no whit of this force was missing. I had sprung up at the moment of his entrance, and now I stood there battling with a fear not unmixed with loathing which he inspired; and I knew that his power resided in a tremendous intellect, for it shone out like a beacon from those strange green eyes, feverishly brilliant in cavernous shadows.

He spoke.

The effort of speech was terrifying. It came to me suddenly as a conviction that Dr Fu Manchu was very near his end. It was as though a magician had conjured back a soul into a body dead for generations.

"I trust that you are conscious of no nausea or other unpleasant aftereffects. My fellows are adept with their knives and strangling cords but clumsy when employing more subtle methods."

One clawlike hand, the nails long and pointed, resting on the plate glass which covered the bench, he watched me for a few moments; and I felt, as of old, as if he read every record printed upon my brain.

I plunged my hand into my pocket; it was a gesture of resignation—but my fingers touched the automatic. . . . I had not been disarmed!

"You seriously inconvenienced my plans, Mr Kerrigan, when you shot Companion Oster. Doctor Oster was a licentiate of Heidelberg and held also a minor London degree. His qualifications, therefore, were limited. Nevertheless he was useful. Your own powers of observation being not entirely undeveloped, no doubt you noted that his skin displayed unusual pigmentary characteristics?"

That intolerable gaze brooked no denial; I replied:

"He was yellow as a lemon."

I was clutching the Colt and saying to myself, "You did not hesitate in the case of the lesser scoundrel; why hesitate now?"

"Exactly. This was due to the nature of the experiments which he had carried out under my direction. Be good enough to glance into the cabinet on your right—but avoid crossing the red line which you may have seen painted on the floor."

I had not seen the red line, but I saw it now: an inch-wide band extending from wall to wall just beyond the cabinet which contained the anatomical specimens and dividing the long narrow room into equal parts. I moved forward; it suited me to do so: it brought Dr Fu Machu into a range at which I could not possibly miss him.

"The hands of the Negro," he went on, his voice low and sibilant, "are of particular interest. Do you agree with me?"

Conquering nausea which threatened to return, I looked at those gruesome fragments. One of the hands was clenched convulsively, and I wondered how the black man had died; the other was rigidly open. But a certain characteristic they shared in common: on close inspection it became apparent that they were not true black nor even brown, but rather of that deep purplish green which is present in some cultivated tulips. I became fascinated.

"Note the white forearm. It is that of a lascar. The bright yellow hand, labelled G, was contributed by a blond Bavarian youth. . . ."

I suppose it was a belated recognition of the meaning of his words, a sudden hot understanding of the fact that human beings, black, white and brown, had been sacrificed to some unimaginable scientific experiment, which prompted my action; but, turning to Dr Fu Manchu, I snatched the Colt from my pocket, took deliberate aim and fired, not at his head but at his heart. . . . To make doubly sure of ridding the world of a monster I fired twice!

In a life which, for one of my years, had been notable for action I think that those dragging seconds which followed the two shots epitomized all the wonder, all the terror and all the acceptance of laws beyond human understanding which any man has known.

Dr Fu Manchu smiled!

He revealed a row of small, even, yellow teeth. It was as though a mummy of one who had lived when the world was young jeered at me. He spoke, but his words sounded as words spoken at the end of a long tunnel.

"They were live cartridges: they had not been exchanged for blanks. I wished you to attempt to add me to your bag, but I observed that you aimed at my breast. The brain, Mr Kerrigan, and not the heart, is the seat of power. The ancient Egyptians knew . . ."

But I had turned away. I tossed the Colt onto the settee and dropped down beside it. I had witnessed a miracle, and I was shaken to my soul. Only the manner of my death remained in doubt.

That odd, indefinable vibration which I had noted at the moment of his entrance suddenly ceased as Dr Fu Manchu's voice again broke through the blanket of stupor which had settled upon my brain.

"A consciousness of cerebral pressure is relieved, no doubt? You experience a sense of restful silence. The explanation is a simple one. If you will be good enough to leave your automatic where it lies and accept this chair, we can approach the real purpose of our present interview."

I stood up and faced him. His eyes were filmy, contemplative; they lacked that emerald lustre which I could never face unmoved. One clawlike hand was stretched across the bench, indicating a metal chair.

With some of the feelings of a whipped cur I rose and moved forward. At the red line I paused.

"You may cross safely."

I crossed and dropped down in the chair facing Dr Fu Manchu. Save for the hissing sound of the burner the room was silent. Dr Fu Manchu rested his chin upon one skeleton hand; his proximity imparted a sense of chill, as though I had sat with a corpse.

"You observe, Mr Kerrigan, that I am employing those primitive methods here which gave Paracelsus such excellent results and by means of which Van Helmont performed his transmutations. But before we proceed to the subject of my present experiments—a subject of some personal interest to yourself"—at those words my heart grew cold—"it is only fair to explain why your bullets failed to reach me."

I clenched my teeth.

"When you were very young Doctor Sven Ericksen died, and the newspapers of the world were filled with stories of the Ericksen ray which that distinguished physicist had never perfected. Although legally dead, he has since completed his inquiries with some slight assistance from myself."

This statement evoked ghastly memories, but I remained silent.

"The so-called 'ray' is in fact a sound wave or chord. Ericksen discovered that a certain combination of incalculably high notes, inaudible to the human ear, could reduce nearly any substance to its original particles. It was a problem of pure physics: that of disturbing harmonic equilibrium. A belt or curtain of these sound waves can be thrown across this room by merely depressing a switch. Continued exposure to such vibrations, however, is highly injurious. Therefore I have disconnected the apparatus."

I looked up quickly and as quickly down again. Dr Fu Manchu was watching me, and even when veiled contemplatively I could not sustain the regard of those magnetic eyes.

"Your bullets are still present, not in the form of lead and nickel but in that of their component elements: they are disintegrated. The importance of this discovery it would be difficult to exaggerate. I am acquainted with only one substance capable of penetrating a zone protected by Ericksen chords——"

I heard a faint buzzing sound—and all the lights went out!

1 / The River Gate

MY FIRST IDEA, naturally enough, was that Dr
Fu Manchu had given some signal, unobserved, for
my dismissal; that I was to be despatched in darkness. The
burner hissing under the retort and its gruesome contents
became silent. I sprang to my feet. At least I could go down
fighting. Out of impenetrable gloom came the imperious voice,
guttural now:

"Pray remain seated. Owing to certain extemporised meas-
ures, power in the laboratory is controlled from an outside
switchboard—and it has been cut off. This means an air-raid
warning, Mr Kerrigan, but it need not disturb you."

An air-raid warning? Then a terrifying idea which I had
been grimly repelling—an idea that unconsciousness had
lasted for a long time; that this secret laboratory was situated
perhaps far away from England—need disturb me no more.
However, I remained standing, and with courage greater than
I had ever known in the visible presence of Dr Fu Manchu:

"You appear to be dangerously ill," I said.

And the ghostly voice replied:

"I have brought myself close to death. Science is my mistress, and I serve her too well. You may have noticed a small
lamp (it is extinguished now) producing a violet light. The
condition in which you find me is due to my experiments with
this lamp. The green jacket I wear affords some slight pro-
tection, but I can discover no formula to reinforce the human
economy so that it may cancel its deleterious effects. Doctor
Oster, my assistant in these inquiries, developed opacity of
the crystalline lens accompanied by other notable pigmentary
changes; and although—a fact to which the specimens you
have inspected bear witness—racial types react variously,
none can sustain these emanations without suffering perma-
nent injury. . . . But you remain standing."

I sat down.

Whether it was imagination or whether, as I had sometimes suspected, the eyes of Dr Fu Manchu possessed a
chatoyant quality, I thought that I could see them watching
me—shining greenly in the dark like the eyes of a great cat.

"I have submitted certain proposals to Sir Denis Nayland
Smith," he went on. "Although, thanks to my recovery of the
chart found by Sir Lionel Barton, I can take suitable precau-
tions, any interference with my plans in the Caribbean may
alter the world's history. You are my hostage. If Sir Denis

refuses to pay your ransom (I gather that you hold a minor science degree), I shall invite you to take the place of Companion Oster—of whose services you deprived me—and to carry on those inquiries, under my direction, which his death has interrupted."

It is beyond the power of my pen to convey any idea of the cloud of horror which swept down upon me as I listened to his words. Before my mind's eye they appeared, those ghastly fragments of men who had died martyrs to the lust for knowledge which animated this devil in human shape. To their tormented company I was to be added!

How I should have acted, what reply I should have made to that monstrous statement, I cannot say. Although I had detected no movement, Dr Fu Manchu had retired from his place on the other side of the glass-topped bench, for when he spoke again it was from beyond the hidden doorway:

"I must leave you for a time, Mr Kerrigan. I strongly urge you to remain seated. Many of the objects here are lethal. I will arrange for the lamps to be relighted. You may smoke if you wish."

A faint sound indicated that the door had been closed.

I was alone—alone with the violet lamp which blinded, which changed men from white to yellow, which had shattered the supernormal constitution of its Chinese creator; alone with the amputated remains of some who had suffered that this dream of Dr Fu Manchu might be realised. What was the purpose of these merciless experiments? What power resided in the lamp?

Fumbling in my pocket, I learned that my torch remained undisturbed. Any fate was preferable to the fate ordained by the devil doctor. I flashed a ray about that awesome room, that silent room which smelled like a mortuary.

It glittered momentarily upon my Colt lying on the couch. It brought to life the head of the Negro grinning in a big jar and lent uncanny movement to those discolored hands which forever had ceased to move.

I stepped towards the red line.

"Consciousness of cerebral pressure" mentioned by Dr Fu Manchu was not perceptible; the Ericksen apparatus remained disconnected. I cross the red line and took up my automatic. At the moment that I retrieved the Colt an abnormally tensed sense of hearing told me that the sliding door had been opened.

In a flash I had turned, a ray focused on the wall behind the bench, my finger alert on the trigger.

No doubt the mystery of the lamp had inflamed my imagination, but I thought that by magic a djinn had been summoned. Although I had the apparition covered by my pistol, consternation threatened me as the torchlight wavered on a gigantic figure framed in the doorway. It was that of a herculean man who wore a white robe and a red sash, a tarboosh on his head. His thick lips, flattened nostrils and frizzy hair were those of a Nubian—but his skin was white as ivory!

Common sense dispersed fantasy. The man was a strangler sent by Dr Fu Manchu to dispatch me. . . .

"Put up your hands!" I ordered.

Blinking in the light, the white Negro obeyed, raising thick, sinewy blond hands, and:

"Not so loud, sir," he said hoarsely. "You spoil your chances if you speak so loud."

That he spoke English, and spoke with an American intonation, provided a further shock; his seeming friendliness I distrusted.

"Who are you? What do you want?"

"My name Hassan, sir. I want help you——"

"Why?"

"White Lady wishes." He touched his brow as he spoke. "When White Lady wishes Hassan obeys."

And now my heart gave a great leap.

"The White Lady—Ardatha?"

Hassan touched his brow again.

"Her family I serve, and my father, his father before; long long time before. White Lady's order more high than Master's order, more high than any but God Almighty. Follow Hassan."

A hundred questions I longed to ask, for this man perhaps held the clue to that torturing mystery never far from my mind; but a quick decision was imperative—and I made it.

"Lead the way," I said, and stepped forward. "I will use my torch."

"No light," he whispered, "no light. Come close and take my hand."

It was in no spirit of childish confidence that I grasped the muscular white hand, but as I had reached the Nubian's side and finally switched off my torch those blinking eyes had told me the truth: Hassan was blind.

"No sound," he said in a low voice. "Hassan see with inner eye. Trust Hassan. . . ."

Along a short passage apparently covered in rubber he led me. Another silent door he opened and closed. The peculiarly nauseating smell of the laboratory was no longer perceptible; the air was cool. We crept up a stone stair and stood at the top for a while. I thought that Hassan was listening. I could detect no sound, no glimmer of light.

His grip tightened suddenly, and he dragged me sharply to the right for three paces and then stood still again.

Faint footsteps sounded—grew nearer—louder. A beam of yellow light shone past an arched opening not ten feet from where we hid. I watched, holding my breath. The moving rays revealed a stone passage. And now came the bearer of the light—a short, stocky brown man (one of Dr Fu Manchu's Burmese bodyguard). He carried a hurricane lamp. He passed. Behind him came two others—they bore a body on a stretcher.

They, too, passed; the sound of footsteps faded, the light grew dim; complete darkness returned.

The most dreadful premonitions attacked me; I grew sick with dread. Whose was the muffled body? What place was this, with its stone-paved passages, which Dr Fu Manchu had chosen for his lair? As if Hassan divined how near I was to speech:

"Ss!" he hissed—and led me on.

Our route lay in that direction from which the bearers had come, and just as I thought I detected a faint light ahead a sound echoed hollowly through the stone passages, a sound which robbed me almost of my last spark of courage. It was the note of a gong!

Hassan stopped dead; he bent to my ear.

"That call for me," he whispered. "Must go. Listen very careful. Straight before is opening—wide and high. River below—very far below. But iron ladder straight under opening. Take much care, sir. Barge lie there; tide rising. If someone is on barge—shoot. Then wade through mud to wooden steps beyond bows——"

A second gong stroke reverberated through the building.

"Hurry!" Hassan whispered. "Hurry!"

He released my hand and was gone.

The prospect was far from pleasing, but I preferred a broken neck to the fate in store for me at the hands of Dr Fu Manchu. I set out towards that distant glimmer. I had formed a mental picture of the "opening—wide and high," and, having no desire to plunge headlong into the mud of the Thames, ventured to use my light. At sight of what lay before me my hopes were dashed.

This was an old warehouse. The passage led to wide double doors beside which I saw rusty winding gear. There was an iron-barred opening in each of the doors—which were closed and locked. . . .

I was trapped!

Although my spirits had touched zero, I went on to the doors and tried the heavy padlock. It was fast. Cold, damp air came through the grilles as I stared out, hopelessly. So dark was the night, so far below the river lay, that I could have formed no impression of the scene if searchlights had not helped me. The blackness was slashed by swords of silver. They formed a changing pattern in the sky, and this was reproduced in the oily mirror of the river far beneath.

From the distance of buildings dimly discernible on the further bank, which I assumed to be the Surrey shore, I judged that I was well below bridges and in the heart of dockland. But that great heart pulsed slowly tonight. A red glow here, a vague iridescence there, and an uneasy hum, like that of a vast hive imprisoned, alone represented the normal Wagnerian symphony of London. Above, the questing searchlights; below, a pianissimo in the song of industry until the hawk's shadow should pass.

Turning with a smothered groan. I looked back along the passage.

At a point which I estimated to be beyond that at which Hassan and I had hidden a bar of yellow light lay across the stone floor. Action was imperative. Walking softly, I approached this bar of light. Apart from fears of a personal character I was filled with the wildest apprehensions concerning Smith. A theory to account for my presence in this deserted warehouse had occurred to me, for I had recalled that the Regent Canal came out at Limehouse.

Along that gloomy waterway, with its cuttings and tunnels, I had been transported from the house in Regent's Park. . . . The body I had seen borne on a stretcher had followed the same route. . . .

I stumbled, stifled an exclamation and managed to fall softly.

There was a gap in the stone paving, and I lay still for a while; for I had fallen not two feet from the bar of light, and as I had tripped I had seen a shadow move across it!

Someone was in the place from which the yellow light shone.

The next few moments covered long agonies of doubt. But apparently I had not been detected. Carefully moving my hands, I tried to find out what lay between me and the light. A discovery soon came. I had tripped and fallen on a square stone landing from which steps led down to a sunken door. It was from an iron-barred window beside this door that the light was shining.

Inch by inch I changed my position until, seated on the steps, I could look into a cellarlike room illuminated by a hurricane lamp set on a crate. From this position I saw a strange thing. Because of the imperfect illumination and my angle of vision, at first I could not altogether make out what it was that I saw.

A pair of sinewy hands were working rapidly upon some mysterious task. Bare wrists and forearms I could see, hairy and muscular, but of the head and body of him to whom they belonged I could see nothing. A faint tearing sound and a sort of hiss gave me the clue at last. The man was stitching something up in sailcloth; I could just make out a shapeless bundle.

Now I felt far from master of myself, but in the almost silent activities of this man who had such powerful arms there was something indescribably malignant.

Who was he, and what was he doing in the cellar?

Observing every precaution, I slightly changed my position again until I could see quite clearly the nature of the bundle which the sailmaker stitched.

It contained a human body!

The worker had started at the feet and had completed the shroud of sailcloth up to the breast.

I closed my eyes for a moment, clenched my teeth. Then I mover further down. The body lay on a stout bench, and from my constrained position it was still impossible to see more than the arms, up to the elbows, of the worker.

But I saw the face of the dead man. . . .

8 / Limehouse Police Station

AT THE MOMENT that I obtained my first glimpse of the face of the man whose body was being sewn up in sailcloth I saw, also, that his arms were crossed on his breast.

Both hands had been amputated.

A spasm of anger, revulsion, nausea, swept over me. I half withdrew the automatic from my pocket; then sanity conquered. I sat still and watched. Lowering my head inch by inch, I presently discerned the pock-marked features of the stitcher. I had seen that hideous mask before: it belonged to one of Dr Fu Manchu's Burmese killers. The yellow lantern light left the sunken eyes wholly in shadow and painted black hollows under prominent cheekbones.

Ss! hissed the thread drawn through canvas—*ss!* as those sinewy fingers moved swiftly upon their task. My dreadful premonitions were dismissed.

The dead man was not Nayland Smith but Dr Oster.

In some incomprehensive way Fu Manchu's servants had smuggled the body from the house in Regent's Park. I suppressed a sigh of relief. The movements of the dacoit cast grotesque shadows upon walls and ceiling of the cellar as I crouched staring at the mutilated remains of the man I had shot.

Horror heaped on horror had had the curious result of inducing acute mental clarity. During the few minutes—not more than three—that I remained there I conceived, and rejected, plan after plan. The best, as I still believe, was to rush the Burman, stun him and await a new arrival—for palpably he could not complete the business of disposing of the body without assistance. Under cover of my automatic I would compel whoever came to lead me to an exit.

This plan was never put into operation.

I was calculating my chances of getting through the doorway and silently overpowering a formidable adversary when I was arrested by a sound of light rapid footsteps which approached from beyond the luminous band from that end of the passage which I had not explored. I was too late. Now I must act quickly if I were to escape detection.

Twisting sideways, I began to crawl back up the steps. I gained the passage above and on hands and knees crept into the shadows. Nor did I win cover a moment too soon. A gigantic figure, wearing only a dark vest and trousers, passed, with the swift, lithe tread of a panther, down the steps and into the cellar not two yards away. It was Hassan, the white Nubian!

I stood up, my back pressed to an icy cold wall, automatic in hand, listening.

"Master order fix weights quick." (Hassan spoke in his odd English, presumably the only language he had in common with the Burman.) "Must move sharp. I carry him. You bring lamp and open river door."

On hearing those words yet another plan occurred to me: if I could follow the funeral procession undetected, this river door to which Hassan referred might serve a living man as well as a dead one. Success or failure turned upon the toss of a coin.

Which way were they going?

If I remained where I was and the cortege turned left, I could not fail to be discovered; if I moved quickly to the other side of the bar of light and they went to the right, then my fate would be sealed.

I determined to remain in my present hiding place and, if

the Burman saw me, to shoot him and throw myself upon the mercy of Hassan.

Much movement, clang of metal and smothered muttering reached me from the cellar, the husky bass of Hassan's voice being punctuated with snarling monosyllables which I judged to represent the Burman's replies. At last came a significant shuffling, a deep grunt and a sound of approaching footsteps. The blind Nubian had the corpse on his back and was carrying it out. Fate had spun a coin; which way would it fall?

First came the Burman, holding the hurricane lantern. As he walked up the stone steps I tried to identify myself with the shadows; for although he presented a target which I could not have missed, although he was a professional assassin, a blood-lustful beast in human form, I shrank from the act of dispatching him.

He turned to the right.

Every movement he had made from the moment of his appearance at the base of the steps had been covered by my Colt. The giant figure of Hassan followed, stooping, Atlas-like, under his gruesome burden. He followed the lantern bearer.

I had not been seen.

And now, as that death march receded into the distance of the long, echoing passage, I stooped, rapidly unlaced my shoes and discarded them. Silently I followed. The cold of the stone paving numbing my feet, I crept along, preserving a discreet interval between myself and the corpse bearer, a huge, crouching silhouette against the leading light. His shadow, and the shadow of his load, danced hellishly upon the floor, upon the walls. upon the roof of the corridor.

The lantern disappeared. The Burman had walked into some opening on the left of the passage, for I saw a rectangular patch of light upon the opposite wall; I saw the burdened figure, bent under its mortal bale, turn and vanish too.

I pressed on to the corner. There were descending steps. Preserving a suitable distance from the moving lamp, I followed and found myself in a shadow-haunted place, a warehouse, fusty as some ancient vault to which the light of the sun had never penetrated, in which, picked out by the dancing yellow light, I saw stacks of cases through an aisle between which the lantern led me.

At the end of this aisle Hassan dropped his load. The muffled slump of the handless corpse was a sound which I was destined too often to remember.

"Open the door." He was breathless. "Got to be quick. We have to make our getaway too."

42

The supernormal clarity of brain remained. The place was about to be abandoned; presumably Dr Fu Manchu had already made good his escape. Visualising the Thames as I had seen it through the grille from the floor above, I determined that the door which the Burman was already unlocking must be close to water level. My course was clear: the issue rested with me.

A gust of damp air swept into the fusty stagnation of the warehouse; followed a subdued clangour. The lantern had been set on top of a crate, but dimly I discerned an opening and I knew what it represented. Whereas loads were hoisted to the upper floor, they were discharged to barges from the warehouse by way of this gangway which projected over the river at tidal level. From here the remains of Dr Oster were to be consigned to old Father Thames and held fast in his muddy embrace until mortal decay cast fragments upon some downstream shallow, fragments which no man should identify.

I could see no searchlights; nevertheless I could see the opening. I heard laboured breathing—creaking feet which supported striving bodies . . . dimly I heard the splash.

Then, Colt in hand, silent in shoeless feet, I rushed.

Silent, I say? Not silent enough for the blind Nubian. I was almost on the drawbridge, I had passed the Burman . . . when an arm like a steel band locked itself about me!

"Inshâllâh!"

Never had I experienced such acceptance of complete inertia. I am no weakling, but I know when I am mastered. The automatic was wrenched from my hand; I became crushed to that herculean body, a limp, useless thing. I divined, rather than perceived, that the dacoit stood behind me, knife raised. My brain, my brain alone, remained active.

"Hassan!" I panted. "Hassan, let me go!"

That unbreakable hold relaxed. Inexorably I was jerked forward. A stinging in my left shoulder and a sense of moisture told me how narrowly I had escaped death from the Burman's knife.

A thud—a snarl—the sound of a fall, and then:

"Take your chance," Hassan whispered. "No other way."

Lifting me above his head as Milo of Crotona might playfully have lifted a child, he hurled me into the river!

"WHO'S THERE?"

Breathless, all but spent, I swam for shore. There was a wharf, I remembered, and steps. That plunge into icy water had nearly defeated me. I had no breath with which to answer the challenge. A blue light shone out. I headed for it.

And as I laboured frantically a swift beam from the river picked me up. I heard shouted orders, the purr of an engine . . . my feet touched bottom; I staggered on towards the shore.

"Down the steps, Gallaho! There's someone swimming in. Douse that searchlight out there!"

Nayland Smith!

The light behind—it must have come from a river-police craft—shone on wooden steps and painted my own shadow before me. Suddenly it was shut off. The blue light ahead moved, came nearer, lower. I waded forward and was grasped and held upright—for I had come to the end of my endurance.

"It's Kerrigan," I whispered. "Hang onto me. I'm nearly through. . . ."

Chief Inspector Gallaho, a friend of former days, helped me to mount the steps. His lamp he extinguished, but I had had a glimpse of the familiar stocky figure, enveloped in oil-skins, of a wide-brimmed bowler, a grim red face.

"This *is* a surprise, Mr Kerrigan," he said as though he had unexpectedly met me in Piccadilly. "It will be first-class news for Sir Denis. You see, you being in their hands made our job a difficult one."

As we stepped onto the wharf:

"That you, Kerrigan?" came Smith's crisp voice.

"Yes, by heaven's mercy! Winded and drenched, but still alive."

"Straight through to the car," Smith went on rapidly. "Show a light, someone. A brisk rubdown and a hot grog at Lime-house Police Station will put you right."

Clenching my teeth, which displayed a tendency to chatter, I followed a lozenge of luminous blue which danced ahead along a gravel path.

"Here we are. Get in, Kerrigan. I leave you in charge here, Inspector. See that nothing, not even a rat, comes out; but make no move without orders from me."

Feeling not unlike a half-drowned rat myself, I tumbled into a car which stood there in the darkness, and Smith joined me.

"Limehouse Police Station," he said to the driver. "Step on it."

We set out along some narrow riverside street in which not one speck of light was visible. Then Nayland Smith re-laxed. He threw his arm around my shoulders, and in a voice quite unlike that in which he had been issuing orders:

"Kerrigan," he said, "this is a miracle! Thank God you're

44

safe. Even now I find it hard to believe. But first—are you hurt?"

The emotion betrayed by that man of iron touched me keenly.

"I'm sorry to have been such a nuisance, Smith," I replied awkwardly. "It was my own folly that gave you all this trouble. I'm all right, though I don't deserve to be. A knife scratch on my shoulder; nothing, I assure you."

"But you are chilled to the bone. Try to tell me all you can. Time is on the side of the enemy."

As the driver, whom I suspected to be Sergeant Sims of the flying squad, whirled us headlong through Limehouse darkness I told my story; I held nothing back, not even my belief that Ardatha had betrayed me to Fu Manchu's thugs.

"Probably wrong there," Smith commented staccato fashion. "But no matter at the moment. I followed the doctor to the garage—and was cleverly locked inside!—Place nearly soundproof. When the raid squad arrived, managed to attract their attention. While they were breaking in, Fu Manchu's gang smuggled Oster's body away and smuggled you away too. Barge on canal with auxiliary motor. House formerly belonged to certain foreign diplomat—hence peephole behind china cupboard . . ."

The brakes shrieked. I was all but thrown from my seat; a headlight shot out. I had a momentary glimpse of a narrow thoroughfare and of an evil-looking yellow man who staggered aside from the bonnet.

"Try thinkee where you go!" the driver shouted angrily. "Hophead!"

And we were off again.

"Barton made the only capture of the night——"

"What?"

"Doctor Fu Manchu's marmoset! It was for the marmoset Ardatha came back, Kerrigan. While we were searching the house—and little enough we found—the phone rang. I answered it . . . and Doctor Fu Manchu issued his ultamatum——"

"In person?"

"In person! Won't bore you with it now. Here we are!"

The car was pulled up in its own length.

"How did you get on my track?"

"Later, Kerrigan. Come on."

He dragged me into the station. . . .

A vigorous towelling before the open fire and a piping hot grog quite restored me. The scratch on my shoulder was no more than skin-deep—a liberal application of iodine soon staunched the bleeding. Wearing borrowed shoes and underwear and the uniform of a district inspector (which fitted me very well), I felt game again for anything. Smith was now wild with excitement to be off; he could not stand still.

"What you tell me unties my hands, Kerrigan. This hideout of Fu Manchu's is an old warehouse, marked by the local authorities for demolition but still containing a certain amount of stock. Lacking clear evidence, I dared not break in. The manager of the concern, a young German known to the police (he is compelled to report here at regular intervals), may or may not be a creature of the doctor's. In either case he has the keys. Point is that the officer who keeps the alien register if off duty; he has taken it home to do some work on it, and nobody knows the German's address!"

"But surely——"

"I have done that, Kerrigan! A police cyclist set out half an hour ago to find Sergeant Wyckham. But now I need not wait. You agree with me, Inspector?"

For a moment I failed to understand, until the laughter of the real inspector who had supervised my grooming reminded me of the fact that I was in uniform.

"For my part," said the police officer, "I don't think this man, Jacob Bohm, is a member of the gang. I think, though, that he suspected there was something funny going on."

"Why?" snapped Smith, glancing irritably at the clock.

"Well, the last time he came in, so Sergeant Wyckham told me, he hinted that he might shortly have some valuable information to offer us. He said that he was collecting evidence which wasn't complete yet but——"

A phone buzzed; he took up the instrument on his desk.

"Hullo—yes? Speaking. That you, Wyckham?" He glanced at Smith. "Found him, sir. . . . Yes, I'll jot it down." He wrote. "Jacob Bohm, 39B Pelling Street, Limehouse. And you say his landlady's name is Mullins? Good. The matter's of some importance, Sergeant. What was that you mentioned last week about the man? . . . Oh, he said he was putting the evidence in writing? He thought that what? . . . That there were cellars of which he had no keys but which were used after dark? I see. . . ."

"Kerrigan," snapped Smith, "feel up to a job?"

"Anything you say, Smith."

"There's a police car outside, as well as that from the Yard. Dash across to Pelling Street—the driver will know it—and get Jacob Bohm. I'm off. I leave this job to you. Bring him back here. I will keep in touch."

He turned whilst the inspector was still talking on the phone, but I grabbed his arm.

"Smith—did you find any trace——"

"No." He spoke over his shoulder. "But Ardatha called me two minutes after Fu Manchu. She was responsible for your finding me where you found me tonight. Jump to it, Kerrigan. This German may have valuable information."

He had reached the office door, the inspector had hung up the receiver and was staring blankly after him, when again the phone buzzed. The inspector took up the instrument, said, "Yes—speaking," and then seemed to become suddenly tensed.

"One moment, sir!" he cried after Smith. "One moment!"

Smith turned, tugging at the lobe of his ear.

"Well—what is it?"

"River police, sir. Excuse me for a second."

He began to scribble on a pad, then:

"Yes—I follow. Nothing on him in the way of evidence? No—I will act at once. Good-bye."

He hung up again, staring at Smith.

"They have just hauled Jacob Bohm out of the river off Tilbury," he said. "A ship's anchor caught him. He was sewn up in sailcloth. Both hands had been amputated."

9 / 39B Pelling Street

OF MY DRIVE to Pelling Street, a short one, I remember not one detail except that of a searchlight which, as we turned a corner, suddenly cleaved the dark sky like a scimitar. I had thought that the man's death rendered the visit unnecessary. Smith had assured me that it rendered it more than ever important.

"He was putting the evidence in *writing*, Kerrigan. We want his notes. . . ."

I mused in the darkness. It was Ardatha who had saved me! This knowledge was a burning inspiration. In some way she had become a victim of the evil genius of Dr Fu Manchu; her desertion had not been a voluntary one. Then as the police driver threaded a way through streets which all looked alike I found myself considering the fate of Jacob Bohm, the strange mutilation of Dr Oster, those ghastly exhibits in the glass case somewhere below the old warehouse.

"Note the yellow hands"—I heard that harsh, guttural voice plainly as though it had spoken in my ear—"they were contributed by a blond Bavarian. . . ." Could I doubt now that the

47

blond Bavarian was Jacob Bohm? I should have been Fu Manchu's next ember thrown to that Moloch of science before whom he immolated fellow men as callously as the Aztec priests offered human sacrifices to Quetzacoatl. . . .

Number 39B was identical in every way with its neighbours. All the houses stood flush to the pavement; so much I could make out; all were in darkness. In response to my ring Mrs Mullins presently opened the door. A very dim light showed (I saw that some sort of black-out curtain hung behind her), but it must have enabled her to discern my uniform.

"Oh, good God!" she exclaimed, "have the Germans landed?"

Her words reminded me of the part I had to play.

"No, ma'am," I replied gruffly. "I am a police inspector——"

"Oh, Inspector, I haven't shown a peep of light! Truly I haven't. When them sirens started howling I put out every light in the house. Even when I heard the all-clear I only used candles."

"There's no complaint. Are you Mrs Mullins?"

"That's my name, sir."

"It's about your lodger, Jacob Bohm, that I'm here."

The portly figure, dimly seen, appeared to droop.

"Oh!" she whispered. "I always expected it."

I went in. Mrs Mullins closed the door, dropped the curtain, which I recognised for an old counterpane, and turned to face me in a little sitting room, candle-lighted, which was clean, tidy and furnished in a way commemorated by *Punch* artists of the Edwardian era. She was a stout grey-haired woman and no toper, but tonight her abode spoke of gin. She extended her hands appealingly.

"Don't say Little Jake was a spy, sir!" she exclaimed. "He was like a son to me. Don't tell me——"

"When did you see him last?"

"Ah, that's it! He didn't come home last night, and I thought to myself, that's funny. Then tonight, when the young lady from the firm called and explained it was all right——"

"What young lady—someone you know?"

"Oh no, sir—I've never seen her before. But she was sure he'd be back later and went up to wait for him. Then that air-raid warning came and——"

"Where is this——"

I ceased speaking. A faint sound had reached my ears, coming from beyond a half-opened door. Someone was stealing downstairs!

In one bound I reached the door, threw it open and looked up. Silhouetted against faint light from above, a woman's figure turned and dashed back! With springs in my heels I followed, leapt into a room a pace behind her and stood squarely in the doorway.

She had run towards a curtained window, and I saw her in the light of a fire, sole illumination of the room, and that which had shone down the stair. She wore a dark raincoat and a small close-fitting hat from beneath which the glory of her hair cascaded in iridescent waves. Dancing firelight touched her face, more pale than usual, and struck amethyst glints from her lovely eyes. But my heart had already prepared me to meet "the young lady from the firm."

"It seems I came just in time, Ardatha," I said, and succeeded in speaking coolly.

She faced me, standing quite still.

"You!" she whispered. "So you *are* of the police! I thought so!"

"You are wrong; I am not. But this is no time to explain." I had formed a theory of my own to account for her apparent ignorance of all that had passed between us, and I spoke gently. "I owe you my life, Ardatha, and it belongs to you with all else I have. You said you would try to understand. You must help me to understand too. What are you doing here?"

She took a step forward, her eyes half fearful, her lips parted.

"I am obeying orders which I must obey. There are things which you can never understand. I believe you mean all you say, and I want to trust you." Prompted by some swift impulse, she came up to me and rested her hands upon my shoulders, watching me with eyes in which I read a passionate questioning. "God knows how I want to trust you."

Almost I succumbed; her charm intoxicated me. As her accepted lover I had the right to those sweet, tremulous lips. But I had read the riddle in my own way, and, clenching my teeth, I resisted that maddening temptation.

"You may trust me where you cannot trust yourself, Ardatha," I said quietly. "I am yours here and hereafter. Shake off this horrible slavery. Come with me now. The laws of England are stronger than the laws of Doctor Fu Manchu. You will be safe, Ardatha, and I will teach you to remember all you have forgotten."

But I kept my hands tightly clenched at my sides; for, once in my arms, all those sane resolutions regarding her would have been swept away and I knew it.

"Perhaps I want to do so—very much," she whispered. "Perhaps"—she glanced swiftly up at me and swiftly down again—"this *is* remembrance. But if such a thing is ever to be, first I must live. If I came with you now I should die within one month."

"That is nonsense!" I spoke hotly and regretted my violence in the next breath. "Forgive me! I would see that you were safe—even from *him*."

Ardatha shook her head. The firelight, which momentarily grew brighter, played wantonly in dancing curls.

"It is only with him that I can be safe," she replied in a low voice. "He is well served because no one of the Si-Fan dare desert him."

"Why? Whatever do you mean?"

Her hands clutched me nervously; she hid her face.

"There is an injection. It produces a living death—catalepsy. But there is an antidote, too, which must be used once each two weeks. I have enough for one month more of life. Then —I should be buried, for dead. Perhaps he would dig up my body: he has done such things before. No one else could save me . . . only Doctor Fu Manchu. And so, you see, with so many others, I am just his helpless slave. Now do you begin to understand?"

Begin to understand? My blood was boiling, yet my heart was cold. I remembered how I had tried to kill the Chinese ghoul and realised that had I succeeded Ardatha would have been lost to me forever, that she . . . But sanity forbade my following that train of thought to its dreadful conclusion.

Such a wild yearning overcame me, so mad a desire to hold and to protect her from horrors unnameable, that, unwilled, mechanically, my arm went about her shoulders. She trembled slightly but did not resist.

"You see"—the words were barely audible—"you must let me go. Forget Ardatha. Except by the will of Doctor Fu Manchu I can be nothing to you or to any man. I can only try to prevent him harming you." She raised her eyes to me. "Please let me go."

But I stood there, stricken motionless, gripped by anguish such as I had never known. My very faith in a just God was shaken by this revelation, by recognition of the fact that a fiend could use this perfect casket of a human soul as a laboratory experiment, reduce a beautiful woman, meant for love and happiness, to the level of a beast of burden—and escape the wrath of Heaven. I wondered if any lover since the world began had suffered such a moment.

Yet Fu Manchu was mortal. There must be a way.

50

"I shall let you go, my dearest. But don't accept the idea that it is for good. What has been done by one man can be undone by another." I continued to speak quietly and as I would have spoken to a frightened child. "Tell me first why you came here."

"For Jacob Bohm's notes that he was making to give to the police," she answered simply. "I have burned everything. Look—you can see the ashes in the fire."

As she spoke I understood why the fire had burned up so brightly. A glance was sufficient to convince me that not a fragment could be recovered.

"And when you leave here where are you going?"

"It is impossible for me to tell you that. But there are servants of the Si-Fan watching this house." (I thought of the yellow-faced man whom we had nearly run down.) "Even if you were cruel enough to try, you could not get me away. I think"—she hesitated, glanced swiftly up—"that tonight or in the early morning we leave for America."

"America!"

"Yes." She slipped free—for I had kept my arm about her shoulders. "I just could not bear to . . . say good-bye. Please look away for only a moment—if you really care for my happiness: I beg of you!"

There was abandonment, despair, in her pleading voice. No man could have refused, and after all I was not a police officer. I looked long and hungrily into those eyes which tonight were like twin amethysts and walked across to the fire.

"I will try, I will try to see you again—to speak to you."

Only the faintest sound, a light tread on the stair, told me that Ardatha was gone. . . .

10 / Barton's Secret

"I DON'T BLAME YOU, KERRIGAN," said Nayland Smith; "in fact, I cannot see what else you could have done."

"Damn it, nor can I!" growled Barton.

We were back in my flat after a night of frustration for which, in part, I held myself responsible. Barton had admitted us. He had returned an hour earlier, having borrowed my key. The police had forced a way into the old warehouse; they were still searching it when I rejoined the party. The room, the very bench on which Dr Oster's corpse had lain, fragments of twine, they had found, but nothing else. The river was being dragged for the body.

That laboratory which smelt like the morgue was below river level; it had been flooded. Only by means of elaborate pumping operations could we hope to learn what evidence still remained there of the nature of the doctor's mysterious and merciless experiments.

"Infernally narrow escape for both of us, Kerrigan," said Sir Lionel; and, crossing to the buffet, he replenished his glass. "Good shot, that of yours." He squirted soda water from a syphon. "I owe my life to you; you owe yours to Ardatha. Gad, there's a girl! But what an impossible situation!"

Smith stood up and, passing, grasped my shoulder.

"Even worse situations have been dealt with," he said. "I am wondering, Kerrigan, if you have recognised the clue to Ardatha's loss of memory?"

As he began to pace to and fro across my dining room:

"I think so!" I replied. "That yellow devil decided to reclaim her, and it was he who destroyed her memory!"

"Exactly—as he has done before, with others. I said to you some time ago Fu Manchu once had a daughter——"

"Smith!" I interrupted excitedly, "it was not until I saw Ardatha in Pelling Street that the meaning of those words came to me. If he did not hesitate in the case of his own flesh and blood to efface all memories of identity, why should he hesitate in the case of Ardatha?"

"He didn't! Ardatha remembers only that she is called Ardatha. Fu Manchu's daughter, whom once I knew by her childish name of Fah-lo-Suee, became Koreâni. You can bear me out, Kerrigan; you have met her."

"Yes, but——"

"Ardathas and Koreânis are rare. Doctor Fu Manchu has always employed beauty as one of his most potent weapons. His own daughter he regarded merely as a useful instrument when he saw that she was beautiful. He found Ardatha difficult to replace; therefore he recalled her. Oh, she had no choice. But she has the proud spirit of her race—and so he bound her to him by this damnable living death from which there is no escape!"

He was pacing the carpet at an ever-increasing speed, his pipe bubbling furiously, and something which emanated from that vital personality gave me new courage. I was not alone in my fight to save Ardatha from the devil doctor.

"Smith," said Sir Lionel, leaning back against the buffet—for even his tough constitution had suffered in the night's work and he was comparatively subdued—"this infernal thing means that if I saw Fu Manchu before me now I couldn't shoot him!"

"It does," Smith replied. "He was prepared to hold Kerrigan as a hostage; he overlooked the fact that whilst Kerrigan lived Ardatha served the same purpose."

Barton plunged his hands in his trouser pockets and became lost in reflection. His deep-set blue eyes danced queerly.

"We both know the Chinese," he murmured. "I don't think I should give up hope, Kerrigan. There may be a way."

"I'm sure there is—there must be!" I broke in. "Doctor Fu Manchu is subject, after all, to human laws. He is supernormal but not immortal. We all have our weaknesses. Mine, perhaps, is my love of Ardatha. He must have his. Smith! We must find Koreâni!"

"I found her two months ago."

"What!"

"She was then in Cuba. Where she is now I cannot say. But if you suppose that Fu Manchu would turn a hairsbreadth from his path to save his daughter, you are backing the wrong horse. Assuming that we could capture her, well—as an exchange for Ardatha (freed from the living death; for I have known others who have suffered it but who live today), she would be a worthless hostage. He would sacrifice Koreâni without a moment's hesitation!"

I was silent.

"Buck up, Kerrigan," said Sir Lionel. "I said there might be a way, and I stick to it."

Smith stared at him curiously, and then:

"As for you," he remarked, "as usual you are an infernal nuisance."

"Don't mention it!"

"I must. Your inquiries in Haiti last year, followed by your studies in Norfolk and, finally, your conversations with the War Office, attracted the attention of Doctor Fu Manchu."

"Very likely."

"It was these conversations, reported to me whilst I was in the West Indies, that brought me back post haste——"

"Fu Manchu got here first," Barton interrupted. "There were two attempts to burgle my house. Queer-looking people were watching Abbots Hold. Finally I received a notice signed 'President of the Seven,' informing me that I had twenty-four hours in which to hand over certain documents."

"You have this notice?" Smith asked eagerly.

"I had; it was in the stolen bag."

Smith snapped his fingers irritably.

"And when you received it what did you do?"

"Bolted. I was followed all the way to London. That was why I phoned Kerrigan and came here. I didn't want to be alone."

"You were right," said Smith, "but you came to your senses too late. I am prepared to hear that the fact of Fu Manchu's interest in your affairs did not dawn upon you until you got this notice?"

"Suspected it before that. These reports from the Caribbean suggested that something very queer was afoot there. It occurred to me that bigger things than a mere treasure hunt were involved, so I offered my services to the War Office——"

"And behaved so badly that you were practically thrown out! Let me explain what happened. Your earlier correspondence with the War Office, although obscure, was considered to be of sufficient importance to be transmitted in code to me—I was then in Kingston, Jamaica. I dashed home. I went first to Norfolk, learned you had left for London and followed. That was yesterday morning. I was dashing about town trying to pick you up. I practically followed you into the War Office, and what you had said there convinced me that at all costs I must find you."

"The War Office can go to the devil," growled Barton, refilling his glass.

"I say," Smith went on patiently, "that I tried to tail you in London. I still have facilities, you know!" He smiled suddenly. "I gathered that you had gone to the British Museum——"

"Yes—I had."

"I failed to find you there."

"Didn't look in the right room."

"Possibly not. But I looked into one room which offered certain information." He paused to relight his pipe. "You have been working for years hunting down the few clues which remain to the hiding place of the vast treasure accumulated by Christophe of Haiti. You know your business, Barton; you haven't your equal in Europe or America when it comes to archaeological research."

"Thank you," growled Barton. "You may join the War Office and also go to the devil, with my compliments."

Through chinks in the blinds the first spears of dawn were piercing, cold and grey in contrast with the lamplight.

"Your compliments might prove to be an admirable introduction. But to continue: You, ahead of them all, even ahead of the Si-Fan and Doctor Fu Manchu, got onto the track of the family to whom these clues belong. You traced them by generations. And you ultimately obtained from the last bearer of the name certain objects known as The Stewart Luck, amongst them Christophe's chart showing where the bullion lies. I do not inquire *how* you managed this."

"It isn't necessary," Barton blazed. "I have my own methods. Buried history must be torn remorselessly from its hiding place and set in the light of day. Once I have established facts I allow nothing to stand in my way."

"You are not enlightening me," said Smith drily. "My experiences with you in Khorassan, in Egypt and elsewhere had already convinced me of this. Your latest discovery from the Portuguese of Da Cunha (you see, I did not entirely waste my time in the British Museum) added enormously to your knowledge——"

Sir Lionel appeared to be about to burst into speech, but he restrained himself; he seemed to be bewildered. Smith paused, pulled out a notecase and from it extracted a piece of paper. Switching on the green-shaded lamp on the desk, he read aloud:

"Da Cunha says that there is 'a great and lofty cave in which a fleet might lie hid, save that the way in from the sea, although both deep and wide and high, is below the tide, so that none but a mighty swimmer could compass the passage.' . . . He adds that the one and only entrance from the land has been blocked but goes on: 'Failing possession of Christophe's chart, no man can hope to reach the treasure.' "

Sir Lionel Barton was standing quite still, staring at Smith as one amazed.

"That quotation from a rare Portuguese ms. in the manuscript room," said Smith, placing the fragment in his case, the case in his pocket, and turning to look at Barton, "you copied. The curator told me that you had borrowed the ms. Since the collection is closed to the public at present, you abused your privileges and were vandal enough to make some pencil marks on the parchment. I said, you will remember, that I was unable to find you there. I did not say that I failed to find your tracks."

Barton did not speak, nor did I, and:

"It was knowing what you had discovered," Smith continued, "which spurred my wild dash to find you. The bother in the Caribbean is explained. There is a plot to bottle up the American navy. Fu Manchu has played a big card."

"You are sure it *is* Fu Manchu?"

"Yes, Barton. He has a secret base in or near Haiti, and he has a new kind of submarine. No one but you—until tonight—knew of this other entrance to the cave. It is shown in that chart which was stolen from you by agents of Doctor Fu Manchu. . . ."

"Suppose it is!" cried Barton; "what I should like you to tell me, if you can, is how, if Fu Manchu is using this place as a base, he gets in and out. You don't suppose he swims? Granting that small submarines can pass through under water, small submarines can't carry all the gear needed for a young dockyard!"

"That point is one to which I have given some attention," said Smith. "It suggests that 'the one and only entrance from the land,' referred to by Da Cunha, is not the entrance shown in the chart."

"You mean there are two?"

"Quite possibly."

"Then why should these Si-Fan devils go to such lengths to get hold of my chart?"

"Surely that is obvious? They feared an attack from this unknown point. They knew that the intelligence services of two countries were making intensive inquiries, for whilst that 'great and lofty cave' remains undiscovered it is a menace to us and to the United States."

"It's to the United States," said Barton, "that I am offering my services. My own country, as usual, has turned me down."

"Nevertheless," rapped Smith, "it is to your own country that you are offering your services. Listen. You retired from the army with the rank of major, I believe. Very well, you're lieutenant colonel."

"What!" shouted Barton.

"I've bought you from the War Office. You're mine, body and soul. You're Lieutenant Colonel Sir Lionel Barton, and you lead the expedition because I shall be in comparatively unfamiliar territory. But remember, you act under my orders."

"I prefer to act independently."

"You've been gazetted lieutenant colonel and you're under the orders of the War Office. There's a clipper leaves for the United States on Monday from Lisbon. I have peculiar powers. Be good enough to regard me as your commanding officer. Here are your papers."

11 / The Hostage

I DREW THE BLINDS and stared down at Bayswater Road, dismal in the light of a wet grey dawn. Sleep was out of the question. Two men stood talking over

56

by the park gate—the gate at which Ardatha had reappeared in my life. Although I heard no one enter the room behind me, a hand was placed on my shoulder. I started, turned and looked into the lean, sun-baked face of Nayland Smith.

"It's rough on you, Kerrigan," he said quietly. "Really, you need rest. I know what you were thinking. But don't despair. Gallaho has set a watch on every known point of departure."

"Do you expect any result?"

He watched me for a moment, compassionately, and then:

"No," he replied; "she is probably already on her way to America."

I stifled a groan.

"What I cannot understand," I said, "is how these journeys are managed. Fu Manchu seems to travel a considerable company and to travel fast. He was prepared to include Barton and myself in the party. How is it done, Smith?"

"I don't know! I have puzzled over that very thing more times than enough. He returned from the West Indies ahead of me, yet no liner carried him and no known plane. Granting, for it is true, that he commands tremendous financial resources, in wartime no private yacht and certainly no private plane could go far unchallenged. I don't know. It is just another of those mysteries which surround Doctor Fu Manchu."

"Those two men are watching the house, Smith."

"It's their job: Scotland Yard! We shall have a bodyguard up to the moment that we leave Croydon by air for Lisbon. This scheme to isolate the United States navy is a major move in some dark game. It has a flaw—and Barton has found it!"

"But they have the chart——"

"Apart from the fact that he has copied the chart Barton has an encyclopedic memory—hence Fu Manchu's anxiety to make sure of him."

London was not awake; it came to me that Nayland Smith and I alone were alive to a peril greater than any which had ever threatened the world. In the silence, for not even the milkmen were abroad yet, I could hear Barton breathing regularly in the spare bedroom—that hardened old campaigner could have slept on Judgment Day.

My phone bell rang.

"What's this?" muttered Smith.

I opened the communicating door and went into the writing room. I took up the receiver.

"Hullo," I said. "Who wants me?"

"Are you Paddington 54321?"

"Yes."

"Call from Zennor. . . . You're through, miss."

My heart began to beat wildly as I glanced towards the open door where Nayland Smith, haggard in grey light, stood watching.

"Is that—you?" asked a nervous voice.

I suppose my eyes told Smith; he withdrew and quietly closed the door.

"Ardatha! My dear, my dear! This is too wonderful! Where are you?"

"I am in Cornwall. I have risked ever so much to speak to you before we go, and we are going in an hour——"

"But, Ardatha!"

"Please listen. Time is so short for me. Hassan told me what had happened. I knew your name and found your number in the book. It was my only chance to know if you were alive. I thank the good God that you are, because, you see, I am so alone and unhappy, and you—I like to believe that I have forgotten now, because otherwise I should be ashamed to think about you so much!"

"Ardatha!"

"We shall be in New York on Thursday. I know that Nayland Smith is following us. If I am still there when you arrive I will try to speak to you again. There is one thing that might save me—you understand?—a queer, a silly little thing, but——"

"Yes, yes, Ardatha! What is it? Tell me!"

"I risked capture by the police to try to catch Peko—Doctor Fu Manchu's marmoset. That was when . . . we met. This strange pet, he is very old, is more dear to his master than any living thing. Try to find out——"

Silence: I was disconnected!

Frantically I called the exchange, but all the consolation I received from the night operator was:

"Zennor's rung off, sir."

"Smith!" I shouted and burst into the dining room.

Nayland Smith was standing staring out of the window. He turned and faced me.

"Yes," he said coolly; "it was Ardatha. Where is she and what had she to say?"

Rapidly, perhaps feverishly, I told him; and then:

"The marmoset!" I cried. "Barton caught it! What did he do with it?"

"Do with it!" came Sir Lionel's great voice, and he appeared at the other end of the room, his mane of hair di-

shevelled. "What did it do with *me?* After the blasted thing
—it's all of a thousand years old, and I know livestock—had
bitten me twice last night I locked it in the wardrobe. This
morning——"

He raised a bloodstained finger; there was a shrill, angry
whistle, and a tiny monkey, a silver grey thing no larger
than a starling, shot through the doorway behind him, paused,
chattered wickedly and sprang from the buffet onto a high
cornice.

"There's your marmoset!" cried Barton. "I should have
strangled him if I hadn't known Chinese character! I said,
Kerrigan, there might be a way. This is the way—there's
your hostage!"

12 / *The Snapping Fingers*

"THE UNACCOUNTABLE ABSENCE of Kennard
Wood," said Nayland Smith, staring out of the window, "is most disturbing. These apartments, Kerrigan, have
been the scene of strange happenings. It was from here that
I opposed Doctor Fu Manchu when he tried and nearly succeeded in his plan to force a puppet president upon the United
States."

I stood beside him looking out over the roofs of New
York from this eagle's nest on the fortieth floor of the Regal
Athenian Hotel.

A pearly moon regarded us from a cloudless sky, a moon
set amidst a million stars which twinkled above a Walt
Disney city. One tall tower dominated the foreground of the
composition. It rose, jewelled with lights, from the frosty line
of an intervening roof up to the pharos which crowned it.
The river showed as a smudge of silver far below; an approaching train was a fiery dragon winding in and out of
mysterious gullies.

In that diamond-clear air I could hear the sound of the
locomotive; I could hear a motor horn, the hoarse whistle of
some big ship heading out for the open sea. Lights glittered
everywhere, from starry heavens down to frostily sparkling
buildings and the moving head lamps of restless traffic.

"Bit of a contrast to London," I said.

"Yes." Smith pronounced the word with unusual slowness. "The fog of war has not dimmed the lights of New
York. But you and I know who is responsible for those
rumours and those missing men in the Caribbean; and although, according to your account, the doctor is a sick man,

we dare not underestimate potentialities. Even now he may be here."

As always, the mere suspicion that the dreadful Chinese scientist might be near induced a sense, purely nervous no doubt, of sudden chill. We had been delayed unexpectedly at Lisbon and again later; it was possible that Fu Manchu was approaching New York. If Ardatha's words had been true, he was already here. . . .

Ardatha! She had promised to try to see me again. I continued to stare out at the myriad twinkling points. From any one of the constellation of windows Ardatha might be looking as I looked from this.

"I am getting seriously worried about Kennard Wood," said Smith suddenly. "According to his last message from Havana he and his assistant, Longton, were leaving by air. They are long overdue. I don't understand it."

Colonel Kennard Wood, of the United States Secret Service, had been left in charge of the Caribbean inquiry when Smith had hurriedly returned to England; we had been expecting him all day. In fact, Barton had been compelled to go to Washington that morning in Smith's stead owing to the importance of the anticipated interview.

There were times when I felt as one who dreams, when, seeing a double newspaper headline, "Great naval battle in Skagerrak," I asked myself what I was doing here at an hour when England and France grappled with a world menace. It was Smith who always supplied the answer: "An even greater menace, one which threatens the entire white race, is closing around the American continent."

The phone buzzed.

Smith turned swiftly and crossed to the instrument.

"Yes—speaking. . . . *What?*"

The tone in which he rapped out the last word brought me about. His eyes glittered metallically, and I saw—those prominent jaw muscles betrayed the fact—that his teeth were clenched.

"Good God! You are sure? Yes . . . at once."

He banged the receiver back and stared at me, suddenly haggard.

"Smith! What has happened?"

"Longton—poor Longton has gone!"

"What!"

"They have just brought his body in from the river. Inspector Hawk of the homicide bureau recognised him in spite of——"

"In spite of what?"

"Of his condition, Kerrigan!" He dashed a fist wildly into his other palm. "Fu Manchu is here—of that we may be sure, for no one but Fu Manchu could have brought the horror of the Snapping Fingers to New York."

"The Snapping Fingers?"

But he was already running towards the door.

"Explain on the way. Come on!"

Seated in a chair in the lobby, the chair tipped back so that he could rest his feet on the ledge above a radiator, was a short, thickset man whose clean-shaven red face, close-cropped dark hair and bright eyes had at first sight reminded me of my old friend Chief Inspector Gallaho of Scotland Yard. As Smith came charging out the man righted his chair, sprang up and began spluttering. Following Smith's example, I hurriedly put on my topcoat. An unpleasant regurgitating sound drew my attention to the man on guard.

"Say, mister," he said, "what's the big hurry?" He began to chew, for in this respect also he resembled Gallaho, except that Gallaho's chewing was imaginary. "Nearly make me swallow my gum——"

"Listen," Smith broke in; "I'm going out. There may easily be an attempt to get into this apartment tonight——"

"Say—*I'm* here."

"I want to make sure," said Smith, "that you don't stay there. These are your instructions: Having made sure that all windows are secure——"

"What, on the fortieth?"

"As you say, on the fortieth: having made sure of this, patrol every room in the suite, including the bathrooms, at intervals of fifteen minutes. If you find anything alive—except, of course, the monkey in a cage in Sir Lionel's room—kill it. This applies to a fly or a roach. Do I make myself clear?"

"Sure, it's clear enough, chief——"

"Do it. If in doubt, call headquarters. I count upon you, Sergeant Rorke."

Throwing the door open, he ran to the elevator and I followed.

"SMITH!" I said as we were whirled in a police car through kaleidoscopic streets, "what has happened to Longton—and what did you mean by the Snapping Fingers?"

"I meant a signal of death, Kerrigan. Poor Longton—whom you don't know and will never know now—may have heard it."

"I saw how the news affected you. Is it—something very horrible?"

Propped in a corner of the racing car, he began to load his pipe.

"Very horrible, Kerrigan. Some foul things have come out of the East, but this thing belongs to the West Indies. Of course it may have a Negro origin. But at one time it assumed the size of an epidemic."

"In what way? I don't understand."

"Nor do I. It remains a mystery to the scientists. But it began, as far as I can make out, in the Canal Zone. A young coloured man, employed on one of the locks, was found in his quarters one morning bled white."

"Bled white?"

"Almost literally." He lighted the charred briar. "He was dead, apparently from exhaustion. There were queerly discoloured areas on his skin—but there was practically no blood in his body——"

"No blood?" I cried over the noise of the motor and the Broadway traffic. "What do you mean?"

"He had been reduced to a sort of human veal. Something had drained all the blood from his veins."

"Good heavens! But were there no traces—no bloodstains?"

"Nothing. He was the first of many. Then, unaccountably, the terror of the Zone disappeared."

"Vampire bats?"

"This was suspected, but some of the victims—and they were not all coloured—had been found in rooms to which a bat could not have gained access."

"Was human agency at work?"

"No. Conditions, in certain cases, ruled it out."

"But—the Snapping Fngers?"

"This clue came later. It was first reported when the epidemic struck Haiti; that is, just before I arrived there. A young American whose name escapes me—but he had been sent from Washington in connection with the reports of unknown submarines in the Caribbean—died in just the same way."

"Significant!"

"Very! But there were singular features in this case. It occurred at a hotel in Port-au-Prince. One odd fact was that a heavy service pistol, fully charged, was found beside him."

"Where was—the body?"

"In bed. But the mosquito net was raised as though he had been on the point of gettting up. Here occurred the first

62

reference to Snapping Fingers. It seems that he opened his door at about eleven o'clock at night and asked another resident who happened to be passing if he had snapped his fingers——"

"Snapped his fingers?"

"Yes—it's queer, isn't it? However, he was found dead in the morning."

"And no trace?"

"None. But I have a hazy suspicion that those in charge of the investigation didn't know where to look. However, the next victim was a German—undoubtedly a German agent. He died in exactly that way."

"At the same place?"

"The same hotel but not in the same room. But the case of the German differed in one respect: *someone else* heard the Snapping Fingers!"

Inside the speeding car was a fog of tobacco smoke; outside the lights of New York flashed by like a flaming ribbon.

"Who heard it?"

"Kennard Wood! He occupied the next room. I had just reached Port-au-Prince at the same time, although I was putting up elsewhere; so that I know more about the case of Schonberg—that was the German's name. After Schonberg had retired that night it appears that Kennard Wood became curious about what he was doing. From the end of one balcony to another was not a difficult climb, and with the exercise of a little ingenuity it is easy to peep through a slatted shutter. He crept along. The German's room was in darkness. He was about to climb back when he heard a sound like that of someone snapping his fingers!"

"From inside the room?"

"Yes. It was repeated several times, but no light was switched on. Kennard Wood returned. Schonberg was found dead in the morning. His door was locked; his shutters were still closed."

"What did you do when you heard this?"

"I went along at once. I have a pretty strong stomach, but the sight of that heavy Teutonic frame quite drained of blood . . . ugh! Fortunately for the hotel a number of cases occurred elsewhere, not only in Port-au-Prince but as far north as Cap Haitien. A story got about amongst the coloured population that it was voodoo, that someone they call the Queen Mamaloi (a fabulous woman supposed to live in the interior) was impatient for sacrifices. A perfect state of panic developed; no one dared to sleep. My God! To think that the fiend, Fu Manchu, has brought *that* horror to New York!"

"But what *is* it, Smith? What *can* it be?"

"Just another agent of death, Kerrigan. Some unclean thing bred in a tropical swamp. . . ."

13 / *What Happened in Sutton Place*

"IT IS MORE than I can bear, Smith," I whispered and turned away. "Although I didn't know Longton, it is more than I can bear."

"Probably painless, Mr. Kerrigan," said Inspector Hawk. "Cheer up, sir."

But there was nothing cheerful in his manner, his appearance or his voice. He was a tall, angular, gloomy person, depressingly taciturn; and he gave to each of his rare remarks the value of a biblical quotation. Under the harsh light of suspended lamps Longton lay on a stone slab. In life he had been slightly built; he had scanty fair hair and a small blond moustache. . . . There was a sound of dripping water.

"What have you got to say, Doctor?" asked Smith, addressing a stout red-faced man who beamed amiably through green-rimmed spectacles.

"A very unusual case," the police doctor replied breezily, "very unusual. Observe the irregular rose-coloured spots, the evidences of pernicious, or aplastic, anemia. A malarial subject, beyond doubt; but the actual cause of death remains obscure."

"Quite," snapped Smith; "most obscure. I am sorry to seem to check your diagnosis, Doctor—but James Longton had not suffered from malaria, and a month ago he was freshly coloured as yourself. Have you heard, by chance, of the minor epidemic which recently appeared in the Canal Zone and later in Haiti?"

"Some short account was published in the newspapers, but I don't believe medical circles paid much attention to it. In any case, there can be no parallel here."

"I fear I must disagree again: the parallel is exact. I suggest that anemia, however advanced, could never produce this result. The body is drained like that of a fly after a spider has gorged its fill." Smith turned abruptly to Inspector Hawk. "The man is nude. How was he found and where?"

"Found just as you see," the gloomy voice replied. "Brought in from West Channel, right below Queensborough Bridge. Kind of caught up on something; shone in the moonlight, and a river patrol made contact. I was once detailed to take care of Mr. Longton; recognised him right away."

"How long dead?" Smith asked the doctor.

"Well," he replied—and I detected a note of resentment—"if my views are of any value, I should say no more than four hours. Hypostasis had only just appeared and there is little rigidity."

"I agree," said Smith.

"Thank you."

Some further formalities there were, and then once more we sped through the bright lights of New York. Smith was plunged in such a mood of dejection that I did not care to interrupt it. We were almost in sight of the Regal Athenian before he spoke.

"Where did Longton die?" he exclaimed. "Why was he in New York without my being notified—and where is Kennard Wood?"

"It's all a dreadful mystery to me, Smith."

There was a momentary pause; we were whirling, issuing warning blasts, past busy night traffic when Smith suddenly leaned forward.

"Slow down!" he cried.

Our speed was checked; the police driver leaned back.

"Yes sir?"

"Go to 39B Sutton Place."

"Mrs Mendel Hammett's?"

"Yes. Move."

We were off again.

"But what is this, Smith?"

"A theory—and a hope," he replied. "Longton's body was found below Queensborough Bridge. Making due allowance for its unusual condition, I assume that it was thrown in near that spot some time tonight. Now how was a body transported and thrown into the river in that state? I suggested to myself that there must have been special conditions —and then I thought of Mrs Mendel Hammett——"

"Who is Mrs Mendel Hammett?"

"She is a relic of the past, Kerrigan, an institution: a patron of promising talent and a distant relation of poor Longton. I suddenly remembered his telling me that he had an apartment in her home which he was at liberty to occupy at any time. Now the garden of 39B Sutton Place runs down to the river; Queensborough Bridge is immediately below!"

"YOU NEED NOT watch me so anxiously, Sir Denis," said Mrs Mendel Hammett. "I am a crippled and weak-bodied old woman but not a weak-minded old woman. May I trouble you to light my cigarette?"

She lay stretched on a couch in a sitting room whose furnishings indicated the world traveller. The bright hazel eyes shadowed by heavy brows were those of a young girl; her skin retained its freshness; so that snow-white curling hair suggested the period of powder and patches.

"You are a wonderful woman, Mrs Mendel Hammett."

"I belong to a tough race," she replied, puffing her cigarette, "and in the company of my late husband I have been in some tough places. So Jim is dead? Well—if I can help you find out who killed him, count on me."

"In the first place," said Smith, speaking very gently, "I have gathered from Miss Dinsford, your secretary, that James Longton was not expected; that he arrived about six o'clock this evening and stated that he wished to use his apartments."

"He did, sir," the vibrant voice replied. "He had come by air from Havana and he said it was important that no one should know that he was here."

"He went up to his rooms," Smith continued, "particularly requesting that he should not be disturbed——"

"He said he was going to take a bath and lie down until dinnertime as he was tired out."

"Quite so. That is most important. Since then, I believe, you had not seen him?"

"I had not."

"Did he bring much baggage?"

"One light suitcase and a large portfolio."

"Who took them up?"

"He took them up himself."

"Then no one else entered his apartments?"

"No one. They were always kept ready for use. Later a maid would have turned down the bed and prepared the room——"

Momentarily the bright eyes clouded; Mrs Mendel Hammett knocked ash from her cigarette.

"People used to find a marked resemblance between Jim and Kennard Wood. I never saw it myself, although they were cousins on Jim's mother's side."

"I had certainly noted it," murmured Smith; "and now that this catastrophe has occurred I must look to the colonel's safety. Before I go up to examine these apartments, Mrs Mendel Hammett, may I ask if James Longton told you anything of Kennard Wood's whereabouts?"

"He told me that they had planned to arrive together;

that they had an important conference with you and some Washington people at the Regal Athenian in the morning. They were on point of leaving Havana by special government plane when Kennard Wood was overtaken by a messenger from the United States minister——"

"So Longton came alone?"

"He came alone. Kennard Wood was to follow as soon as possible, and Jim intended to call his hotel directly he—awoke. For some reason they were travelling in great secrecy."

"*I* know the reason," said Smith grimly. "If you will be good enough to excuse us . . . Come on, Kerrigan."

A grey-haired coloured manservant led the way upstairs, knocked upon and then unlocked a door. We switched on the light inside.

"Mr James' apartment, sir," he murmured.

One analytical stare Smith directed upon the man's face, and then:

"You may go," he said.

We entered James Longton's rooms. The first of these was a sitting room, furnished in a manner which betrayed the hand of a woman. Some of the pictures, however, were obviously autobiographical, and there were college groups and a collection of old pipes on a desk.

Nayland Smith, standing just inside the door which he had closed, began sniffing.

"Do you notice any unusual smell, Kerrigan?"

At that I, also, directed my attention to the atmosphere of the place, and:

"Yes," I replied, "there is a faint but very unpleasant smell. I am trying to place it."

"I have placed it!" said Smith. "I have come across it before. Now for the bedroom——"

He opened a door, found the switch and led the way into a small but adequately equipped bedroom. Beyond, on the right, I saw a curtained recess in which presumably there was a bath. The place had a spartan quality which may have reflected the character of the dead man, so that, noting a handsome Chinese casket on a table beside the bed—an item which seemed out of place—I was about to examine it when:

"Don't touch it!" snapped Smith. "Touch nothing. I am walking in the dark and taking no chances. The unusual smell is more marked here?"

Startled by his abrupt order, I turned from the box.

"Yes, it certainly seems to be. You have seen that the bed is much disarranged?"

"I have seen something else."

He crossed to the draped recess, went in and came out again.

"Longton undressed in the bathroom," he said; "his clothes are there. He had a bath and then lay down. It is clear that he was tired out. His suitcase you see there on a chair, unopened. He just got into bed as he was and fell into a deep sleep. Now you note a chill in the air?"

"Yes."

"Unless I am on a wrong track we shall find a window open."

He crossed and jerked the draperies aside. I saw moonlight glittering on water.

"Wide open!" he exclaimed; "a balcony outside."

And as he stood there peering out and flashing a torch, in a moment of perhaps psychic clarity I saw him against a different background: I saw the bloody horror of Poland, the sullen sorrow of Czechoslovakia, that grand defiance of Finland which I had known; and I saw guns blazing around once peaceful Norwegian fiords. An enemy pounded at the gates of cilivisation, but Nayland Smith was here; therefore here, and not in Europe, the real danger must lie. . . .

Smith turned and stared at the disordered bed.

"Observe anything unusual?" he snapped.

"It is all terribly untidy."

"Really, Kerrigan, as a star reporter you disappoint me. A hostess of Mrs Mendel Hammett's calibre does not expect a guest to lie on a blanket. The undersheet is missing!"

"Good God! You're right!"

He stared at me for a moment.

"They used it to lower his body to the garden," he said slowly. "I can see the rope marks on the balcony rail! There is an old, strong clematis growing up the wall below. One of Fu Manchu's thugs climbed it whilst Longton was in the bath; he may or may not have forced open the window. He returned later, bundled up the body and lowered it to an assistant waiting in the garden. Miss Dinsford showed me over the ground-floor rooms; unlikely that anyone should hear: these fellows work silently as stoats."

"But what killed him?" I cried. "There may be some clue here——"

I had turned to the disordered bed when:

"Stand back, Kerrigan!" Smith said sharply. "Touch nothing. Leave the search to me."

Arrested by his words, I stood there whilst he stripped the bed, opened the Chinese box (which contained nothing more lethal than cigarettes), explored every bookcase, cabinet, nook and cranny in the room. He was as painstaking in the other rooms, and from amongst Longton's possessions he selected the key of the suitcase, opened the case, examined its contents. And all the time he was sniffing—sniffing like a hound on a half-lost scent.

"The smell is fading?" he jerked. "You note this? I can spare no more time. But the room must be sealed: it is imperative. You have no doubt remarked that the large portfolio, mentioned by Mrs Mendel Hammett, has disappeared. . . ."

14 / We Hear the Snapping Fingers

AS I HURRIED PAST the hall porter's desk in the main entrance to the Regal Athenian a boy came running after me. Smith had been detained, but he was anxious that I should establish contact with Sergeant Rorke.

"Urgent message for you, Mr Kerrigan."

At sight of the handwriting on the envelope my heart skipped a beat; the message was from Ardatha! I tore it open, there where I stood, and read:

Please do not recognise me unless I am alone. I think I have been followed. I am in the main foyer: you can see me as you come up the steps. If there is anyone with me, go up to your apartment and I will try to call you.

The note was not signed.

Thrusting it into my pocket, I started up the imposing flight of carpeted stairs which had always reminded me of the palace scene in a Cinderella pantomime and surveyed the vast foyer. That cosmopolitan atmosphere for which the Regal Athenian was celebrated tonight was absent, but there was a considerable ebb and flow of after-theatre supper seekers. I saw Ardatha at once.

She was seated on a divan not five yards away, deep in conversation with a sallow-faced man. She wore a perfectly simple blue evening frock which outlined her slender figure provocatively, exposing her lovely arms and shoulders so that her head, poised proudly, with its crown of gleaming hair, set me thinking of a cameo by some great master. She did not so much as glance in my direction. But I knew that she had seen me.

Resolutely I walked along to the elevator and went up to our apartment. The knowledge that the presence of the sallow man alone had denied me at least a few stolen moments with Ardatha was a bitter pill to swallow; I could gladly have strangled him.

I opened the door to find Sergeant Rorke standing just inside. On recognising me his tense attitude relaxed and he began to chew again.

"Anything to report?"

"No sir—except that a lady calls up ten minutes ago. She won't leave her name. I just say you are out."

"Nothing from Sir Lionel Barton?"

"No sir. I'm a gladder man when he's back here. Feeding wild animals is no part of a police officer's duty." He displayed a bandaged finger. "There's one dead monkey on the books if I have my way."

But I went into the sitting room, lighted a cigarette and began to walk to and fro beside the telephone. Ardatha was here! She had tried to get in touch with me. She had been followed, but she would try again. That the fact of her presence meant also that Dr Fu Manchu could not terrorise me tonight. Ardatha was here; soon, perhaps, I should hear her voice. If I had ever doubted what she meant in my life (and certainly I had known always, for I had wanted to die when I believed that she had left me), tonight that swift vision of her dainty loveliness, her aloof, always mysterious personality, had confirmed the fact that without her I did not want to go on.

How long I wandered up and down the carpet, how many cigarettes I smoked, I cannot say. But at last the phone buzzed.

So utterly selfish was my mood, so completely was I absorbed in my dreams of Ardatha, that had the caller been Smith, or even the missing Kennard Wood, I know that I should have been disappointed. But it was Ardatha. . . .

"Please listen very carefully." Her adorable accent was unusually marked. "First, for someone else—a man called Colonel Kennard Wood will be killed tonight at some time before twelve o'clock. I cannot tell you how, and I do not know where he is, except that he is in New York. These—murders horrify me. Try to save this man."

"Ardatha——"

"Please, I beg of you! At any moment I may be discovered. We are setting out for Cristobal later tonight—as soon, I think, as Colonel Wood is dead. Tell me now if you found in London any trace of Peko, Doctor Fu Manchu's marmoset. He mourns him as one mourning a lost child."

"He's here, darling! We have him!"

70

"Ah!" The word reached me as a wondering sigh. "Please God you keep him safe! Tell me again. I cannot believe it: you have him?"

"We have him, Ardatha."

"He may mean escape for me—the end of the living death. Come to Cristobal . . . Bart. When you reach the Panama Canal——"

"Ardatha! It's more than I can suffer! Give me the word and I will see Doctor Fu Manchu now and test the value of this hostage!"

"Stop! It is impossible, I say! Listen: you can get in touch with me at the shop of Za——"

The line was disconnected.

"SO MUCH and yet so little!" said Smith.

He was pacing restlessly up and down, surrounding himself with a smoke screen of pipe fumes.

"One thing at least is clear," I declared: "Kennard Wood is doomed!"

"Don't say that, Kerrigan! The idea drives me mad. Longton gone—and Kennard Wood next, whilst I stay idle! I wish I had been here when Ardatha called you. However, my delay with the police resulted in another clue, but a baffling one——"

"What clue?"

"The sheet—the sheet in which Longton's body was thrown into the river—has been recovered."

"Well?"

"It is bloodstained all over!"

"But——"

"Don't tell me there were stains on the blanket, because I looked for them. Not a trace." He turned suddenly. "You have noticed no evidence here of the peculiar smell?"

"None. But I have placed it. I know of what it reminded me: a charnel house!"

"Exactly. Hullo! Who's this?"

The phone had buzzed, and he had the receiver off in a second.

"What! Kennard Wood? . . . Thank God! Quick, man—where are you? . . . At the Hotel Prado. No, no! Listen to me: I cannot explain now. But you simply must not dream of going to bed! Leave all lights on in your apartment, remain fully dressed and wait until I join you!"

Running out to the lobby, he gave rapid instructions to Sergeant Rorke.

"You understand?" he said finally: "Inspector Hawk is

downstairs. Tell him he is to start now, get this report and stand by at the Prado. Move."

As Sergeant Rorke went out Smith ran to the phone and called police headquarters. He was through in a matter of seconds. . . .

"I want a raid squad outside the Prado in five minutes. They may not be needed, but I want them there. Is it clear? Good." He hung up, and: "Come on, Kerrigan!" he cried.

A few minutes later we were hurrying through the foyer, but Ardatha was not there. We ran down the steps. A car belonging to the police department was always in attendance, so that without a moment of unnecessary delay we were off for the Hotel Prado. Somewhere a clock was chiming midnight.

I looked out from the speeding car, striving to obtain a glimpse of the faces of travellers in other cars, of those who entered and left restaurants. Had Ardatha been detected by the spy set to watch her? Had she risked a ghastly punishment in communicating with me? But such speculations were useless and selfish. Resolutely I fought to focus my mind on the drama of Kennard Wood.

Here, amid the supermodernity of New York, surrounded by millions of fellow creatures, a man lay in the shadow of a death which surely belonged to primeval swamps and jungles; already, in his apartment at the Prado, most up-to-date and fashionable Park Avenue hotel, Kennard Wood might even now have heard the Snapping Fingers!

As if he had divined my train of thought:

"It is possible," said Smith, "that some other method will be used against Kennard Wood. We cannot be sure. It is also highly probable that the doctor's watchdogs will be in the foyer." He leaned forward. "I am not familiar with the Prado, driver. Is there a staff entrance?"

"Sure—right on the corner of the block."

"Stop there—but not directly outside."

"It's one way, so we turn up here. . . ."

When Smith pushed open a revolving door I followed him into a place, tiled and brightly lighted, where a number of men and women in white overalls were moving about busily. I heard the rattle of dishes and in the distance caught sight of a man wearing a chef's cap. Another man, who wore evening dress, came towards us.

"Perhaps you have made a mistake," he began.

"No mistake," rapped Smith. "Police department. Inspector Hawk should be somewhere in the hotel. Send him a message to stand by near the main entrance and get me a house detective or anybody who is well acquainted with the building."

The authority in Smith's voice was unmistakable.

"It will save time if you will follow me, gentlemen."

Our guide led us through a maze of service rooms and kitchens which the normal guest at such a hostelry never sees, presently emerging in an office where a big dark-jowled man sat at a desk smoking a very short fragment of a very black cigar. As this man stood up:

"Oh, Sergeant Doherty," said our guide, "these police officers want a word with you."

From under heavy brows suspicious eyes regarded us.

"My name is Nayland Smith," explained my friend rapidly, indeed irritably. "Inspector Hawk is here?"

A swift change appeared upon Doherty's truculent-looking face.

"Why, surely, sir! I was puzzled for a moment, but I was here waiting for you. At your service, sir."

"Good." Smith turned to our guide. "Will you take my message to Inspector Hawk at once?"

"At once."

The man went out.

"Now, Sergeant Doherty, I want to go up to Colonel Kennard Wood's apartment without entering the public rooms."

"Easy enough. The waiters' elevator is just outside. This way."

As we came out of the office:

"What is the house detective's report?" asked Smith.

Sergeant Doherty closed the elevator door and pressed button 15.

"It's kind of funny," he replied. "The Prado is a smart place for supper these days, and Pannel—the house detective on duty—says that when the supper mob was coming in he got an idea somebody had a large dog."

"Large dog? I don't follow."

"Well, he says he hunted around, thinking some crazy deb, maybe, took a thing like that along to parties—and animals aren't allowed in the Prado. But except for that one glimpse he saw nothing of it again, whatever it was."

As we reached the fifteenth floor and stepped out of the elevator:

"Is Pannel a reliable observer?" asked Smith.

"Sure." We were following Doherty along a carpeted passage. "Used to be with us. Mind you, he doesn't swear it was a dog and he doesn't swear he wasn't mistaken, but what he told me is what I tell you."

"When did Colonel Kennard Wood arrive?"

"He checked in around that time." Sergeant Doherty pressed a bell. "Colonel Kennard Wood's apartment."

A moment later, as the door was opened:

"Stay in sight of this room," Smith ordered.

Colonel Kennard Wood faced us. He was—a fact for which I had been prepared—superficially like James Longton, but I judged him to be ten years Longton's senior. In build I could see that the dead man, normally, must closely have resembled his cousin. Kennard Wood was greying, sunburnt and wore a single eyeglass.

"Smith! You are very welcome."

We went in, and the colonel closed the door. I saw that he bore all the marks of overstrain and deep anxiety, but he placed chairs and proffered drinks.

"Thank you, but no," said Smith. "The matter which brings myself and my friend, Bart Kerrigan, here at this hour is one of life and death."

"I had hoped," Kennard Wood confessed wearily, "to enjoy a few hours' rest. I have had little enough during the past few days. So that the moment I got in I notified you and proposed to go to sleep——"

"You would never have awakened," said Smith grimly.

Kennard Wood, dropping into an armchair, stared haggardly.

"You mean—I have been traced here?"

Smith nodded.

"As James will have told you," the colonel went on, "I was recalled at the very moment I was about to leave Havana. Some new and startling facts had come to hand. But knowing of tomorrow's conference, I sent James ahead with all material to date. You have this, no doubt?"

Smith stood up abruptly.

"I speak to a soldier," he said, "and so I can be blunt. Your cousin James Longton——"

"Not——"

"I am sorry—yes."

Kennard Wood crossed to a small buffet and steadily poured out a drink.

"As I decline to drink alone, Smith," he said quietly, "no doubt Mr Kerrigan and yourself will reconsider your decision?"

"Of course—but time is precious. *You* are marked as the next victim!"

"As to that," said the colonel, turning—and his features were set in a coldly dangerous mask—"we shall see."

He served us, drained his own glass and set it down.

"How—was it done?"

"Details must wait, but no doubt you recall the Snapping Fingers deaths in Port-au-Prince?"

"The Snapping Fingers! You don't tell me that James——"

"Unfortunately, yes. He went to Mrs Mendel Hammett's undoubtedly believing that he would be safe there——"

"We both had reason to fear for our lives. There had been numerous attempts."

"So I gather."

"But this horror—here in New York!"

"Unless I am quite wrong, here in this hotel! First, where is your baggage?"

"In the bedroom. I will show you."

As we followed Kennard Wood Smith began sniffing suspiciously. I, too, sought traces of the vilely carnal odour which evidently betokened the presence of the thing called the Snapping Fingers. I could detect nothing. In the bedroom Smith stood quite still for a moment, looking around. It was an ordinary if luxurious hotel bedroom. The bed was turned down, and folded pyjamas were laid out; a travelling clock and some books were on a side table; a suitcase stood on a rack against one wall. Smith stepped into the bathroom. Toilet articles were disposed on a dressing table and on glass shelves.

He turned to Kennard Wood; the colonel had paled under his tan.

"Who brought up the baggage?"

"The hotel porter."

"Were you here when he arrived?"

"As a matter of fact, no. I was at the desk below, asking for messages."

"And who unpacked and set out?"

"The valet. I was in my apartment. The man knows my ways; I have stayed at the Prado several times. If I understood what it is that you apprehend, Smith, I might be able to help. But we are on the fifteenth floor of a modern New York hotel, not in Haiti!"

"Harsh to remind you, Wood, but poor Longton was in his own quarters in the home of Mrs Mendel Hammett. Forgive me if I seem to take liberties, but I must examine your gear closely." As Kennard Wood moved forward: "Be good enough to touch nothing!"

While the stricken colonel and I stood by, inert, watching, Nayland Smith made a rapid but efficient examination of every foot of the apartment; frequently he sniffed. High above the supper crowds, above the fashionable activities of Park Avenue, I thought that we were isolated, alone as though Fate had cast us together on an uninhabited island. Indeed, a man may be as hopelessly alone, as far from human aid, in the midst of a million fellows as one in the heart of the Sahara. The death mark of Fu Manchu was set upon Kennard Wood's door; he knew.

"I have found absolutely nothing," said Smith at last, "if I except these remnants of some kind of wrapping which, however, you may be able to place."

He displayed what looked like a tattered piece of grease-proof paper.

"No." Kennard Wood shook his head. "Nothing of mine was wrapped in that: possibly a relic of some former occupant."

"Possibly," Smith murmured and set the fragment aside. "Now for the acid test. I warn you, Wood, that I am submitting you to an ordeal of which I know nothing. But its outcome may be the solution of the mystery of the Snapping Fingers, an explanation of Longton's death."

"Give me my orders."

"I must add that nothing may be attempted. Possibly the agents of Fu Manchu responsible for your dismissal know that you are not alone. Both windows are open; the attack may come from either of them. In order to steel you for what may be a nerve-racking task let me say that I believe that Longton was mistaken for yourself——"

"And died in my place?"

"I may be wrong, but I think so. Did you ever stay at Mrs Mendel Hammett's?"

"Yes."

"Then I am right! But they know now. The material in the portfolio contained new facts?"

"New facts! Smith, there's a conspiracy aimed against this government which has no parallel in history!"

"I know," said Smith quietly; "that is why Longton died, why so many have died, why I am here. Now, Wood, I am going to ask you to lie down on the bed, and then I am going to turn out every light in the apartment. This thing always strikes in the dark."

"Very well."

Kennard Wood threw himself on the coverlet, taking an automatic from his pocket as he did so.

"No shooting!" snapped Smith. "Yours is the harder, the passive part. Is it agreed?"

"As you say."

76

"Just here by the door, Kerrigan. Do nothing without the word from me."

He moved. I heard several clicks. The whole place was plunged in darkness. Then came Smith's voice:

"Steady, everybody. Be ready for anything."

In the sudden darkness and complete silence, the buzz of that sleepless hive which is New York rising from far below, I became aware of a sense of impending peril which, as I knew at that moment, I had experienced before. Agents of Dr Fu Manchu were near. Even had I been uninformed of the fact I should have known it; every nerve in my body proclaimed it, was a herald announcing, psychically, the approach of some lethal thing.

Quite distinctly, from no more than a stride away, came a faint clicking sound.

"My God!" breathed Kennard Wood, "it's here!"

"The Snapping Fingers!" whispered Smith. "Stand fast!"

15 / *Nayland Smith Fires Twice*

THE SUDDEN KNOWLEDGE that here, in the darkness of the room, some nocturnal creature which drained one's blood was already questing victims imposed a test upon my nerves which I found hard to meet. Kennard Wood breathed rapidly.

True, I shared the horror and the peril; but recalling that story by the house detective, his strange account of something which might have been the "phantom hound of Peel," I had a stiff struggle with my imagination. Since Smith had examined almost every foot of the apartment it was not admissible that such a creature could be hiding there, but I remembered that windows were open and I visualised a giant vampire bat at this very moment entering stealthily: a hybrid horror created in the laboratories of Dr Fu Manchu. The suspense of those tense moments was almost unendurable.

A repetition of the snapping sounded very distinctly—on this occasion, I thought, from near the bed. A third time I heard it. . . .

"It's utterly uncanny!" muttered Kennard Wood. "What is it, Smith? What *is* it?"

"Ssh!" Smith warned. "Don't stir."

Twice again in quick succession it came—*snap! snap!*

"Now," cried Smith, "we shall know!"

He was standing near the door, and as he cried out he turned up all the lights.

What I had expected to see it is impossible to state—some ghoul of mediæval demonology, I believe. What I actually saw was Kennard Wood crouching on the bed, automatic in hand, staring wild-eyed about him, and Smith beside me looking right and left in ever-growing amazement.

Nothing whatever was visible to account for the sounds!

"It's supernatural!" groaned the colonel. "We all heard it."

"Nothing touched you in the dark?" Smith asked.

"Nothing."

"You, Kerrigan?"

"Nothing at all."

"Yet it's here!" Smith cried angrily. "It's here!"

Crossing the room, he jerked the draperies aside and stared out. I could see twinkling lights and a rectangular patch of starry sky. The windows were wide open. He turned, tugging at the lobe of his left ear.

"Defeated," he said quietly. "Get your kit together quickly, Wood. We will lend a hand. Must have you out of this!"

Kennard Wood went eagerly to work, and as we gathered up his belongings and hastily stacked them in the suitcase I could hear the hum of traffic rising from Park Avenue. When finally we opened the door and deposited case, topcoats and other gear out in the corridor Sergeant Doherty came doubling up.

"All's well," I said. "The colonel is changing his quarters."

Smith, last to leave, switched off the lights and brought the key.

"Get all this stuff downstairs, Sergeant," he said. "Colonel Kennard Wood will be coming with us. I will give the management instructions about this apartment in a moment."

But as we moved towards the elevator his preoccupied manner was so marked that I was on the point of saying something about it when:

"Kerrigan," he snapped and pulled up dead, "did you observe a flower vase in the bedroom?"

"Yes—I believe there was a vase of flowers."

"The management," Kennard Wood explained wearily, "decorates the apartments of incoming guests in this way."

Without another word Smith turned and began to run back.

"Smith!" I cried and followed; "what is it?"

"A bad show for Nayland Smith!" he replied. "I examined everything else, but I did not examine the flowers."

"But surely——"

"Slipshod methods are fatal"—he was unlocking the door —"in dealing with Doctor Fu Manchu."

Throwing the door open, he stood still for a moment.

"Quiet! Listen!"

I almost held my breath, but all that came to me out of the dark and ominous apartment was the subdued roar of Park Avenue rising from below.

He switched the lights up, and I followed him through the sitting room into the bedroom. We both looked at a round table set between the windows. Here had stood a glass flower vase.

"Good God!" Smith shouted, "it's gone!"

For my own part I was so dazed by this inexplicable incident that I began seriously to wonder if the Haitian Negroes had been right, if the Snapping Fingers were pure voodoo; if, in short, we were faced with supernormal phenomena.

Smith's reaction was strictly positive.

Running forward, he dropped down on his knees and scrutinised the carpet under the round table.

"Water spilled here!" he reported.

Springing up, he stepped to one of the windows and craned out. He appeared to be looking down into the avenue. Then, twisting sideways, I saw him staring upward, and suddenly:

"Hang onto me, Kerrigan!" he cried.

Frantically I leapt forward and grasped him; I thought that violent vertigo threatened his precarious balance. But before I could speak and at the moment that I gripped him he leaned right out and raised his arm. I saw the flash of his pistol in the moonlight.

He fired twice, upward and to the left.

Hot on the second shot came a high thin scream which seemed to grow swiftly nearer and then to fade away into silence. From far below there arose a muted uproar: cries, a cessation of the immediate traffic hum, a shrill whistle . . .

We rushed out no more than a few moments after the police had dragged something onto the sidewalk. They were holding back a crowd of morbid onlookers, many in evening dress. Inspector Hawk elbowed a way through for us. A heavy truck was drawn up near by, and the driver, an Italian, was excitedly explaining to a stolid policeman that he had had no chance to pull up.

"I tella you he falla from the sky!" he was shouting.

We stood hushed, looking down at what had been a small brown-skinned man.

"As I thought," said Smith: "one of the doctor's devils."

And as he spoke and I turned away—for the spectacle was horrifying—a suspicion crossed my mind that here lay the origin of the strange story told by the house detective. The dead brown man wore a kind of jersey almost of the same hue as his skin and trousers of a similar colouring; his footgear consisted of rope sandals. But the outstanding characteristic was his disproportionately long arms: he had the arms of a baboon. One broad tire of the truck had crushed him as he fell right in front of the moving vehicle.

"He was dead when he landed, Inspector," said the patrolman to Hawk. "Must have come a long way down. He had some kind of a satchel hung over his shoulder, and it was filled with glass or something. The front tire just ground it all to powder. . . ."

16 / Padded Footsteps

"KENNARD WOOD is safe—for the time being."

Smith faced me in our sitting room. He was smoking at top speed. Wood was asleep in an apartment near by, a man worn out. Rorke remained on duty in the lobby but would be relieved at four o'clock.

"Now that Wood has got in touch with you," I said, "the mischief is done—from Fu Manchu's point of view. Probably he will leave him alone."

"I agree. In this case Fu Manchu has failed. Wood has much to tell me, but he is too desperately tired for further exertion tonight. By the same token we have failed too."

"How? It's true that poor Longton died a horrible death, but you saved Kennard Wood——"

"And when I shot the Negrito I lost the only clue to the Snapping Fingers! Yes, it was one of the doctor's pygmies, whether from the Andamans or Sumatra I cannot say. You have had some experience of these little devils, Kerrigan. Undoubtedly he slipped in tonight amongst the crowd. The man Pannel, the house detective, evidently had a glimpse of him; but these creatures move like shadows and go as swiftly on all fours as upright."

"But why did he come?"

"He brought the Snapping Fingers! Then he slipped out of a window and crouched somewhere outside to await the end. Anywhere an ape can climb a Negrito can climb. When I saw him he was swarming up an apparently smooth wall from ledge to ledge, making for the roof. He would have come down the fire ladders."

"He carried a satchel——"

"To accommodate whatever causes the Snapping Fingers. When Wood was dead it was the pygmy's job to remove the evidence. He saw that plans had miscarried and so made sure that no trace of the attempt should remain. The thing—whatever it is—was in that flower vase! I failed there, badly."

I was silent for a while, watching him pacing up and down.

"The—characteristic smell was missing," I said.

Smith turned and stared at me.

"The characteristic smell is present not before but *after* the feast," he replied. "Now I am going to bed. This delay is madly irritating, and I know just how you feel about it; but we have to meet the government representatives in the morning, and there is no escape. Kennard Wood is on the spot, and Barton is returning with the people from Washington. Take my advice and turn in."

It was sound advice and, having bade Smith good night, I tried to act upon it.

But I found that sleep was not for me. That quiet which comes upon New York only in the very late small hours had fallen now. Dawn was not far away. The hivelike humming of this sleepless city was at its lowest ebb. Yet I could not rest. A score of problems bombarded my mind: Where was Ardatha? How were these strange journeys of the Chinese doctor accomplished? Should we be able to keep the marmoset alive until an opportunity arose to trade with the greatest enemy of white civilisation? Would Fu Manchu restore Ardatha? Where was his New York base from which he had operated against Longton and Kennard Wood? What caused the Snapping Fingers?

Groaning, I switched on the lights, got up and reached for my dressing gown. As chronicler of the expedition, my work was badly in arrears; better to arrange my notes than to lie torturing myself with unanswerable queries.

A chilling wave of loneliness swept down upon me. I had to tell myself that I was really in New York, for in some way I seemed to have become removed from it, raised high above into a rarefied but sinister atmosphere, cut off from my fellow men. Although a hotel bedroom is not inspiring, I discovered inspiration of sorts, as a working journalist, in the litter of notes and a portable typewriter standing under a desk lamp. Yes, I must work.

The suite was very silent. . . .

Thoughts of Ardatha haunted me; her image, as I had glimpsed her in the blue dress in the foyer below, persistently intruded between me and my purpose. Her eyes, seen even in that swift regard, had seemed to mirror a shadowy fear.

My thoughts took a new turn.

What was the nature of the gruesome experiments upon which Dr Fu Manchu had been engaged in that deserted Limehouse warehouse? What new secret did he try to wrest from a normally unreadable future? That he had exposed himself to tremendous stresses was a fact manifest in his weakened condition. I endeavoured to visualise that laboratory beside the Thames; the violet lamp; to recall words spoken.

The ghastly horror of the Snapping Fingers was never far from my thoughts, and I was asking myself if the violet lamp might be associated in some way with that agent of death when a sudden stir in the lobby brought me to my feet.

"Who's there?" I heard dimly. "Don't try any funny business!"

Something had aroused Sergeant Rorke.

The room allotted to me was the last but one at the north end of the suite; Sir Lionel's was actually the last, and there was a communicating door. Smith slept at the southern end. I set out to inquire, switching up the sitting-room lights as I went through.

Rorke had the front door open and was peering to right and left along the corridor outside, at that hour only partially lighted. Hearing my footsteps, he turned swiftly.

"Oh, it's you!" he said, and his manner was jumpy.

Once more he peered sharply to left and right, then came in and closed the door. He began to chew.

"What rouses you, Mr Kerrigan?" he asked (he was a present-tense addict). "Hope it isn't me singing out."

"No—I was awake. Did you hear something?"

"Well"—he resumed his seat—"I'm on duty here now quite a while, and this job is kind of monotonous. Maybe I doze off, but certainly I think I hear something—right outside the door."

"What?"

"Now, that's not so easy. No sir. It might be a shuffle, like somebody steals along quietly, or it might be somebody fumbles with the door."

"It didn't sound like—snapping fingers?"

"Snapping fingers?" Sergeant Rorke stared hard and chewed hard. "Why, no. I don't reckon so. Why does anybody snap his fingers?"

"I don't know," I answered wearily. "But you saw nothing?"

"Not a thing."

I went back to my room. Smith had not been awakened, and I was inclined to believe that Rorke had dreamed the episode. The vicious little marmoset (which, nevertheless, meant so much to me) occupied a commodious cage in Barton's adjoining room, and there was nothing to indicate that the animal had been aroused.

My notes engaged my attention for the next few minutes. I was about to take a cigarette when I paused, my hand suspended over the box.

"What was that?" I muttered.

I thought I had detected a faint movement in the sitting room, indefinable but inexplicable. It translated me magically to an apartment at the Prado; I seemed to hear again the ghostly snapping sound, to see the bloodless body of James Longton. Smith had told me often that in dealing with Dr Fu Manchu I must control my imagination.

But I opened a drawer, took out my Colt and slipped it in my pocket.

There was something reassuring in its cool touch, and now I lighted a cigarette. As I dropped the lighter on the desk I caught my breath and listened intently.

I had heard the sound again. . . .

DISMISSING THE IDEA that anyone could have been hiding in the rooms since Smith and I had returned, only one other theory seemed to remain—assuming that my overtired senses were not deluding me. I remembered that Rorke had recently opened the front door and had gone out into the corridor. It was possible, just possible, that during that interval someone had crept in.

Certain secret maps and plans, indispensable to our project, according to Barton, were locked in a steel box in Sir Lionel's bedroom.

I stepped quietly into the darkened sitting room and stood there for a while. I could detect no sound. I switched on the lights. The room was empty. Nevertheless I examined it methodically but found nothing. I believe I missed no possible hiding place, and accepting the fact that there was no one in the room but myself, I experienced a swift reaction of contempt. I returned and once more seated myself at the desk.

"These creatures move like shadows. . . ." Almost I seemed to hear the crisp voice of Nayland Smith. "Anywhere an ape can climb a Negrito can climb."

Had one of Fu Manchu's devilish little brown allies crept into the place in some way?

These devilmen were the bearers of the Snapping Fingers, of the loathsome thing that battened on blood. Yet for all my tremors—and I confess that I was fighting panic—I remained unwilling to disturb Smith unless more concrete evidence presented itself. No sound came from Sergeant Rorke.

I dropped my cigarette in a tray and sat upright, listening. There it was again. . . .

Footsteps, I was prepared to swear—padding footsteps. *Pad, pad, pad*—halting, furtive, but unmistakable.

I sprang up and ran to the door. I had left the lights on in the sitting room.

It was empty.

Yet as I stood there my ears convinced me that soft, padding footsteps were actually receding at the further side!

I took myself firmly in hand. Was my imagination indeed playing ghostly tricks? I walked in the direction of the sound and came to the door which led into the lobby. It was shut, and I paused there for a moment, listening. What I heard determined my next move. Quietly I opened the door and stepped out.

Sergeant Rorke was fast asleep in his chair.

A short passage led to Smith's quarters; I could see his door from where I stood, and I hesitated. I knew that he must be even more weary than Rorke. What I might have decided to do does not matter now: a decision was forced upon me.

From somewhere behind came a weird whistling and thrumming—not loud enough to waken the sleeping police officer but clearly audible to myself. I started wildly, twisted about, my heart leaping, and then recognised the sound: it was the marmoset in its cage! This recognition brought a momentary relief, to be followed by a doubt . . . what had awakened the animal? I turned back into the sitting room. Here the queer sibilant language of the tiny monkey sounded much louder; the creature was excited.

Crossing to my own apartment, right on the threshold I pulled up sharply.

The communicating door, the door which led to Barton's quarters, was wide open: when I had gone out it had been closed!

Determined now that the menace was real, that some clandestine thing, kin of the shadows but a thing physical, which could open doors, which I could shoot, was in the suite, I ran to the dark opening, reached for the switch and turned up the lights. . . .

Perhaps I stood there for as long as thirty seconds, staring, staring into an empty room!

The steel box, with its three locks, remained in its place, untouched. Set on a chest of drawers opposite was the big cage which Sir Lionel had bought to accommodate Peko, the doctor's marmoset. And Peko's behaviour was most remarkable.

Wrinkled forehead twitching, wicked teeth exposed, he tore at the wire bars with tiny eager fingers, pouring out a torrent of angry whistling chatter.

Why?

A door from Barton's room opened directly onto the main corridor, but it was closed. I began to distrust my own judgment; I listened almost eagerly to sounds rising from the city below, sounds of motor horns, of a moving train: sounds which spoke of human activity of a normal kind: of people who did not explore the dark and sometimes evil secrets of nature but were just ordinary human beings.

Resolutely I turned my back on these phenomena which had no visible cause, returned to my room and mixed myself a stiff drink.

I had left the door open, and even as I set my glass down on the desk I heard again but very softly . . . *pad, pad, pad.* The marmoset whistled furiously and tore at the bars.

And then I grew terribly afraid—afraid not of this invisible menace but afraid of myself. I could see again the thoughtful eyes of the Harley Street doctor who had assured me that I must not think of active service for at least three months. I wondered what he had feared; perhaps that the poison in my system might in some way reach my brain.

It was a horrible thought, worse than any physical danger. But even as that dread crossed my mind, and as I raced across and stared into Barton's room, it was dispelled by an unassailable, a physical fact.

I saw that the outer door was wide open. . . . It closed, and I heard the snap of the lock!

Almost hurling myself forward, I reopened it and sprang out. So precipitate was my action that Sergeant Rorke, who had evidently awakened and had come along the outside corridor, was nearly bowled over.

"Go easy, Mr Kerrigan," he spluttered. "Gee! What's doing?"

"Quick! It's important, Sergeant! Did someone come out just ahead of me?"

"Come out? No sir. I'll say someone goes in! I wake up—oh, I'm asleep all right—and I get a hunch there's another door to these apartments. Seems to be kind of something doing along here. I move right away. I see the door shut just as I step up to it. Then it opens again and you come out like the Gestapo's after you."

"But you are *sure*"—I grasped his arm—"that the door opened before *I* opened it?"

He resumed chewing, regarding me stolidly.

"That goes in my report, Mr Kerrigan."

"Thank God!" I whispered. "Because, you see, Sergeant Rorke, no one came in. I was just behind the door. And you know that no one came out!"

"Someone is coming out!" a snappy voice announced. "It's impossible to sleep through all this chatter!"

Turning, I saw Nayland Smith.

"Smith!" I exclaimed, "I did not want to wake you, but something very strange is going on."

"So I gather."

Rapidly, in a very gabble of words, I told him of the incident of the padding footsteps, of the remarkable behaviour of the marmoset and of the opening door.

"And I'll say," Rorke interpolated, "that nobody comes out."

"As you say," Smith murmured thoughtfully, "no one comes out."

He stared at me very hard, and in the sudden silence I knew that he was listening.

"I shall be glad," he added, "when the conference is over, Kerrigan. In New York we are beseiged by enemies who fight with strange weapons. . . ."

11 / Christophe's Chart

"I SHALL BE OBLIGED, Sir Lionel," said Mr Hannessy, "if you will tell us now in your own way the circumstances which have led you to believe that you hold a clue to what may prove to be a secret submarine base in the Caribbean. We are told by our navy—represented here by Commander Ingles—that, allowing for underwater craft belonging to belligerent nations, there is still a big surplus around those waters belonging to no nation which so far we have been able to identify. Valuable lives have been lost in trying to plumb the mystery. One"—he glanced at Kennard Wood—"right here in New York, only last night. The credentials borne by Sir Denis Nayland Smith"—he nodded in Smith's direction—"are sufficient proof that your theory has a concrete basis. We are all anxious to hear the facts."

We sat around a long table in our sitting room. On my right, at one end of the table, was Nayland Smith; facing me, Commander Ingles and Kennard Wood; on my left the celebrated Mr Wilber Ord, expert adviser to the White House on international relations. Facing Wilber Ord, John Hannessy, the speaker, white-haired, fresh-coloured, vigorous, stood for that monument which is sometimes called republican and sometimes democratic but which always stands for freedom. From the other end of the table Sir Lionel Barton dominated everybody. The steel box lay before him.

He was in his element. Those dancing blue eyes under shaggy brows told how much he was enjoying himself. He glanced around at everybody, and then:

"I might remark, sir," he said, addressing Mr Hannessy, "that the credentials borne by *myself* are a sufficient proof that my theory has a concrete basis. But I will not stress this point. To be brief: There had been for many years an heirloom in a branch of the Stewart family known as The Stewart Luck. It consisted of a silver-mounted pistol to which a small object was attached by a piece of catgut."

He paused, looking about again from face to face.

"The family met with misfortune. I had great difficulty in tracing the survivor—last of the Stewarts of that branch. From her—she is a very old woman—I acquired The Stewart Luck."

Opening the steel box, Barton took out an old duelling pistol.

"This," he said, "with the object attached, is The Stewart Luck. Now this pistol was almost certainly manufactured in Edinburgh about 1810–14. The fact is significant. It is fitted with a Forsyth percussion lock: an early example. It was designed, of course, to fire a ball. How it came into the possession of that remarkable character to whom I am about to introduce you I leave to you, gentlemen, to decide. Myself, I think I know. But his crest was added by a later hand."

He pointed to a crest engraved upon the mounting.

"The 'attached object'—a piece of silver resembling a small pencil case—called for my special skill. For a long time it defeated me. Only by identifying the monogram on the pistol was I enabled to grasp the real character of this mysterious object. After many failures I deciphered the monogram. The monogram mystery solved, my next conclusion was obvious . . . the small silver object was almost certainly the first *conical bullet* ever used in the history of arms!"

Sir Lionel was warming to his subject. His great voice boomed around the room; he no longer looked at us in stressing his points; he glared.

"My discovery was revolutionary. I had satisfied myself that the device, monogram or crest embodied a date in

Roman numerals. That date was 1811 A.D. Together with the monogram and the silver bullet it was sufficient. This pistol had been the property of Christophe—that great Negro who built the Citadel, perhaps the most majestic fortress in the world; who expelled Napoleon's troops; who made of cowering slaves from the interior of Africa prosperous and useful citizens. Yes, gentlemen—Henry Christophe, crowned in 1811 King of Haiti!"

No one interrupted. Barton had his audience enthralled.

"King Christophe, that noble Negro, at the height of his power was betrayed, deserted; and it is common knowledge that he fired a silver bullet into his own brain!"

John Hannessy stared around, nodding in confirmation to the others present.

"The first conical bullet in history was fired into the brain of King Christophe by his own hand. He was a Negro genius; possibly the bullet was of his own invention, made for him by some skilled workman brought to Haiti for the purpose. This point of my inquiry reached—what did I ask myself?"

"I cannot imagine, sir," said John Hannessy in a hushed voice.

"The question I asked myself was this: Why should so many persons—myself included—incur great risk and expense to recover the pistol and the bullet with which King Christophe possibly committed suicide? I replied: A great treasure—jewels, bullion, variously estimated at five to seven million pounds sterling—was hidden by the Negro king during his lifetime, searched for after his death—but never found!"

By now I was keyed up as tensely as the others. This strange story was not wholly new to me, but I understood at last the importance of the steel box which Sir Lionel had guarded so jealously from the outset. I was not prepared, however, for what was to follow.

Barton continued:

"I found myself to be much intrigued by the fragment of catgut which formerly had attached the bullet to the pistol. Catgut is uncommon stuff. It suggested (a) a fiddler, (b) a surgeon——"

"I don't believe, sir," John Hannessy burst in, "re catgut, that catgut ligatures were in use circa 1811."

"And I don't care a damn, sir! Some later owner may have tied the bullet to the pistol. But I had my clue! You see, I knew that King Christophe had a resident medical attendant—Duncan Stewart, a Scots physician."

"Good heavens!" Smith murmured. "You certainly know your own game, Barton."

"I knew that he, Doctor Stewart, was probably the last man to see the black king alive. Later the body was thrown into a pit in the courtyard of Christophe's great fortress, the Citadel, on the crest of the mountain. But"—he spoke slowly and emphatically, punctuating each word with a bang of his fist on the table—"before that event took place Doctor Stewart had extracted the bullet and had seized the pistol, which I suspect to have been his own present to the black king!

"We must assume that Doctor Stewart was ignorant of the secret—assume that he retained these gruesome relics for purely sentimental reasons. It remained for me to discover that the historical silver bullet was *hollow!*

"I submitted it to microscopical examination. It was one of the most beautifully made things I have ever handled—the work of an expert gunsmith. There was a pin in the base. This being removed, it became possible to unscrew the shell —for a shell it was! I extracted a roll of some tough vegetable fibre, no larger than a wooden match."

Nayland Smith was staring hard at Sir Lionel, who had now taken from the steel box a tiny piece of papyrus set under glass. The expression upon Barton's sun-wrinkled, truculent face was ironical.

"I should be glad, Mr Hannessy," he said, "if you would examine this and then pass it on."

He handed the fragment to John Hannessy.

"A glance was enough. Christophe had had a chart—a minute chart—made of his treasure cave and had hidden it in his own skull at the instant of death!"

There was a momentary silence—an awed silence—as Mr Hannessy passed the chart to Commander Ingles.

"It can be read only by aid of a powerful lens," Barton went on, "but it shows an enormous cavern in which the cache is marked by a red cross. Further inquiry—you know something about it, Smith—led to the discovery that this cavern, which has an underwater outlet to the sea, was big enough to hide a battle fleet!"

"I am prepared to hear, Sir Lionel," said Commander Ingles, studying the chart through a magnifying glass, "that you have identified the location of this cave: you know its exact bearings?"

"Commander Ingles—I know my way there as well as I know the way from my town house (now sold) to my club! And listen, Smith: the passage from Da Cunha's manuscript in the British Museum was copied by Doctor Fu Manchu, in person, as long as a year ago! I have evidence to prove that. But I have beaten him to it this time. Wilton of Drury Lane, the best manuscript faker in Europe, made me a duplicate of Christophe's chart.

"Wilton's duplicate was exact in every particular—except that the treasure cache and the exact bearings of the entrances to the cave from land and sea were slightly altered. It was Wilton's chart that was stolen by Doctor Fu Manchu. *This* is the original!"

Nayland Smith was tugging at one ear.

"There's your secret submarine base, gentlemen. It will be my privilege to——"

"Who's there?" cried Commander Ingles and glanced back over his shoulder.

He had been absorbed in study of the chart. Now his lens clattered onto the table.

"I heard nothing," snapped Nayland Smith.

"Nor did I. But, nevertheless, something *touched* me!"

"Touched you?" Barton began to chuckle. "Perhaps it was my story!"

"I insist that someone bent over my shoulder whilst I was examining the chart."

We all sat perfectly still, listening. Commander Ingles was not a man whose self-possession is easily ruffled, but it was plain to see that he was disturbed.

The ceaseless voice of the city came up to us from the streets far below; dazzling sunshine shone in at the windows —yet I, my brain working feverishly, became possessed of an uncanny sense that some thing, some supernormal thing, had joined our council. Then:

"Who opened that door?" Nayland Smith demanded sharply.

Those with their backs to the door indicated turned in a flash. We all looked in that direction.

The door leading to my room was half open—and suddenly the marmoset, in Barton's quarters beyond, began to whistle shrilly!

Smith exchanged a swift glance with me and then sprang up. He reached the open door first, but I was not far behind him. Everybody was up now. As we dashed through to Sir Lionel's room I saw at a glance that the outer door, that which led to the hotel corridor, was wide open. . . .

Smith muttered something under his breath and went running out. We came behind him in a pack.

The corridor outside was bare from end to end. Neither

elevator was moving. Several of the party began to talk at once, but:

"Silence!" rapped Smith angrily. "I want to listen."

Silence fell, save for the whistling chatter of the monkey, and we all listened.

We all heard it:

Pad, pad, pad . . .

Soft footsteps were moving along the corridor, far away to the left. But no living thing was visible.

"RUSH TO THAT STAIRCASE, Kerrigan!" rapped Smith. "Bar the way to anything—visible or invisible."

And as I dashed off a conviction seized my mind that he, too, had grasped the possibility, hitherto incredible, which indeed I had regarded as inadmissible: that some thing— some thing which we could not see—had been amongst us, and not for the first time.

I raced headlong to the end of the corridor, trusting to my considerable poundage to sweep anything from my path. However, nothing obstructed me.

Coming to the head of the staircase which forty floors below gave access to the foyer, I stood still, breathing heavily and listening.

Smith's snappy orders had followed me in my rush:

"You, Barton—that way! Watch all the doors. If one opens, rush for it. Commander, cover both elevators. Allow no one and nothing to enter, whoever comes out. . . ."

Fists clenched, I stood listening.

That sound of padded footsteps was no longer audible. No elevator was moving, and apart from a buzz of excited voices from our party along the passage I could hear nothing; so that as I stood there the seeming insanity of the thing burst upon me irresistibly. We were all victims of some illusion, some trick. . . . Its object must have been to get us out of the apartment!

As this idea seized me I turned from the head of the staircase and began to run back.

"Smith!" I shouted, "it's a ruse! Someone should have stayed in the room."

"Don't worry." Smith was standing there on guard. "I have stuck here, and Barton's door is locked."

But we found no one and heard no one. The shadow had come—and gone.

Completely baffled, we reassembled in the sitting room and resumed our places about the table. Nayland Smith solemnly deposited before Barton the ancient pistol, the silver bullet and the chart.

"You left them behind. I picked them up for safety."

We stared rather blankly at one another for a moment, and then:

"It seems to me, gentlemen," said John Hannessy, "that the experience which we have just shared calls for a consultation."

Everybody was in tacit agreement with the speaker. Commander Ingles replied in his crisp way:

"I give my testimony here and now, without hesitation, that something, something palpable, touched my shoulder at the moment that I called out. Something or someone we could not see was in the room at that time. We all know that a door was open which had not been open when this session began; we all know that the communicating doors were closed. And I think I am right"—he looked around—"in saying that we all heard the sound of soft footsteps in the corridor outside. . . ."

He paused suddenly, staring down at some notes on the table before him. His silence was so unexpected and his expression so strange that:

"What's wrong?" growled Barton, leaning forward. "What have you found there?"

Commander Ingles looked around from face to face, and I saw that he held a sheet of paper in his hand.

"Just this . . . I will read out what is written here:

" 'FIRST NOTICE——' "

"What!" snapped Smith and was on his feet in a moment.

"I will repeat: 'FIRST NOTICE.

" 'The Council of Seven of the Si-Fan is aware of the aims of an expedition led by Sir Lionel Barton and Sir Denis Nayland Smith. In view of the fact that the council is in a position to negotiate with the government of the United States regarding a matter of first importance, this is a warning, both to the government of the United States and to Sir Denis Nayland Smith and those associated with him. The mobility of the United States navy is seriously threatened, but the council is in a position to nullify the activities both of a certain Eastern neighbour and also those of a Western power. This is to notify all whom it may concern that you have two weeks in which to decide. An advertisement in a daily newspaper consisting of the words "Negotiate. Washington" will receive prompt attention.

" 'President of the Seven.' "

"BETTER LUCK today, Kerrigan," said Nayland Smith.

"Thanks," I replied. "I can do with it."

Cristobal—I was at last in Cristobal (or more exactly in Colon), where I had confidently expected to meet Ardatha again. Yet for two days and the greater part of one night I had combed the towns and their environs without success. Recollections of how that last conversation with Ardatha had been abruptly terminated haunted my mind. Had Fu Manchu detected her in the act of phoning to me—and changed his plans?

The essential clue had been partially lost as the line was disconnected, but at least I knew that news of her was to be had at the shop of someone whose name began with Z. Although Z is comparatively unusual as the index letter of a surname, my quest had led me nowhere.

I sat beside Smith in a cane rocking chair on the terrace of the hotel. An avenue of mastlike coconut palms stretched away before us to the gate. The hotel was crowded; even at this early hour nearly all the chairs were occupied. There were elderly men studying guidebooks, younger men reading newspapers but looking up whenever a new arrival passed along the terrace; one kindly old lady there was who made a point of conversing with everybody, and there were several very pretty women who all seemed to be travelling alone. The major languages of Europe were represented.

"Never, in a long government career," said Smith, glancing at a dark-eyed Spanish girl who seemed willing to be talked to, "have I met with so many political agents in any one building."

"How do you explain it?"

"I explained it a long time ago when I mentioned the fact that the Panama Canal has two ends. Kennard Wood, as you know, found indisputable evidence pointing to a plot by a certain power to close the canal at an opportune moment. We sit on a potential front line, Kerrigan. All the advance units are here."

"And I spend my time looking for Ardatha!"

"Why not? She is a most valuable ally; I am concerned about her almost as deeply as you are. A link with the enemy is not lightly to be broken."

"Utterly fantastic, Smith, but true, that her safety, her

very existence, may depend on the life of that wretched little animal——"

"The doctor's marmoset? Yes, Barton says the creature cannot last much longer unless he can discover something that it will consent to eat. As it is reasonable to suppose that Fu Manchu knows now of our capture, what has puzzled me is the doctor's silence——"

"And our immunity!"

"That is less surprising. I know from experience that a cessation of hostilities usually follows the delivery of a Si-Fan ultimatum until the date has expired. We may hope for another week's safety."

Nevertheless I had suffered wakeful hours, hours when I had lain listening for soft footsteps, for the coming of that shadow which had been amongst us in New York; and I had known, on many a sleepless night, the dread of the Snapping Fingers.

"If only I could find that accursed shop!" I exclaimed. "I am beginning to despair."

But Smith was plunged in sudden reflection: I doubted if he had heard me. And I was looking about aimlessly at the varied types of humanity represented on the terrace when he jerked:

"Did Ardatha state expressly that Z—— was to be found in Cristobal?"

"Why, yes—that is, let me think."

To recall the exact words—to recall almost any words Ardatha had spoken to me since our strange reunion in London—was not difficult.

"Smith!" I spoke excitedly. "I believe I have been wasting precious time! She said that they were setting out for Cristobal but then added, 'When you reach *Panama!*'"

"That's it!" snapped Smith, standing up. "Panama! Barton and I have our hands full, as you know, but in any case this is a job you can do better alone. I will notify the Zone police. An officer will meet you. The sooner you start the better, Kerrigan. I suspect that Z—— is in Panama. . . ."

Indeed, I required no urging; ten minutes later I was on my way. . . .

Storage tanks and other anachronisms left behind, my journey swept me straight into the jungle. Through dense shadows of tropical foliage I could see, with my mind's eye, Morgan and his leather-skinned fighting men marching on Panama. Alligators basked in the pools, unfamiliar birds flitted from branch to branch; and I saw here at last a curtain against which the drama of Dr Fu Manchu might fitly be played. On this, the Gold Road across the Isthmus, Spaniard and buccaneer had clashed in many a bloody conflict which the narrow belt had known.

Just beyond the mirror of the waters, beyond festoons of flowering vines, lay hundreds and hundreds of miles of primeval jungle, forest and mountain, much of it untrodden by a white man's foot; places never yet explored, inhabited by humans, beasts, birds and insects so far unclassified.

When the train (surely one of the strangest under Uncle Sam's control) pulled into Panama I was thinking that somewhere in the secret swamps beyond Dr Fu Manchu had found the horror called the Snapping Fingers. . . .

Sergeant Abdy of the Zone police met me, a man from the Middle West but leather-skinned and truculent as any that followed Morgan in the days of the Gold Road.

"All the stores with phone numbers have been checked up, Mr Kerrigan. I guess there's not much news for you."

My heart fell.

"You mean there are no names beginning with Z?"

"Just that, except for 'Zone.' But listen—there's the market stalls and the *playa* on the water front. We've done some; I broke away to meet you. I plan to explore that section. What I suggest is this: while I do the market—a bit late now —you do the streets between water front and Central; they're full of little stores. Meet me at the Marina Hotel."

Further details were all agreed as we walked along together and Sergeant Abdy gave me my bearings. When we parted I confess that the size of the job rather staggered me: only by sheer good luck could I hope to find Z.

But Fate (I often think with the Arabs) has us in leading strings. Parting from Sergeant Abdy, I set out more or less at random down a crooked, cobbled, narrow street which transported me in spirit to Clovelly in Cornwall. I doubt if I had proceeded twenty paces on my downward path before, on the corner of a shadowy courtyard, I saw above a shop which appeared to be even more ancient than its neighbours, the name:

ZAZIMA

I pulled up sharply, my pulse beating faster. Through a dirty narrow-paned window I stared at some of the queerest objects ever assembled. There were two voodoo masks of repellent appearance, some fragments of antique pottery and a piece of grotesque mural decoration which might have come from a Yucatan temple. I saw a leather bowl filled with tarnished coins, backed by a partly unrolled Chinese carpet which even my unpractised eye told me to be almost priceless. There were two cracked and battered tea chests, a number of lopsided and primitive wine bottles; but set right in front of the window, so that it was no more than an inch removed from the dirty glass, was the strangest exhibit of all.

It was a human head!

The head was that of a bearded old man, reduced by the mysterious art of Peruvian head-hunters to a size no greater than that of an average orange. The shrivelled features still retained the personality of the living man. One expected him at any moment to open those sunken lids and to look out with tiny, curious eyes upon a giant world.

This repellent thing was mounted and set in a carved mahogany box having a perfectly fitting glass cover resembling a clockcase; and as I stared at the ghastly relic, for my inspection of the window of Zazima had occupied only a matter of seconds, I became aware that from the black shadows of the shop beyond someone was watching me.

The face of the one who watched was so like that in the mahogany box, magnified, that horror touched me and I know that I bent forward and peered more closely into those dim shadows.

Faintly I could discern a bent old man sitting upon cushions which were piled upon a high-backed wooden chair. He wore a robe or dressing gown. And as I peered in over the shrivelled head in the window a thin hand was raised. I was invited to enter.

I opened the door of the shop. A bell jangled as I did so, and from an ancient church somewhere further down the street a clock chimed the half hour.

Immediately, as the door closed behind me, I became aware of an indescribably fusty atmosphere: I had stepped out of the Panama of today into a crypt in which were preserved age-old memories of the Panama which had seen rack, death by fire, Spanish swords countering English; or into an even earlier Panama worshipping strange gods, a city unknown to the Inquisition or to the England of Francis Drake.

It seemed at first glance that the bulk of Zazima's offerings were displayed in the window. There were some carpets on the walls and some faded charts and prints. A few odds and ends lay about the untidy place. But it was upon the face of the proprietor, for so I assumed the old man in the high-backed chair to be, that my attention was focussed.

He was, as I have indicated, yellow and wrinkled, with fragments of scanty hair and beard clinging, colourless, to the parchment of his skin. He sat cross-legged upon the cushions, and for one moment, looking into his sunken eyes, a vague apprehension touched me. I had met a strangely penetrating glance. When I spoke I was staring over his head.

"You have some attractive wares for sale."

I glanced back at him. He was nodding, and I saw now that he held a common clay pipe in his left hand and that the peculiar odour of the place was directly traceable to the tobacco which he was smoking.

"Yes, yes!" He thrust the stem of the pipe into an apparently toothless mouth. "As you say. But business is very slack, Mr Kerrigan."

I don't know if it was the perfect English in which he addressed me or his knowledge of my name which more greatly surprised me, but I can state with certainty that his confirmation of my hopes, that here indeed was a link with Ardatha, made my heart beat even faster than it was already beating.

"Why do you call me Mr Kerrigan?"

"Because that is your name." He smiled with a sort of naïve cunning. "Of course I was expecting you."

"But how did you know me?"

"By three things. The first: your appearance, of which I had been advised; the second: your behaviour. Those two things, conjoined to the third, assured me of your identity."

"And what was the third?"

"I could see your heart beating under your coat when you looked up and read the name Zazima."

"Indeed?"

Sans the clay pipe the aged philosopher might have been the immortal Barber of Baghdad.

"Yes, it is true. I cannot think why you have been so long in coming."

"How was I to know you were in Panama? I have been searching in Colon and Cristobal."

"But why in Cristobal? I, Zazima, have been here in Panama for forty years."

"This I did not know."

I was beginning now to wonder about the nationality of Zazima, and I decided that he was some kind of Asiatic, certainly a man of culture. Behind him on the wall hung a piece of Moorish tapestry, faded, worn, but from a collector's point of view probably of great value; and I saw Zazima as an Eastern oracle, sitting there, cross-legged, inscrutable.

He removed the clay pipe from his shrunken lips, and:

"Recite to me the message which the lady delivered," he said, "since here is some mystery. I know you bear it in your memory, for I have lived and loved myself."

Doubtful, always suspecting treachery, for if I had learned anything during my association with Nayland Smith it had been that the power of the Si-Fan was everywhere, I hesitated. I have had occasion before to refer to a sort of lowering of temperature, a sense of sudden chill, which subconsciously advised me of the presence of Fu Manchu; I knew others who had shared this experience. And as I stood there, watching the strange old man in the high-backed chair, I became aware of just that sensation.

No doubt I betrayed myself, for Zazima spoke again: he spoke gently, as one who seeks to soothe a nervous child.

"Those who oppose the Master fight with the elements. You are in no danger. If you are sensible in this, my humble shop, of a greater presence, have no fear. Beneath my roof you are safe. Danger is to the lady you love. Tell me, if you please, what message she sent to you."

A moment more I hesitated, and then:

"She told me," I said, "that I should have news of her at the shop of Za—— There her words were cut off."

I watched Zazima closely. His sunken eyes were closed; he seemed to be in a state of contemplation. I decided that the Moorish tapestry covered a doorway. But presently those piercing eyes regarded me again.

"We who work for the Master work unafraid. The lady's message, Mr Kerrigan, should have run 'at the shop of Zazima in Panama look for the head in the window.' I sorrow to learn that you have sought in vain. However, it is not too late."

"Quick! Tell me!" My hand shot out in supplication. "Where is she? Where can I find her?"

"It is not for me to answer, Mr Kerrigan."

He alighted from the chair; I cannot state that he stood up—for I realised at this moment that he was a dwarf! Clay pipe in hand, he passed me, crossed to the window, pulled aside the folds of the Chinese carpet and, straining forward, reached the box which contained the shrivelled head. With this he returned.

"It is twenty dollars," he said, "which is a stupid price."

"But"—I shrank back—"I don't want the thing!"

"The lady's message should have concluded with these words: 'Look for the head in the window. Buy it.'"

I stared down at him suspiciously. Was I becoming involved in a cunning web spread by Dr Fu Manchu? For of the fact that the Chinese doctor, if not present in person, dominated this scene I was convinced. Yet—for now I was cool enough—I saw that I must trust Zazima. Ardatha had asked me to seek him out. Dark, sunken eyes watched me, and I thought that there was an appeal in them.

"As you say, it is a stupid price."

I handed twenty dollars to Zazima, and he surrendered to me my strange purchase.

"Have you nothing else to tell me?"

"Nothing. I have sold you the head. A great Chinese philosopher has written: 'When the cash is paid words cannot restore it.' The matter is concluded."

I turned to go. Zazima had reseated himself on the high-backed chair.

"Do not open the box," he added softly, "until you are alone."

And he seemed to speak as one who is prompted. . . .

19 / *Flammario the Dancer*

AS I SAT outside a café which Sergeant Abdy had recommended to me I was far from easy in my mind. Having first wrapped my strange possession in a newspaper, I had bought a cheap attaché case which now stood on the table before me; it contained the shrivelled head. A halt for refreshment had proved to be imperative, and in any case I had to wait for a train. My luncheon dispatched, I lingered over an iced drink.

It was cool beneath the awning; before me rose ranks of royal palms seeming to mount guard along the tiled paths. Coloured boys had given up pestering me to have my shoes cleaned, to buy postcards, tickets for bullfights and other things which I didn't want. Dark-eyed señoritas transported me in spirit to Spain as they moved on jutting iron balconies of ancient stone houses. *Coches* rattled lazily along the cobbled streets. It was pleasantly hot and the sky looked unreally blue.

But I had much to think about.

I could not fail to remember that the most delicate operation in the murders due to the Snapping Fingers was that of introducing the unknown agent of death. Suppose (I argued) I carry in the mahogany box such an agent; suppose I am being used, cunningly, to destroy my friends and myself!

It was not outside the bounds of possibility. In Zazima's shop I had been acutely aware of a hidden presence. Against this was the indisputable fact that Ardatha had directed me to go there—that I had been expected.

Ardatha! What had my journey availed? I knew no more than I had known before I had set eyes on the strange dwarf called Zazima. And there was something else.

As I had come out into the cobbled, sloping street, carrying my purchase, an idea had been strong upon me that I was watched—not by someone inside the shop but by someone *outside;* that this person was following me at a distance. So strong did this conviction become that as I turned into Sixth Street I paused for a moment and then turned back.

I almost fell over a slim, sallow-faced man who was on the point of rounding the corner!

Muttering an apology, he hurried on; but his appearance had set me a problem. Where had I seen that sallow face before? A wide-brimmed hat had somewhat obscured his features, but nevertheless I knew that this was not the first time that I had seen him. . . .

Abstractedly selecting a cigarette from my case, I watched a *coche* which slowly approached, hood up, for the noonday sun was hot. In any more objective mood I might well have failed to note the passenger, but now his sallow features imprinted themselves upon my passive brain with medallike accuracy. He had removed the wide-brimmed hat and lay back in the shadow of the hood, but I knew him, knew him for a spy—for the man who had followed me as I left Zazima's shop. . . .

More, that fugitive memory was trapped: he was the man who had been with Ardatha in the foyer of the Regal Athenian!

The carriage clattered past at some little distance from the café and turned into a side street just beyond an ancient church whose huge iron-studded doors probably dated back to the days when Drake met the Spaniards in Nombre de Dios Bay.

I was closely covered. What was the purpose of this espionage?

The link with Ardatha was established; its implications horrified me. My anxiety to examine the head grew so intense that for a moment I thought of hiring a room in the restaurant merely for that purpose.

Sergeant Abdy's reappearance induced wiser counsels. He dropped down on a chair facing me.

"Checked up on Zazima," he reported. "Nothing against him. He has contacts in the Chinese quarter, and it's suspected some of his stock is stolen and the rest smuggled. If so, he's clever. But he's never given any trouble. . . ."

BOTH NAYLAND SMITH and Sir Lionel were out when I returned, but Smith had left a message which read:

"Back for late dinner. Don't go out until I join you."

I passed through the foyer with its arcades and lighted showcases and, for all my distracted frame of mind, could not fail to notice that I was an object of interest to a number of visitors lounging about in a seemingly aimless fashion. Indeed, it did not call for a newspaper training to see, as Smith had seen, that Colon was a hotbed of foreign agents, each watching the other but all bent upon some common purpose.

What was the purpose?

I wondered if this gateway of a sea lane which joined two oceans was normally beset by spies; that cryptic remark of Smith's, "the Panama Canal has two ends," recurred to me again and again.

One graceful brunette seemed bent upon making my acquaintance: she was tall, slender, but despite her light brown skin, the colour of which might have been due to sun bathing, had that swaying carriage which betrays African ancestry. Her brilliant amber eyes, shaded by long curling lashes, fixed upon me, she conveyed so frank an invitation that I found it embarrassing. As I stepped into the elevator:

"Who is that dark girl?" I asked the man.

"Oh, that's Flammario, the dancer from The Passion Fruit Tree."

"Does she live here?"

"No sir; and if you're thinking she's man hunting—you're wrong. Did you check up on the emeralds? That girl is a good little businesswoman; I guess she owns about half the town."

This information made Flammario's behaviour even more hard to understand, but by the time that I reached the apartment I had dismissed her from my mind: someone else occupied it exclusively.

I set the carved wooden box on the table in the sitting room and stared through the glass at that dreadful exhibit.

Who had he been, this old man who had met death by decapitation? What tragedy of the Peruvian woods was locked up in my strange possession, and, paramount thought, why had Zazima forced the thing upon me?

The idea that this fragment of dreadful mortality formed a link with Ardatha was one I was anxious to dispel, yet I clung to it. Lighting a cigarette, I considered the relic, and suddenly an idea occurred to me. I wondered that it had not occurred to me before.

The reason for so roundabout a method was not clear, but Zazima may have known himself to be spied upon. That someone else had been concealed at the back of his shop I had felt quite certain, some servant of Fu Manchu—possibly the doctor himself. I must suppose that the hidden watcher had good reasons for remaining hidden. The answer to the problem must be that vital information of some sort was hidden in the box!

I anticipated no difficulty in opening it; the front was secured by a catch similar to that of a clockface. Yet I hesitated; I loathed the idea of touching that little shrivelled head mounted upon a block of some hard black wood. I peered in through the glass, expecting to find a note there. But I could see nothing. The box was decorated with carving, some kind of native work, and I thought it possible, noting the thickness of the wood, that part of the base might conceal a secret drawer. Another possibility was that the head was hollow, that if I took it out I should find something hidden inside.

Conquering repulsion, I was about to open the glass front and examine that shrivelled fragment of a long-dead man when abruptly I desisted.

I had heard a rap, short but imperative, at the outer door!

Hastily I placed the shrivelled head in its mahogany casket in a bureau. I was anxious that none of the staff should see it: I mistrusted everyone where Dr Fu Manchu was concerned. As I locked the bureau and slipped the key into my pocket rapping on the outer door was repeated, this time more insistently. I thought it might be Barton, but I could not imagine why he did not ring the bell.

Swift dusk was falling, and as I opened the door the lights in the passage outside had not yet been switched up.

A woman stood there.

Because of the darkness, because she was graceful and slender, a pang of joy stabbed me. For a moment I thought . . . Ardatha. Then the visitor spoke:

"I have had to come because I want to help you—I *must* speak to you."

It was Flammario the dancer!

BRILLIANT AMBER EYES looked into mine: they were beautiful, but their beauty was of the jungle.

"Please, no, do not turn up the light. I promise you, I declare to you, that I am here to be of help. It is that your interests are mine. I know that you—look for someone——"

She preceded me into the rapidly darkening room, for dusk falls swiftly in the tropics, and seated herself in an armchair not far from the door. Her movements had a wild animal grace which might have been a product of her profession or have been hereditary. She was very magnetic, an oddly disturbing figure; I was far from trusting her. And now (she had a velvety, caressing voice):

"Will you please promise me something?" she asked.

"What is it?"

"There are two other ways out of here. Is it true?"

"Yes."

"If Sir Denis Nayland Smith comes, or Sir Lionel Barton, will you help me to escape?"

I hesitated. My thirst for knowledge, knowledge that might lead me to Ardatha, prompted me to accept almost any terms, and Flammario had said, "I know that you look for someone." Yet I distrusted her; I suspected her to be a servant of Dr Fu Manchu, an instrument, a mouthpiece; otherwise from what source had she gained her knowledge of my companions? But my longing for news of Ardatha tipped the balance.

"Yes, I will do my best; but why are you afraid of them—and how do you come to know their names?"

"I had a friend—he is now my enemy." The huskily musical voice came to me from a shadowy figure. "He, my friend, is a member of a secret society called the Si-Fan. You know it, eh?"

"Yes. I know it."

"He told me much about it—far more than he should have told to anyone, and because I seem to know about the Si-Fan I think that those others might——"

"Might hold you as a suspect?" I suggested.

"Yes." The word came in a whisper. "It would not be fair. And so"—she had the quaintest accent—"will you promise me that I am not arrested?"

A moment longer I hesitated, and then:

"Yes," I said.

She laughed softly, a trilling, musical laugh.

"You Englishmen are so sweet to women—so are American men. It is foolish, but sometimes it pays."

She was now a dim shape in the armchair.

"You mean that until we have been tricked we expect women to play the game?"

"Yes, perhaps that is it. But I have something to ask you

and something to tell you, and the time is short. First—you look for the girl called Ardatha?"

"And you believe that she is with Doctor Fu Manchu?"

"Yes!"

"Of course."

"She is not."

"What do you say?"

"She is with—my *friend*. Please let me go on. The name of this dear friend of mine is Lou Cabot. He is part owner of The Passion Fruit Tree where I am hostess. He is also the chief agent of the Si-Fan in the Canal Zone. He was sent to New York to bring Ardatha here——"

"Is he a sallow-faced fellow," I broke in savagely, for I was thinking of the man I had seen with Ardatha in the Regal Athenian—the man of Panama; "greasy black hair and semi side whiskers?"

"He might look so to you, but please listen. The society, the Si-Fan, is split into two parts: there is a conspiracy against the president, and Lou is of those who plan his ruin. A dangerous game. I told him—and so he will find it! So far so good. But now, if you please, because he is so sure of himself he has taken her away——"

"What!"

"Please, be patient: she may not have fought so hard; Lou has a charm for women——"

"Enough of that!" I said sharply.

Flammario glided to my side, threw one arm around me and rested her head on my shoulder.

"I am a woman," she whispered; "perhaps I know better than you when a man is fascinating to women. I do not think, myself, that her heart has changed about you. But I know—how well I know—that mine has changed! Listen again—my *friend* has wounded my pride. I know him now for a vain fool. He will surely die when the plot is known."

"Yes, but——"

"Yes, but I wish to *see* him die!" She laughed; it was musical but demoniacal laughter. "And if I can show you these two together I am sure that you will kill him. . . ."

Flammario was undeniably beautiful in an exotic way, but as she pronounced those last words I thought of a puma, a sleek, satiny, lithe, dangerous beast.

"I assure you I shall do my best! But where is she? Where is she?"

"I think I know. Later tonight I shall be sure."

"Then—quickly: what am I to do?"

She drew away from me; it was now nearly quite dark, and she appeared as a phantom.

"I will tell you—for someone must be here soon. You will make your friends promise—about me, and then be at The Passion Fruit tonight before twelve o'clock. You must be prepared to *act*——"

"How? Tell me."

I heard the elevator stop at our floor, heard the gate clang; I saw the phantom figure of Flammario drawn swiftly upright.

"Quick! Which is the better way?" I hesitated. "You promised—I trusted you. You can say I was here, but first let me go!"

"This way."

I led her through to Barton's room and opened the outer door.

"Tonight, before twelve—I shall expect you. . . ."

20 / *The Shrivelled Head*

AS I CLOSED THE DOOR after Flammario footsteps passed by outside. Whoever had come up in the elevator was not bound for our apartment. In a few more precious moments I might have learned so much, but now it was too late. . . . Ardatha in the hands of the sleek, sallow scoundrel I had seen in Panama! The mere idea made my blood boil. In some way I regarded the Chinese doctor as one might have regarded a disembodied spirit, although a spirit of evil; a sexless supermortal; but Lou Cabot . . . Could it be true?

Switching up the light, I turned and looked at a large cage which stood on a side table. Its occupant lay in the sleeping box, only a tiny grey-whiskered head drooping disconsolately out. I saw a bowl of food, untouched, upon the sanded floor. Peko the marmoset was near his end.

I approached the bars, staring in anxiously. Wicked little eyes regarded me, teeth were bared, and there was a faint whistling chatter. Peko might be moribund, but he could still hate all humanity. I returned to the sitting room, lighted up and took out the head in its mahogany box.

Shrivelled, hideous thing it was, and upon it (as again, overcoming my repulsion, I studied it more closely) there still rested the shadow of a distant agony. Was this no more than a trap? Why should I trust Zazima? Yet because the fate of Ardatha meant more to me, nor do I deny it, than the success or failure of the expedition upon which I was engaged I knew that I was prepared to believe in his sincerity—prepared to believe Flammario. I was mad with apprehension.

Opening the case, I peered inside eagerly. I could see nothing concealed there. Perhaps I must remove the head; perhaps some message was hidden in the shrivelled skull itself. But as I held the box by its carved and crudely coloured base I made a discovery which induced an even greater excitement. One of the painted knobs moved slightly. . . .

I was about to attempt to pull it from its place . . . when the head began to speak!

When I say that it began to speak I do not mean that any movement of those wasted features became perceptible; I mean that a low, obscene whispering proceeded from it.

I all but dropped the box. I was appalled; I think that any man must have been appalled. But I set it on the table. Then, as that high sibilance continued, I clenched my fists and forced myself to listen.

"So it befell—so it befell . . ." The whispering was in English! "Ica I was called—Ica . . . Chief was I of all the Quechua of Callao. But the *Jibaros* came: my women were taken, my house was fired, my head struck off. We were peaceful folk. But the head-hunters swept down upon us. Thought still lived in my skull, even when it was packed with burning sand. . . . My brain boiled, yet I knew that I was Ica, chief of the Quechua of Callao . . ."

The uncanny whisper died away. I stood there rigidly, staring at the head, when again a voice spoke from the box:

"Such is the brief obituary of Ica, chief of the Callao Quechuas."

And this voice was the voice of Dr Fu Manchu!

"If I address Mr Bart Kerrigan," it continued, "be good enough to press the red indicator on the right of the box once."

A sort of icy coolness, which in my case sometimes takes the place of panic, came now to my aid. Bending forward, I pressed the red knob which I had already discovered.

"The grotesque character of the receiving set before you," that high distant voice resumed, "was designed for a special purpose. It is otherwise similar to the example which Sir Denis deposited in Scotland Yard's Museum rather more than a year ago but which is no longer of any use. Listen attentively. If Sir Denis or anyone else joins you, press the blue indicator on the left of the box. The safety of Ardatha depends upon your obedience."

Almost I ceased to breathe.

"What I have to say must be said briefly: it is for you to employ it to good purpose. Your Western world is locked in a stupid clash of arms. You have created a situation resembling those traffic blocks which once were a feature of London. The shadow of Russia, that deformed colossus, frightens the children of Europe, none more so than the deluded Germans; but since one cannot wield the sword at the same time as one guides the ploughshare, nations far distant tremble for their trade. This is where East meets West. The more equally the scales be weighted, the more certainly a decimal of a gramme added to one of them must tip it."

The voice ceased; I feared that that which I most particularly wanted to hear was to be denied to me, but:

"I hold such a decimal of a gramme in my hand," the cold guttural voice continued. "That dangerous meddler, Sir Lionel Barton, dreamed of outwitting me. He failed. Mention to him that Haiti, and not Panama, is the home of the Snapping Fingers. He captured Peko, the marmoset who shares all my secrets, including that of longevity. You are unaware of the fact, but I have twice attempted to recover him and twice have been unsuccessful. In holding Peko I confess that you hold my heartstrings. In the wooden base upon which the head of Ica is mounted you will find a small phial containing a heavy liquid resembling chartreuse. Press the red indicator twice when you have found it."

Without hesitation (I wondered if anyone had ever disobeyed Dr Fu Manchu) I removed the shrivelled head, the base of which I found to be fixed in two grooves so that it could be pulled out from the box. I inverted it and saw that there was a sliding lid. Inside the cavity lay a phial and a tiny tortoise-shell snuffbox packed in cotton wool.

I reclosed this strange casket, replaced the head and followed instructions.

"You have in your hand," the imperious voice responded, "that which means the life not merely of an animal. One minim, no more, is to be added to one gill of fresh goat's milk. This must be given to the marmoset at once. Afterwards the milk once daily, with the liqueur only on every third day. An added fragment of the powder in the snuffbox will induce him to eat any suitable food. Press the red indicator once if you understand; otherwise twice."

When I had signified that I understood:

"See that Peko lives," the distant voice went on. "I am prepared to exchange Ardatha for Peko—when I have recovered Ardatha. There is a schism in our ancient ranks: an usurper seeks to be president, one who believes that the Nazi blunderers, who have recently approached me, can be used to our advantage. Here, in acting for yourself, you act also for me. There is a creature called Lou Cabot who has joined my enemies. So far he has escaped me. He is hiding in Colon; Ardatha is with him. You have Sir Denis and the Zone police; I have my own methods. Seek for this reptile. If you should chance to kill him it would save me trouble."

Again the voice ceased. I was in a state of intense nervous tension, but at last:

"Find Cabot," the voice added, now faintly and from far away. "Delay may be dangerous. . . . Take care of Peko. . . . I will restore . . ."

The voice ceased entirely.

21 / *Concerning Lou Cabot*

"IT WILL BE INTERESTING to learn," said Nayland Smith, "whether the Zone police, Doctor Fu Manchu or a jealous woman first discovers the whereabouts of this man Lou Cabot. However well hidden he may be, I may add that I do not envy Lou Cabot."

The hour grew late, and with every moment that passed my impatience grew hotter. Somewhere, perhaps within call of the balcony outside our windows, Ardatha was imprisoned at the mercy of the sallow-faced, sleek-eyed scoundrel who had tracked me in Panama! Smith relighted his pipe, shooting a quick glance in my direction.

"I do not necessarily believe the woman Flammario," he added, puffing vigorously.

"What could her object be?"

"Assuming it to be revenge—and your description depicts a woman whom it would be unwise to offend—it does not necessarily follow that her construction of the situation is the correct one. What I find hard to believe is this: that a member of the Si-Fan, presumably a senior official and therefore one well acquainted with their methods and efficiency, should, for a mere infatuation, invite the terrible penalties which must follow."

"I see your point," I replied miserably; "but if there is any truth at all in Flammario's story, what other explanation can there be?"

"One which occurred to me immediately," snapped Smith. "You had it from Fu Manchu himself. In one respect the doctor stands unique amongst all the villains I have known:

he never lies. Civil war has broken out in the ancient order of the Si-Fan: the man Cabot has joined the rebels. This, Flammario told you. I assume that Cabot is acting under the orders of the opposition leader."

"You mean that his interest in Ardatha is not personal, as Flammario thinks?"

"I mean just that. She, as a woman, would naturally think otherwise. Ardatha is in some way useful to the rebel members, and so they are endeavouring to smuggle her away. This is not the first time, Kerrigan, that strife has broken out in the Council of Seven. The last rebel who endeavoured to assume control of that vast and dreadful organisation——"

He ceased speaking and began to pace up and down restlessly.

"Yes?" I prompted.

"A train of thought, Kerrigan—possibly an inspiration."

He was still promenading, plunged in a brown study, when the door opened and Barton came in.

"Fu Manchu is undeniably a wizard physician," Sir Lionel declared. "The treatment he prescribed seems to have taken years off that beastly little marmoset. It is now as full of fight as a bulldog."

"I am glad," I said and spoke with sincerity. "I was afraid we were going to lose the thing."

"Any more messages from the Talking Head?" he inquired in his loud, facetious way.

"No." Smith suddenly emerged from some maze of speculation in which he had been lost. "We have tried pressing the red control—and, as you see, the door of the box is open."

"I am prepared to believe that it is a receiving set and not some kind of hypnotic machine," growled Barton, "when I have actually heard it for myself. It isn't connected up in any way; there is no battery in it; it's just an empty box— except, of course, for the shrivelled head."

"No doubt I should be as skeptical as you," Smith admitted, "if I had not had previous experience of this amazing apparatus. The head, of course, has nothing to do with the matter. Fu Manchu lacks a true sense of humour, but he has a strong sense of the baroque. Sometime when you are in London and have an hour to spare I must take you along to the Scotland Yard Museum. One of these receivers is there. European experts have overhauled the mechanism and have unanimously declared it to be without equipment for receiving and transmitting sound waves—yet it did, as Kerrigan can testify. My dear Barton, Doctor Fu Manchu is many generations ahead of others in nearly all the sciences.

I have never been able to make you understand that he has at his disposal many first-class brains other than his own."

"The facts of that *zombie* business are not too clear to me either," I confessed.

"If, as I suspect," said Smith rapidly, "Haiti or its neighbourhood prove to be the doctor's new headquarters, it is possible, Kerrigan, that you may learn more of this matter in the near future."

His gaze became abstracted again, and:

"What were you thinking about, Smith," I asked eagerly, "with regard to the internal troubles of the Si-Fan?"

"I was thinking," he replied and spoke with unwonted slowness, "of the woman feared by the whole of the Negro population of Haiti, the woman known as Queen Mamaloi. . . ."

"THERE HAS BEEN a thorough checkup on this man Cabot," said Beecher of the Zone police. Captain Jacob Beecher was tall, had a square frame and a square face. He looked efficiently dangerous. "We have a considerable *dossier Cabot* already; in fact, at one time there was a movement to throw him out of the area."

"What for?" asked Smith.

"Well, in that gin cellar of his he's sitting pretty to pick up information, and it was thought, but it couldn't be proved, that he was Fifth Column man for one of the dictator teams. Personally, I still think he is. He has a lot of money and substantial interests around Panama; but although The Passion Fruit Tree is a dividend maker, I don't believe all his money comes from there."

"Where does this bird roost?" asked Barton.

"Well, sir, he has ritzy quarters right on the premises, and I guess the villa where Flammario lives (she's his partner) is Lou's property anyway."

"But," I asked, "where is he now? Have you any information on that point?"

"No sir. We know he went to New York beginning of last week, and there's some evidence that he came back two or three days ago. But he hasn't been seen in The Passion Fruit or in any of his usual haunts. One thing is fairly certain: his girl friend has soured on him."

"You are sure of this?" snapped Smith.

"Certain. Some of my boys who keep an eye on the place— it's right enough in its way, but at times they've sailed pretty close to the rocks—report that there's another dame in the case. Flammario is out for murder." He looked about with his cold, unwinking eye. "I may add, gentlemen, that although we have never had that pretty on the books, it's known that she doesn't stick at trifles."

"Is the man an American citizen?" I asked.

"Yes—they are both Americans by adoption. Makes it kind of difficult, you see. But whatever the truth may be about Cabot, I have always held that the woman has nothing to do with his political work—if he is really engaged on political work."

"Have you ever heard of a society known as the Si-Fan?" asked Smith.

"Sure. One of the Chinese tongs, isn't it? When I was in the Philippines I came across them once in a while, but, except maybe in the Chinese quarter, I don't think they figure in the Canal Zone."

"Indeed!" murmured Smith. "But I assume you have had no occasion to pursue such an inquiry?"

"None whatever—how would I? It isn't the Chinese we worry about around here. . . ."

"Nor is the Si-Fan exclusively Chinese," said Smith. "But since you can give me no information on this point, we will not pursue it. Let us make our plans for the evening."

"My plans are made," said Barton. "We've been taking chances here. What about the charts? The steel box is in the hotel safe. What about that damned monkey? One of us has always got to be in this apartment until we leave. I don't like missing the fun—but I'll stay on guard tonight."

"As you wish, Barton," said Smith; "I entirely agree with you. And now, Captain Beecher, the position is this: We have to find Lou Cabot, and this woman Flammario has undertaken to tell us tonight where he is hiding."

"If anyone can find out, she can," murmured the police officer. "The Passion Fruit scouts know every sewer in the town."

"Very well. Mr Kerrigan and I propose to go along there immediately. Is the place a restaurant, a cabaret or a club?"

"All three," was the reply, "and plenty expensive. There's a cover charge of five dollars a head, paid as you go in, whether you want supper or not. If you like, I'll come along with you. But I rather thought of standing by with a few of the boys in case any quick action should be called for."

"That would be best," said Smith. "Merely give me full particulars regarding the place and be somewhere within sight of the entrance if I should want you."

"All ready," said Police Captain Beecher. "As the idea is to get in touch with Flammario, I suggest, when you go in, that you sit at a table outside the bar—the balcony, see. Don't go down onto the dance floor. The bar opens right out of the lobby. If you want to leave in a hurry, that's the best place. One of my boys who knows you by sight will be right outside. Maybe I'll come too. . . ."

22 / *The Passion Fruit Tree*

I CANNOT VOUCH for the accuracy of my notes regarding The Passion Fruit Tree. The bare idea of Ardatha being in the power of the man Lou Cabot, of whose private life I had heard much before our arrival, had made me long to have my fingers around his throat. The primary appeal of the resort was to tourists. That puritan spirit which governs the Canal Zone disapproved of the impression which might be carried away by visitors to The Passion Fruit, which twice had been closed and twice reopened again under ostensibly new management.

It did not present a dazzling façade to the world; merely a shadowy doorway above which in illuminated letters appeared the words "The Passion Fruit Tree." A cloudless sky studded with stars dimmed the glamour of the appeal. It was a hot, still night, and a murderous pulse was beating in my temple.

On entering I discovered the lobby to be painted with murals representing jungle scenes, and from a reception office trellised with flowering vines a shrewd-looking old coloured woman peered out. A powerful mulatto in uniform was in attendance, and everywhere one saw pictures of Flammario. We paid the extortionate entrance fee and walked through to the bar. The strains of a dance band reached my ears, and now I saw that one side of the bar opened upon a balcony which overlooked the dance floor.

Subdued lighting prevailed throughout as did the jungle scheme of decoration. I was dimly aware of the presence of people at tables on the balcony, but Smith and I alone sat at the bar over which a coloured attendant presided. When he had ordered drinks:

"I am naturally suspicious," said Smith in a low voice, "when we are dealing with the Si-Fan. Even now I am not satisfied that this may not be a trap of some kind."

"But, Smith, no attempt is likely to be made here!"

"I was thinking more particularly of Barton and of Ardatha."

Our drinks were served; he paid the man, and the latter walked to a chair at one end of the bar.

"Regarding Barton, I see what you mean. It might be an elaborate plan to split up the party?"

Smith nodded.

"But," he added, "Barton is an old campaigner and, as we know, very well capable of taking care of himself. Furthermore, although I have not notified him of the fact, there is a police officer on duty outside our apartment tonight."

"But Ardatha?"

"I am disposed to think"—he spoke in a very low voice—"that she is actually in Colon. All this may be a red herring designed to get us out of the way whilst she is smuggled elsewhere. But in the circumstances we can do nothing but wait for some sign from this woman Flammario."

"I still believe," said I, "that she is sincere."

"Possibly," Smith replied; "at least in her passionate hatred of Cabot. Let us hope so." He glanced at his watch. "Three minutes to midnight. Suppose we go in and survey the scene."

We went out onto the balcony, a place heavy with tobacco smoke and a reek of stale perfume. There were three men at an end table and two women at another. The women were obviously dancing partners. They were smoking cigarettes and drinking coffee; after a momentary professional glance in our direction they resumed a bored conversation. The men, I thought, looked harmless enough; probably passengers from a ship passing through the canal, out visiting the high spots of Colon. We looked down at the dancing floor.

An orchestra concealed under the balcony was serving out swing music, pianissimo and at a very slow tempo. Only three pairs were dancing, and these also bore unmistakable evidence of being passengers ashore for the night. There were supper tables set along a sort of arcade on the left of the floor, but not more than half were occupied. Except for the persistent jungle note it was a scene which had its duplicate in almost any city in the world. A hot irritation possessed me.

"Smith," I said, "this somnolent booze shop is going to get on my nerves. Whenever I think what we are up against—of the fate of Ardatha—this awful inactivity drives me mad."

"The calm before the storm," he answered in a low voice. "Observe the two men at a supper table right at the other end, the table with the extinguished lamp."

I looked in the direction indicated. Two stocky Asiatics whose evening clothes could not disguise their tremendously powerful torsos were seated there. Slitlike eyes betrayed no indication of where or at whom they were looking. But although individually I had never seen the men before, they were of a type with which I had become painfully familiar in the past.

"Good God, Smith!" I exclaimed. "Surely a pair of Fu Manchu's thugs."

"Certainly."

"Then you were right—it *is* a trap. . . . They're waiting for us!"

"Somehow I don't think so," he replied. "I regard their presence as distinctly encouraging. In my opinion they are waiting for Lou Cabot. Our night will not be a dull one, Kerrigan."

THE BAND CEASED, the dancers returned to their places. All the lights went out, and then a drum began to beat with the rhythm of a darabukkeh. A lime directed through a trap in the roof shone across the empty floor and upon the figure of Flammario.

Her costume did not interfere in any way with appreciation of her beauty, and as she stood there for a moment motionless none could have denied that the gods had endowed her with a splendid form. Her briliant eyes were raised to the balcony; and although I doubted if she could see, because of the beam of light, I was convinced that she was looking for us.

To the drumbeat was added a monotonous reed melody, and Flammario began to dance. It was one of those African dances which for my part I regard as definitely unpleasant, but judging from the rapt silence of a now invisible audience I may have been in the minority. She moved languorously along the edge of the arcade where the supper tables were set until at last she was directly beneath us. There for a moment she paused, raised her eyes, and:

"Yes!" she said.

The deep-toned, slightly hoarse voice was clearly audible above the throb of the music, and into that one word Flammario had injected triumph—and a barbaric hatred. As she continued her dance, proceeding now towards the entrance through which she had made her appearance, Smith bent to my ear.

"She has found him! The woman wins. There is not a moment to waste if we are to get there ahead of Fu Manchu's thugs. Now to establish contact."

To a frenzied crescendo the dancer finished. She stood for a moment arms upraised and then stepped back into the shadow behind the limelight. Smith and I were up, tense, ready for action. But the almost complete darkness remained unbroken, and as we waited Flammario reappeared wearing a silk wrap. She acknowledged the applause of her audience.

Again she retired, and as the lights sprang up instinctively I stared in the direction of the end supper table.

The two yellow men had gone.

"Good God!" snapped Smith. "It's going to be touch and go. Somehow, Kerrigan, they have got hold of the information!"

He had started back towards the bar when he was intercepted by a strange figure entering. It was that of a hunchback Negro, emaciated as with long illness, his small, cunning eyes so deeply set in his skull as to be almost invisible.

"Mr Kerrigan, please?"

He looked from face to face.

"Yes," snapped Smith, "this is Mr Kerrigan. What do you want?"

"Follow, if you please. Hurry."

We required no stimulus but followed the stooping figure. As we came into the bar I saw that the attendant had the flags raised at the further end. We hurried through a doorway beyond; the door was closed behind us. Down a flight of stairs we ran and along a corridor not too well lighted. At the end I saw Flammario. She wore a long sable cloak, and as we hurried forward I realised that she stood at the door of a small but luxuriously furnished dressing room.

"Quick!" she cried. Her eyes were gleaming madly. "You are ready to start?"

"Yes. This is Sir Denis Nayland Smith. You have found Cabot?"

"I told you I had found him. I tell you now we must hurry."

"Two agents of the Si-Fan were here a few moments ago," said Smith rapidly. "Did you see them?"

She shrugged impatiently and the fur fell away from one bare shoulder. She snatched it back into place.

"I have to dance again in half an hour," she explained simply. "Of course I saw them." She stepped forward, forcing a way between Smith and myself. "Paulo!" she cried.

I turned and looked along the empty passage. The hunchback Negro had disappeared.

"Do you think they have got the information?" jerked Smith.

"There is no time to think!" cried Flammario. "I tell you we must act. My car is outside. I know the way."

"A police car would be faster," said Smith on an even note. "One is waiting."

Flammario was already running along the passage.

"Any damn car you like!" she shouted. "But hurry! I have only half an hour, and I want to see him killed. Hurry! I show you where he is—and the girl is with him."

POLICE CAPTAIN JACOB BEECHER was waiting
beside a police department car not three paces from
the side entrance to The Passion Fruit Tree.

"All set," he said as we ran out. "Where to?"

"Listen, Big Jake," cried Flammario hoarsely, "this is my
night, and so I give the orders."

Even in this side turning to which moonlight did not penetrate I could see the flash of her eyes.

"I am listening," growled Beecher.

"This is a gentlemen's agreement and I have two gentlemen
with me. You and your boys just cover us. Leave the rest to
me and my friends."

"But where in hell are we going?" growled Beecher. "Tell
me and I'll make arrangements."

"We are going right to Santurce, and we are moving fast.
Do you know the home that used to belong to Weisman, the
engineer they fire from the canal service—eh?"

"Sure I know it."

"That is where we go."

"It was hired to somebody else."

"Somebody else we are looking for."

Then, Nayland Smith and a police driver in front and I
and Flammario at the back, we set out through a velvety
tropical darkness sharply cut off where a brilliant moon
splashed it into silver patches. Santurce, as a residential
suburb, I had deliberately overlooked in my recent quest for
the shop of Zazima, so that soon, leaving more familiar parts
of Colon behind, I found myself upon strange ground. Flammario clutched my arm, pressed her head against my shoulder
and poured out a torrent of words.

"It is Paulo who finds him. Paulo can find anyone or anything in the Canal Zone. But Paulo is of the Si-Fan. You
understand—eh?"

"Yes. I expected it."

"Although he would do anything for me, he is terrified of
them. Why does he run away tonight? Where do those two
thugs go? What you think?"

"I think he gave them the information."

"It seem that way to me." She nestled closer. I was aware
of a musky perfume. "You are right about your girl friend.
He has her locked up. But give Lou time and he sets an ice-
berg on fire. No, please, do not be angry. I tell you. I can

overlook so much—why not? But all the town knows he leave me flat—me, Flammario. Queer, eh, how a woman feel about a thing like this? Just as hard as I used to love him—I hate him now." She slipped a bare arm about my shoulder. "You will kill him, won't you?"

With a sincerity which was not assumed I replied:

"Given half a chance, I absolutely undertake to do so."

Flammario's heavily painted lips were pressed to my left ear.

On the corner of a street in which there were detached villas, each surrounded by its own garden, a big black saloon car was drawn up with no lights on. We passed it and swung into a street beyond.

A moment later we, too, pulled up. I had now quite lost my bearings. White-fronted houses with their shuttered windows, young palms shooting tender masts out of banks of foliage, made a restful picture in the tropical moonlight, a picture bearing no relation to the facts which had brought us there. As we scrambled out, Flammario ahead of all, a police officer detached himself from the shadows of a high wall.

"Squad all ready," he reported. "What orders?"

"Do nothing until we are in," Smith replied rapidly, "and keep well out of sight. The signal will be a blast on my police whistle—or shooting. The men are standing by?"

"In the big saloon back there. Captain Beecher worked fast. Making for their posts right now."

Flammario already was running ahead.

"One thing is important," said Smith insistently. "Grab anyone that comes out."

We overtook Flammario racing up a tree-shaded path towards a green-shuttered house from which no lights shone.

"How do we get in?" she panted. "Have you figured that out?"

"I have figured it out," Smith replied, and I observed for the first time that she was carrying a handbag.

The front of the house was bathed in moonlight, but dense shrubbery grew up to it on the left, and here I saw a porched door. We pulled up, watching and listening.

"Listen," said Flammario. "This house is planned by an architect with a one-track mind. He does most of the building around here. Can you count on the police? Because when we break in, if I know Lou, he will run for it."

"The place will be surrounded in another minute," snapped Smith irritably. "This door here in the shadow: does it lead to the kitchen?"

"Yes. And that is our way in. It is half glass. Smash it, and if the key is inside, we are through."

"We could try," muttered Smith.

We advanced, always in shadow, to the porch.

"Show a light, Kerrigan," said Smith.

I shone the ray of a torch upon the door—then caught my breath. The glass panel was shattered to fragments, the door half open . . .

"My God!" groaned Smith, "we're too late!"

THE KITCHEN QUARTERS showed no evidence of disturbance. If utensils recently had been in use, someone had cleaned and put everything away. There was a spotless white-tiled larder. In that immaculate domestic atmosphere the barbaric figure of Flammario, wrapped in her sables, those jungle eyes flashing from point to point, stuck a note truly bizarre.

"They are here ahead of us," she began in a hoarse whisper. "That mongrel Paulo——"

"Quiet!" Smith said imperatively yet in a low voice. "I want to listen."

And the three of us stood here, listening.

Very remotely sounds from the Canal reached me: shipping sounds which transported my thoughts to the early stages of this ghastly business which had led me to Colon. But immediately about us and inside the house was complete silence. I was about to speak when:

"Ssh!" whispered Smith.

Tensely I listened—and presently I heard the sound which had arrested his attention. It was a very faint creaking, and it came from somewhere upstairs.

"They are still here!" exploded Flammario. "Have your guns ready!"

With that she raced out of the kitchen into a passage beyond, switching up the lights as she went—a feat which surprised me at first until I recollected her words about the architect with a one-track mind. I found myself in a dining room very simply furnished. The curtains were drawn along the whole of one side, and to these Flammario darted, wrenching them apart. I saw a garden dappled with molten silver where the moon poured down upon it. There was a terrace outside with cane chairs and tables, but there was no one there.

The atmosphere smelled stale as that of a room unused, and for some reason, in an automatic way, I unfastened the catch of one of the french windows and pulled it open. The perfume of some night-scented flower was borne in upon a light breeze, even as I recognised that I was acting irrationally, that the place would be filled with nocturnal insects, and so reclosed the window:

"There it is again!" said Smith.

We fell silent, listening. . . . Unmistakably there was a sound of movement upstairs.

Smith was already dashing for a door at the other end of the room. Flammario overtook him and switched up a light in a square lobby. We started up a short flight of carpeted stairs so rapidly that I made a bad third. On the landing, the light of which was subdued, three doors offered—and they were all locked.

"This where we want the coppers!" said Flammario huskily. "Blow that whistle of yours."

"Quiet!"

I could hear her rapid breathing as she stood beside me in semidarkness, for the only light was a sort of shaded lantern. One, two, five, ten seconds we waited, but the silence remained unbroken. I pictured Ardatha gagged and bound—I pictured her dead. I think in all my quest of her since she had revealed to me the truth of her slavery to Dr Fu Manchu I had experienced no keener sense of longing to hear her voice, of terror that I should never hear it again.

"Blowing a lock out is not so easy in fact as in fiction," said Smith; "but these are not the good old-fashioned kind of doors—just matchwood and three-ply. See what a hundred and seventy pounds can do with that one, Kerrigan. I'll tackle this."

Pushing Flammario aside, I stood back from the door to within a stride of the staircase and then, shoulder down, hurled myself upon it.

A metallic rattle and a faint creak rewarded my first charge. Smith had attacked that immediately facing the staircase. He had had no greater success.

"Kick a panel out, Kerrigan!" he cried. "There may be a key inside."

I tried, whilst the strange woman from The Passion Fruit Tree urged us on.

"Go to it, boys!" she screamed huskily. "Never weaken! We are here to kill!"

I did some damage to the door which, although stout, was of unseasoned wood. Failing to break through, I cursed under my breath, clenched my teeth and, once more standing back, hurled my weight upon it. So successful was the second attack that the door crashed open and I pitched headfirst into darkness.

Staggering to my feet, breathing heavily, I groped my way back to the doorway to find the switch. As I turned up the light a sound of banging and splintering came from the landing outside.

I was in an untidy office. The drawers of a roll-top desk had been broken open and the place showed other evidences of a hasty search. However, it was empty, and it seemed to possess no other door. I ran back onto the landing just as Smith had kicked his right heel through a panel.

Reaching in, he evidently found a key, for a moment later the door was thrown open. I followed him into what proved to be a small suite, sitting room, bedroom and bathroom, fitted up in an effeminate and luxurious manner.

There were framed pictures of women, mostly cabaret artistes, upon the walls; a deep-cushioned divan; a shaded lamp held aloft by an ivory nymph in a niche behind it. Fine Persian carpets covered the floor; I saw leopard skins and exotic furniture. There was a faint perfume in the place.

"This is Lou's new nest," said Flammario breathlessly. "I know his tracks." She ran into the bedroom. "Not a trace. No one has been here."

"Where is Ardatha?" muttered Smith. "Come on; the third door."

But outside we pulled up at a hissed injunction and stood awhile silent.

"Do you hear it?" cried Flammario. "That rat, Lou, is hiding in the loft!"

"How do we get to the loft?" snapped Smith.

"Through this door. There are two other rooms beyond, and a back stair to the loft."

Turn and turn about, Smith and I hurled ourselves against the third door until at last with a splintering crash it gave. We crowded into a short passageway, rooms right and left; both doors were wide open. In one which had shuttered windows we found the evidence for which we sought. . . .

It was a bedroom with a bathroom attached. The lock of the door had been smashed in. The bed was disordered, but the coverlet had not been turned down: in other words, no one had slept in the bed. Smith ran eagerly from point to point like a hound keen on the scent.

"This is where he had her locked up!" he cried.

"Sure!" snarled Flammario. "These cigarettes in the tray were smoked by a woman."

"You are right! And after the door was crashed in the woman was dragged out. It is easy enough to reconstruct the scene. And, hello! What have we here?"

I saw something glittering at his feet as, stooping, he picked up a ring—a beautifully cut scarab of lapis lazuli set in a dull gold band. At sight of it I knew—and what I knew chilled me. No further possibility of doubt remained.

It was Ardatha's ring.

24 / Flammario's Cloak Slips

"SHE WAS CONSCIOUS when they carried her off," said Smith. "This ring was left as a clue. A consolation to know that they did not drug her."

But Flammario was already out in the passage which, as I saw now, terminated on a landing leading up to a back staircase. The stair ended before a small door.

We ran up. The platform before the door was so narrow as to give little purchase for an attack, but:

"There's no metal surround to this keyhole," said Smith. "The door is fast. I shall try to shoot the lock out. . . . *Ssh!* Listen!"

He and I stood still for a moment, listening again. A subdued scrambling sound which might almost have been made by a rat came to my ears.

"Here goes!" snapped Smith.

It was as he fired once, twice, and muffled detonations echoed weirdly about the place that I thought of Flammario —turned and found that she was not there!

"Smith!" I cried. "Flammario has gone!"

"Can't help that!" he cried. "Those shots will have brought up the raid squad."

I followed him into a storeroom lighted by a single lamp suspended from rafters. It contained nothing more than the usual lumber of suburban households, representing, I suspected, some of the effects of the former occupant. Then I saw something else.

There was one window, a low gable window. That part of it made to open was not wide enough to permit the passage of a man's body, but the frame of the larger part beneath had been forced out of place; fragments of glass lay on the floor, suggesting that, leaning through the opening above, someone who had been in the attic had knocked the glass in from the outside and then forced the sash. As Smith craned out:

"A balcony just below," he reported, "running outside those rooms we have already seen. . . . And, hello!—a stair up to it from the garden!"

He turned and ran to the door.

"You understand, Kerrigan?" he cried. "Fu Manchu's thugs got here before us! The man Cabot, who had Ardatha locked in that room below, bolted up here to save himself. What he had planned to do he has done: forced a way through this window, dropped onto the balcony below and, unless the police catch him—made a clean getaway!"

We were running along the lower passage now, making for the staircase.

A theory to account for the remarkable behaviour of Flammario at the moment that Smith and I had entered the loft had just begun to form in my mind as we ran down the stairs, across and out through the kitchen to the back porch. The balcony from which the fugitive had made his escape ran along this side of the house. As we came into the darkness there Smith, a pace ahead of me, pulled up suddenly and grasped my wrist with a grip that hurt.

A high, piercing shriek, followed by gurgling, sobbing sounds, split the silence frightfully.

As that dreadful cry died away I heard a shout—a sound of running footsteps. The police were closing in. Two paces forward we moved hesitantly, and there, half in shadow and half silhouetted against a silver curtain of moonight, I saw Flammario. She stood at the foot of the steps leading down from the balcony. Her cloak had slipped; she looked like a sculptured Fury.

Hearing us, she turned in our direction. I could see the glitter of her amber eyes. Then, stooping into the shadows at her feet, she retrieved the sable cloak, threw it about her shoulders.

"I reckon that balances our account, Lou," she panted.

Captain Beecher raced up to join us, followed by two other police officers, as a ray from Smith's torch shone fully down upon a man who lay there. He was prone but in falling had twisted his head sideways, as if at the moment that death came he had looked swiftly behind him. Staring eyes held a question, which had been horribly answered.

It was the man of Panama.

His fingers were embedded in the turf on which he lay, and the hilt of a dagger, decorated with silver which glittered evilly in the light, protruded squarely from between his shoulder blades.

Police Captain Beecher glanced from the dead man to the fur-wrapped figure of Flammario, whose tawny eyes regarded him contemptuously.

"So we have you on the books at last!"

"Forget it!" rapped Smith. "She won't run away. The girl, the girl who was captive here, has been carried off. She must not be smuggled out of Colon. Advise the port. Hold all outgoing shipping till further orders. Spare no efforts."

But what with frustrated hopes and new fears, such a cloak of misery had descended upon me that I could not think consistently. There was movement all about; the issuing of rapid orders, men hurrying away. And presently, reaching me as if from a distance, came Smith's words:

"Take care of Flammario. After all, she has done her best for us. Return straight to the hotel."

A hand touched my arm. I looked into brilliant amber eyes.

"Drive me back, please," said Flammario, "or I shall be late for my show. . . ."

Of what she said to me on the way back, this red-handed murderess, I recollect not one word. I know that her arms were about me. I presume it was a normal gesture employed whenever she found herself alone in a man's company. I think, just before we reached the side entrance to The Passion Fruit Tree, that she kissed me on the lips, that I started back. She laughed huskily. I would have left her at the door, but:

"You have lost your girl friend," she said; "you must want a drink." I think in her half-savage way she was trying to be sympathetic. "Go through there to the bar. If you wait, I have a drink with you."

As she ran towards her dressing room I opened the back door to the bar. It was true that suddenly, and only at that very moment, did I realise how badly I needed a stiff brandy and soda. The barman turned swiftly but, recognising me, allowed me to pass.

There was no one in the bar, and he had just placed my drink before me when the lights went out.

Morbid curiosity induced me to walk out onto the balcony. A subdued, excited hum of conversation rose from below; evidently there had been other arrivals. Then, to the muted strains of the unseen band, Flammario entered.

She stood there, picked up by the lime, and slowly began to dance—her lips set in the eternal voluptuous smile of the African dancers of all time, the smile which lives forever upon the painted walls of ancient Egypt.

Fascinated against my will, I watched her, when from behind me I heard the faint note of a telephone bell. A moment later the barman touched me on the shoulder.

"You are wanted on the phone."

Desperation fought to conquer hope within me as I took up the receiver. The caller was Nayland Smith.

"Come back at once. . . . Barton has been knocked out."

"SMITH!" I said, "he's not dying?"

"Thank God, no."

He and I stood looking down at Sir Lionel Barton where he lay livid, his breathing scarcely perceptible. I turned to a man wearing a white jacket who stood at the foot of the bed.

"You are sure, Doctor?"

Dr Andrews nodded, and his smile was reassuring.

"He's had an emetic, and I've washed him out with permanganate of potassium," he replied; "also I've poured coffee down his throat—very strong. Fortunately he has a constitution like a bullock. Oh, he'll be all right. I have given him a shot of atropine. We'll have him round before long."

"But how," I said, looking about from face to face, "did this happen? What of the police officer on duty outside?"

"Went the same way!" replied Dr Andrews. "But not for the same reason, nor is he responding so well."

"How do you account for that?"

"You see"—the doctor took up a tumbler from a side table—"This contains whiskey and also (I have tasted it) a big shot of opium. In other words, Sir Lionel Barton has swallowed the narcotic and I have thoroughly washed him out. But the sergeant of police smoked a drugged cigarette."

"What!"

"Yes," snapped Smith. "I have the remains of the packet; they are all drugged."

"But surely he could taste it?"

"No." The physician shook his head. "Indian hemp was used in this case, and the brand of cigarette was of a character which"—he shrugged his shoulders—"would disguise almost anything."

"But where could the man have obtained these cigarettes?"

"Don't ask me, Kerrigan," said Smith wearily. "As well ask why Barton, alone in these apartments, permitted someone to drug his whiskey."

"But was he alone here when you returned?"

"He was found alone. I was recalled from police headquarters, and from there I phoned you. They had discovered the police sergeant unconscious in the corridor. Naturally the management came in here and found Barton."

"Where was he?"

"In an armchair in the sitting room, completely unconscious, with that glass beside him."

"And . . . ?"

"Yes! We have lost our hostage, Kerrigan. The marmoset has gone."

"But, Smith," I cried desperately, "it doesn't seem humanly possible!"

"Anything is possible when one is dealing with Doctor Fu Manchu. The fact which we have to face is that it has happened. Two men, fully capable of taking care of themselves, fully on the alert, are drugged. Someone, unseen by anybody in the hotel, gains access to these rooms, removes the cage containing the marmoset and lowers it out of the sitting-room window, which I found open, to someone else waiting in the garden below. At that late hour the garden would be deserted; in short, the rest of the matter is simple."

"Thank God old Barton has survived," I said, "but heaven help us all—we are fighting a phantom. . . . Ardatha!"

Smith leaned across the bed on which the unconscious may lay and grasped my shoulder.

"Fu Manchu has recovered her. It may be an odd thing to say when speaking of the greatest power for evil living in the world today, but for my part I would rather think of her with the doctor than with——"

"Lou Cabot? Yes, I agree."

"In taking no part in your conversation, gentlemen," said Dr Andrews, "I am actuated by a very simple motive: I don't know what you are talking about. That there is or was someone called Doctor Fu Manchu I seem to have heard, certainly. In what way he is associated with my two patients I do not know. But regarding Lou Cabot—I presume you refer to the proprietor of The Passion Fruit Tree—you touch upon familiar territory. I have had the doubtful honour of attending this man on more than one occasion——"

"You will attend him no more," said Smith.

"What is that?"

"He's dead," I began.

Smith flashed a silent, urgent message to me, and:

"He died tonight, Doctor, up at Santurce," he explained, "under mysterious circumstances."

"Good riddance!" murmured Dr Andrews. "A more cunning villain never contrived to plant himself in the Canal Zone. The fellow was an agent for some foreign government. Doctors must not tell, but I heard strange things when he was delirious on one occasion."

"Foreign government," murmured Smith, staring shrewdly at the speaker. "Perhaps a foreign *power*, Doctor, but not a government—yet."

SEVERAL HOURS ELAPSED before Barton became capable of coherent speech. The man drugged with hashish cigarettes was causing Dr Andrews some anxiety. Lying back in an armchair, visibly pale in spite of a sun tan on a naturally florid skin, Barton stared at us. It was dawn and to me a wretched one.

No clue, not even the most slender, as to the whereabouts of Ardatha had been picked up. Flammario had forced a confession from the hunchback Paulo. The agents of the Si-Fan had intercepted him as he had returned with the news for which she was seeking. In this way, by less than twenty minutes, the Si-Fan had anticipated our visit to the villa occupied by Lou Cabot, the circumstances of whose death the authorities had agreed to hush up in the interests of the vastly more important inquiry being carried out by Nayland Smith.

"I must be getting old," said Barton weakly. "At any rate I feel damned sick. Definitely I refuse to drink any more coffee."

"Very well," said Smith, "but whiskey is taboo until tomorrow."

"Tomorrow! It's tomorrow already," growled Barton. His blue eyes were rapidly regaining their normal fire. "Naturally you want to know how I came to make such an infernal ass of myself. Well, I can't tell you."

"What do you mean, you can't tell us?"

"I mean I don't know. I had just mixed myself a final and was going out to make sure that the police officer you were kind enough to allot to me (whose presence I had discovered earlier) was awake when I thought I heard that damned padding sound."

"You mean the soft footsteps we have heard before?"

"Yes. Now let me give you the exact facts: I assure you they are peculiar. I had been to take a look at that blasted marmoset. He was asleep. I opened the door of my own room onto the main corridor and glanced along to see if the police officer was awake. He was. He sang out, and I wished him good night; but he is a garrulous fellow and he held me in conversation for some time."

"Your door remaining open?" suggested Smith.

"Yes—that's the point."

"Was the sergeant smoking?"

"He smoked all the time."

"Was his manner normal?"

"Undoubtedly. Never stopped talking."

"And you heard no unusual sound?"

"None whatever. I came in, sat down, lighted a pipe and

was about to take a drink—when I *saw* something. I want to make it quite clear, Smith, that I saw this before I took the drink, and I want to add that it was not a delusion and that I was very wide awake."

"What did you see?"

Barton stared truculently at Smith as he replied:

"I saw *a green hand!*"

"A green hand!" I echoed.

Smith began to pace up and down restlessly, tugging at the lobe of his left ear.

"I saw a human hand floating in space—no arm, no body. It was sea green in colour. It was visible for no more than a matter of ten seconds, then it vanished. It was over by the door there——"

"What did you do?" snapped Smith.

"I ran to the spot; I searched everywhere. I began to wonder if there was anything wrong with me. This prompted the idea of a drink, so I sat down and took one. The last thing I remember thinking is that this hotel sells the world's worst whiskey."

"You mean that you fell asleep?"

"No doubt about it."

Smith kept up that restless promenade.

"A green hand," he muttered, "and those padding footsteps. . . . What *is* it? What in heaven's name *is* it?"

"I don't know what it is," growled Barton, "but I thank God I'm alive. It's Fu Manchu—of that I am certain. But there's no love lost between us. Why didn't he finish me?"

"That I think I can answer," Smith replied. "Several days have yet to elapse before his First Notice or ultimatum expires. The doctor has a nice sense of decorum."

"I gather that he has recaptured the girl Ardatha. You have my very sincere sympathy, Kerrigan. I don't know what to say. I alone am responsible . . . and I lost your hostage."

I bent down and shook his hand as he lay back in the armchair.

"Not a word, Barton," I said, "on that subject. Our enemy uses mysterious weapons which neither you nor I know how to counter."

"Death by the Snapping Fingers," murmured Smith; "the green hand—and the shadow which comes and goes but which no one ever sees. How did Fu Manchu get here? Where did he hide? How does he travel and where has he gone?" He pulled up in front of me. "You have to make a quick decision, Kerrigan. As you know, my plans are fixed. Tomorrow we leave for Port-au-Prince."

"I know," I groaned, "and I know that it would be useless for me to remain behind."

26 / Second Notice

ONLY MY KNOWLEDGE that in war-scarred Europe many thousands suffered just as I was suffering held me up during the next few days. Although I know I dreamed of her every night, resolutely in the waking hours I strove to banish all thought of Ardatha from my mind. As I saw the matter, we had lost every trick so far. In a mood of deadly, useless introspection I remained throughout the journey to Haiti. For the time all zest for the battle left me, and then it returned in the form of a cold resolution. If she were alive I would find her again; I would face the dreadful Chinese doctor who held her life in his hands and accept any price which he exacted from me for her freedom—short of betraying my principles.

Many times I had opened the glass front of the box containing the shrivelled head and had pressed the red control; it had remained silent. But these notes, actually written some time later, bring me to the occurrence which jolted me sharply back from a sort of fatalistic passivity to active interest in affairs of the moment.

We were quartered in a hotel in Port-au-Prince; not that in which the Snapping Fingers had appeared. Nayland Smith habitually eschewed official residences, preferring complete freedom of movement. The beauty of Haiti, its flowers and trees and trailing vines; the gay-plumaged birds and painted butterflies; those sunsets passing from shell pink through every colour appreciated by the human eye into deep purple night: all formed but a gaudy background to my sorrow. And those purple nights throughout which distant drums beat ceaselessly—remorselessly—to me seemed to be throbbing her name: *Ardatha—Ardatha!* Can I ever forget these dark hours in Haiti?

Following such a restless drum-haunted night I came downstairs one morning—a morning destined to be memorable.

One side of the dining room opened upon a pleasant tropical garden in which palms mingled with star-apple trees and flowering creepers which formed festoons from branch to branch and trellised the pillars against one of which our table was set. At this season, we had learned from the proprietor, business normally was slack; but, as in Cristobal, the hotel was full. In fact, failing instructions sent to the American consul,

I doubt if we should have secured accommodation. Even so, our party had been split up; and looking around, whilst making my way across to my friends, I recognized the fact that of the twelve or fifteen people present in the dining room there were at least four whom I had seen in Colon!

Taking my place at the table:

"Are these spies following *us*, Smith?" I asked, wearily shaking out my napkin, "or are *we* following them?"

"The very thing, Kerrigan," said Barton in a whisper audible a hundred yards away, "which I have been asking Smith."

"Neither," Smith replied shortly. "But the position of the Allied forces in Europe is so critical that if action is to come from this side of the Atlantic it must come soon. I don't suggest that the British Empire is in danger; I mean that any other power wishing to take a hand in the game must act now or never. The United States in not impregnable on the Caribbean front. At least one belligerent is watching and possibly a 'neutral.' Doctor Fu Manchu is watching all of them." He pushed his plate aside and lighted a cigarette. "Had a good night, Kerrigan?"

"Not too good. Did you?"

"No. Those infernal drums."

"Exactly."

"I thought I was back in Africa," growled Barton. "Felt that way the first time I landed here."

"It *is* Africa," said Smith shortly. "An African island in the Caribbean. Those drums which beat all through the night, near and far, on hills and in valleys—since we arrived do you know what they have been saying?"

I stared at him perhaps a little vacantly.

"No," I replied; "the language of African drums is a closed book to me."

"It used to be to me." He ceased speaking as a Haitian waiter placed grapefruit before me and withdrew. "But they use drums in Burma, you know—in fact, all over India. In my then capacity—Gad! it seems many years ago—I went out of my way to learn how messages were flashed quicker than the telegraph could work, quick as radio, from one end of the country to another. I picked up the elements, but I can't claim to be an expert. When you and I were together"—he turned to Barton—"in Egypt, and afterwards on the business of the Mask of the Veiled Prophet, I tried to bring my information up to date. But the language of these Negro drums is a different language. Nevertheless I know what the drums are saying."

"What?" I exclaimed.

"They are notifying someone, somewhere, that we are here. Every move we make, Kerrigan, is being signalled."

"To Fu Manchu?" asked Barton.

Smith hesitated for a moment, puffing at his cigarette as though it had been a pipe, then:

"I am not sure," he returned slowly. "I have been here before, remember—my only other visit and a short one. But during the night I used to note the drumbeats. And working upon what I knew of drum language, I ultimately identified, or think I did, the note which meant myself."

"Amazing!" exclaimed Barton. "I have a bundle of notes some three hundred pages long on drum language, but I don't believe I could identify my own name in any of them."

"I say," said Smith, still speaking very slowly, "that I am not sure. But I formed the impression at that time, and later events have strengthened it, that the drummers were not speaking to Doctor Fu Manchu. We can roughly identify the doctor by his deeds: we know, for example, that the Snapping Fingers is operated by Doctor Fu Manchu. We know that the padding footsteps, the shadow which comes and goes, is controlled by him. It was this shadow which penetrated to our quarters in Colon and put opium in your whiskey. The same shadow which, unseen by the police officer, substituted a packet of drugged cigarettes for those which temporarily lay upon a ledge beside him. To these phenomena we must add now the green hand. But more and more I find myself thinking about the woman called Queen Mamaloi. . . ."

He paused, laid his cigarette down, and:

"Good God!" he exclaimed.

An envelope had appeared upon the table beside his plate. No waiter was near; the next occupied table—for Smith had recognised the presence of a number of agents in the hotel—was well removed from ours!

"It came from the garden path there," spluttered Barton. "I positively saw it blow up."

I had merely seen it drop beside the plate. I remained silent, dumbfounded. Smith's jaw muscles became very prominent, but he hesitated only a moment, and then with a table knife he split the envelope. He read aloud in a perfectly toneless voice:

"SECOND NOTICE:
"The Council of Seven of the Si-Fan point out that no reply has been received to its First Notice. Two powers have opened negotiations with the council relative to a readjust-

ment of naval forces in the Caribbean and Panama waters. A copy of this Second Notice has been sent to Washington. You have three days.

"President of the Council."

27 / Father Ambrose

FATHER AMBROSE, S.J., arrived immediately after breakfast. Father Ambrose had been recommended to Smith by Colonel Kennard Wood as one who knew more about Haiti than any other white resident. He was a stout, amiable-looking cleric, wearing glasses and carrying a heavy blackthorn. He had a notably musical voice, its production betraying the trained elocutionist, and his rather sleepy eyes held a profound knowledge of men and their affairs.

The meeting took place in Smith's room—as this was the largest; and he, having cordially welcomed the priest, broached the real business of the interview with a strange question:

"Are you acquainted, Father Ambrose, with the superstition of the zombie? Dead men who are dug up and restored to a sort of life?"

"Certainly," the priest replied in that rich, easy voice. "It is no superstition—it is a fact."

"You mean that?" Barton challenged.

"I mean it. You see, the dead are not really dead; they are buried alive. These people, I mean the exponents of voodoo, are acquainted with some kind of poison, or so I read it, which produces catalepsy. In this condition the victims are buried and their identities lost. They are then secretly dug up again and restored in the form of that dreadful creature—a zombie. Personality has gone; in fact, one would say that the soul had gone. They are entirely under the control of the voodoo doctor."

"You see, Kerrigan," snapped Smith, "Doctor Fu Manchu is not the only man who knows this strange secret."

"I have heard of Doctor Fu Manchu," said the priest, "but to my knowledge he has never been in Haiti."

"That," said Barton, "we shall make it our business to find out."

"The zombie, then, in your view," Smith went on rapidly, "is not just a Negro variety of the vampire tradition but a scientific fact?"

"Undoubtedly. The thing has been practised here in quite recent times—may be practised now." A shadow crossed the speaker's face. "Many of my flock, a large and scattered one,

131

are, I regret to say, both professed Roman Catholics and also secret devotees of voodoo." He shook his head. "I can do nothing to stop it."

"It is the cult of the serpent," growled Barton. "This knowledge of unfamiliar drugs and of hypnotic suggestion has come down from West Africa, but it reached West Africa from ancient Egypt. The recurrence of the Ra symbol and the importance of the snake prove my point, I think."

"I quite agree with you," Father Ambrose replied. "That point has not actually been established, but I hope to establish it before I die." He fumbled for a moment in his pocket, and: "I recovered this from a penitent recently," he added and handed something to Smith.

Smith held it in the palm of his hand, staring down at it curiously. Gaily plumaged birds flew from branch to branch outside the open window; there were strange movements in the crests of the coconut palms; the drums of the night were silent. I stood up to obtain a closer view of the object which the priest had produced. It was the figure of a snake, crudely carved in some soft wood and coloured green.

"Does any special significance attach to this?" Smith asked.

"Yes." The priest nodded gloomily. "You see, this abominable cult, which in my opinion today has its head centre here in Haiti, is divided up into sects; actually it is a kind of heathen religion. Each of these sects has a distinguishing mark or badge; the green serpent is that of a group or lodge to which my penitent belonged, or did belong. I made him swear that he would never attend again."

"But how are the things used?" asked Smith.

"As passports!" said Barton. "They are used as a means of recognition. The analogy may be blasphemous, Father, but the sign of the cross was employed in a similar way amongst the early Christians. Other lodges have other symbols, of course, several of which I possess. In fact, I have a selection with me, thought they might be useful."

"I see," muttered Smith. He laid the little amulet thoughtfully on the table before him. "In your experience are all these people pure Africans?"

"Not at all." The priest shook his head. "Many people who have very little Negro blood are followers of voodoo; some— who have none at all!"

"You amaze me!" I exclaimed.

He gave me a glance of his mild eyes.

"There is undoubtedly power in voodoo," he said sadly, "and to grasp power unscrupulous men will follow strange paths. One who could control this movement would have much power."

"I quite agree," said Smith. "I think I know one who has already done so. Another question, Father. Do you recall recent deaths due to the Snapping Fingers?"

"I recall them very well."

"Would you ascribe them to voodoo?"

The priest hesitated. He had produced a huge curved calabash pipe, and as Smith passed his pouch:

"I have warned you," he said, indicating the enormous bowl, "and I hope you have plenty of tobacco in reserve. Now you have posed me a difficult question, Sir Denis. By the coloured population those deaths were universally accepted as the work of voodoo. In the matter of their direction they may have been. Myself, I always thought they were due to some natural cause."

"You mean some creature," Smith suggested.

"Yes." The last few strands of nearly half an ounce of tobacco had disappeared into the mighty bowl. "Some odd things live here, you know. And owing to the fact that Haiti is not yet fully developed, I imagine that there are others which have not yet been classified."

Smith began to pace up and down, then:

"Just glance at this map," he jerked suddenly.

He opened on the cane table a large scale map of Haiti. Barton's blue eyes danced with curiosity; he, too, stood up as the priest bent over the map.

"Yes," said Father Ambrose, "it is a good map. I know most of the routes."

"You observe a red ring drawn around an area in the north?"

"I had noted it. Unfortunately it is a part of Haiti with which I am imperfectly acquainted. My confrere, Father Lucien, looks after that area."

"Nevertheless," said Smith, "you certainly know it better than I do. I am going to ask you, Father, if you have ever heard of a legend, or tradition, of a large cave along that coast?"

"There are many," the priest returned, puffing out great curls of tobacco smoke. "That rugged coast is honeycombed with caves. Perhaps you are referring to Christophe's Cave, which so many people have tried to find but which I am disposed to think is certainly a legend."

"Ah!" growled Barton.

"It has been suggested to me"—Father Ambrose smiled—"that the object of your present visit, Sir Lionel, is to look for Christophe's treasure. I remember you were here a year or two ago, although I did not meet you then. But I may give you a warning: what information you have it is not my business to inquire, but much gold and some human lives have been wasted during the past century in that quest. Christophe's Cavern has a history nearly as bad as that of Cocos Island."

"You surprise me," murmured Smith, laying the tip of his forefinger upon a point within the red circle upon the map. "But here, I am informed, there is a ruined chapel dating back to French days. Am I right?"

"You would have been a week ago."

"What!"

Barton and Smith were staring eagerly at the speaker.

"The chapel was either stuck by a thunderbolt or blown up by human hands at some time during last Thursday night. Scarcely one stone was left standing upon another. I had a full report, in a letter, of this mysterious occurrence from Father Lucien."

Smith and Barton exchanged glances.

"Perhaps you realise now, Barton," said Smith, "that Doctor Fu Manchu—one morning in New York, if I am not mistaken—took steps to check the chart in his possession from the original which you held. . . ."

The ruined chapel, now demolished, had marked the entrance to Christophe's Cavern!

"QUEEN MAMALOI," said Father Ambrose in a low tone. "Yes, unfortunately, there *is* such a person."

"She is not a myth?"

"Not at all—I wish she were. Who or what she is I cannot tell you. Only selected devotees of voodoo have ever seen her."

"Has there always been a Queen Mamaloi?" I asked.

The priest shook his head.

"Not to my knowledge. One never heard of her in Haiti until about"—he considered—"about 1938, I suppose. She is some very special sorceress, perhaps imported from Africa."

"I thought," said Barton in his coarsely jovial way, "that the Jesuits knew everything."

Father Ambrose smiled.

"We know many things," he replied, "but no man knows everything."

"Are you acquainted"—Smith spoke slowly and emphatically—"with anyone who has seen this woman?"

"I am." Father Ambrose indicated the little amulet on the cane table. "This penitent has seen her. Hence my putting the fear of hell into him and confiscating his charm."

"Did he describe her?"

"He was too excited at the time, I gather—these meetings are orgiastic, you know—to be a credible witness. But one point I established quite firmly. She is not black."

"What!" Smith's eyes glinted with sudden excitement. "You are sure of that?"

"Perfectly sure."

"A white woman?"

Father Ambrose extended his stout palms.

"Probably Negro blood. Some of them, you know, are as white as you or I. I cannot suppose that a European woman could have obtained this hold over the coloured people: it extends, mark you, beyond the boundaries of Haiti. At the great ceremony of the Full Moon——"

"Tomorrow night!" snapped Smith.

"Yes, there is to be a meeting tomorrow night, and many will come over the borders; nor"—he spoke sadly—"will they all be black. We fight phantoms here, Sir Denis, but we shall win in the end."

Smith was pacing up and down again, furiously loading his cracked old briar. Suddenly he turned to Barton.

"You hear, Barton?" he said. "You hear? Two moves are open to us. In one, I fancy, we have been anticipated by Doctor Fu Manchu. I consider it at least equally important that we should see this woman."

"And I assure you," Father Ambrose interrupted, "that it is quite impossible you should see her, whatever your reason may be. Haiti is highly civilised, as you know"—he smiled—"but for any white man, or any white man ignorant of voodoo ritual, to attempt to penetrate to that place would be"—he shrugged his broad shoulders—"shall we say as dangerous as for one to walk into Mecca?"

"You say 'that place,'" Smith remarked.

"Yes."

"Does this mean that you know where it is?"

The priest hesitated, and then:

"Yes, I know," he replied. "But it is contrary to the dictates of my conscience to tell you. Voodoo is undoubtedly the work of Satan. I would encourage no man to touch it. It is, as you yourself have suggested, a survival of pagan creeds older than Christianity. It is the worship of the hidden side of the moon."

There was a brief silence during which Nayland Smith paced restlessly up and down and the bowl of the priest's pipe bubbled unmusically.

"I don't presume, Father, to interfere with your conscience.

But let me make our position a little more clear. For your private information I am not treasure hunting, although it is true that I hope to find Christophe's Cave. I am acting for the United States government and for my own. There are two movements taking place in Haiti: one mechanical, the other psychological. It is my business to investigate both. You say yourself that voodoo has great power. You evidently know a lot about it, more than you have told us. But one thing you do not know. A secret society and a very old one, the Si-Fan——"

"The Si-Fan!" interjected Father Ambrose. "But what has the Si-Fan to do with Haiti? You see"—he smiled apologetically—"I was in Tibet for four years before I came here. Nearly as many of my converts there were members of the Si-Fan as here they are devotees of voodoo."

"No doubt!" said Smith. "The roots of the Si-Fan may not go as deep as those of voodoo, but nevertheless it is an ancient organisation and a very powerful one. It is controlled by a Chinese genius; it includes all races and all creeds—all shades of colour. Personally I cannot say for how long it has included voodoo."

"What!"

"The Si-Fan is almost purely political. I need not emphasise the underground influence which could be set in motion by control of voodoo. But those influences are already at work. There is a concrete danger to the United States government growing hour by hour and day by day in the Caribbean. Several agents who have been sent to investigate have died or have never returned."

"I confess," murmured the priest, "that I know of one myself."

"There have been many. And this woman, the Queen Mamaloi, is undoubtedly an agent of the Si-Fan. I am urged by no idle curiosity. It is my plain duty to see this woman, to establish her identity—to check her activities. Now, I have been making some inquiries myself."

He turned again to the map and rested the point of a pencil upon a spot which appeared to be the peak of a mountain close to the Dominican border. He glanced interrogatively at the priest.

Father Ambrose nodded.

"Yes, that is the headquarters of voodoo in Haiti," he admitted. "Morne la Selle, the Magic Mountain. I cannot deny it; I can see it from my own windows at Kenscoff. But I would point out that if you go with a considerable armed party you will find no one there and that if you go alone you will certainly never return."

Smith relighted his pipe, and:

"You do no more than your duty, Father," he said. "We have heard your warning and we do not take it lightly. But I have a duty as well as you, and I am going to be present at this meeting." He took up the little snake amulet. "Is it consistent with your convictions that I should borrow this?"

The priest's pipe bubbled; great rings of smoke rose from the steaming bowl. At last:

"You place the matter in a new light, Sir Denis," he said. "I believe I shall be justified in withdrawing my opposition."

28 / Drums in the Night

"WE KNOW ROUGHLY what we have to expect," said Nayland Smith, "and I think our plans cover all the possibilities which we can foresee."

"I regret every moment lost in getting to work on the cave," cried Barton. "There's a party of United States marines ready to land; even with their help it may take some time to clear the debris of the old chapel. In the present state of the war over there Fu Manchu's chance might come tomorrow!"

"And tomorrow we set to work," snapped Smith. "Tonight I have another job to do——"

"Which may iron you out altogether!"

"Barton," said Smith, "I regret to have to remind you that I am in charge of this party. Be good enough to listen. Near the top of Morne la Selle, our destination, there is a perfectly flat plateau. As the place is a voodoo holy of holies, the American authorities have contented themselves with aerial survey. But it's a good landing ground. Three army planes are standing by. They are our rear guard, Barton, and you're in command. I am not prepared to trust a soul in Haiti now that I know the Si-Fan is here. Nobody but you knows when those planes start or where they are going."

"Right," growled Barton. "You know you can count on me."

"One thing is important: I *must* see the Queen Mamaloi; and the time of departure I have given you allows for the starting of the ceremony. Don't start a moment earlier. . . ."

It was afternoon before Smith and I set out for the house of Father Ambrose in Kenscoff. We went in the car of the American consul, a saloon; and saloons are rare in Port-au-Prince. The consul's chauffeur drove us. Smith's plans were peculiarly complete, as I was presently to learn; but at the outset he was very silent, filling the interior of the car with clouds of tobacco smoke. I realised as the journey proceeded what he had meant when he had said, "This *is* Africa." The route betrayed a vista of wild, unspoiled beauty. There were magnificent trees, banks of flowers and, once clear of the town, absence of any evidence to show that we were not indeed in tropical Africa.

Although this was a modern road, the dwellings which bordered it might have had their being in Timbuctoo. An all but unbroken file of Haitian women, each with a burden upon her head of vegetables, fruit or other produce, wound its way antlike down to the market place; a returning stream marched upwards. I saw no white faces from the time that we left the borders of the town. But below a wonderful prospect was unfolded.

From above, Port-au-Prince, nestling in a cup between two mountains, reminded me momentarily of Damascus seen from the Lebanon hills. Beyond, seemingly floating on a blue sea, La Gonave, the mystery island, alone disturbed the blue expanse of ocean to the horizon. Little curiosity was displayed by the hundreds of natives we passed. Exceptions were a fierce-eyed old woman riding a donkey and a tall, distinguished-looking mulatto who carried a staff. The interest of this pair, I thought, although they were a mile or more apart, was definitely hostile. As the car passed, the tall mulatto and his fierce glance sought us out in passing.

"We are covered, Kerrigan," said Smith. "Did you note that man?"

"Yes."

"One of the voodoo doctors, beyond doubt. Drums will beat feverishly tonight."

He said no more right up to the moment that we reached the priest's house, a long, low, creeper-clad building, flowers climbing over a verandah which overlooked a tropical garden where hummingbirds hovered and butterflies of incredible colours flitted from flower to flower. As we descended from the car:

"The Father has comfortable quarters," murmured Smith.

We were met by the genial priest and shown into a cool and spacious study. I thought, looking about me at the plain wood shelves laden with works in many languages, at the littered working desk, a typewriter on a side table and a large crucifix upon a white-painted wall, that here, probably, was the headquarters of Rome in its battle against African superstition; an advance post of Christianity all but hemmed in by the forces of ancient and evil gods.

WHEN DUSK FELL Smith and I, with Father Ambrose, were in the garden. I looked into the crimson sunset and wondered what the new dawn would bring. With dramatic suddenness the sky became a mirror of every known colour—light jade, deep purple and a shell-like pink—all merging as I watched into an inverted casket of blue velvet, holding a million diamonds. A queenly moon rode in that serene heaven. . . .

"It is time we went in," said Father Ambrose.

Back in the study, now electrically lighted, for there was a small Kohler engine installed in the garage, I stood staring at Smith and he stared at me. We were heavily sunburned, yet except in the dusk no man, I think, could have been deceived by our substitutes; two trustworthy lads selected by the priest who, wearing our clothes, had gone back in the consul's car and would sleep in his compound that night. It was hoped, in this way, to lead spies to believe that we had returned to Port-au-Prince.

Smith wore an ill-fitting drill suit and a straw hat. I was similarly attired, except that I boasted a scarlet pull-over beneath my jacket. My own headgear was a pith helmet of sorts.

"How many spare rounds in your belt?" Smith snapped.

"Twelve."

He nodded grimly.

"More would be useless."

As he began to load his pipe Father Ambrose closed gauze shutters before the windows.

"The light attracts many nocturnal insects," he explained; "some are beautiful but others are unpleasant."

Smith lighted his pipe and, standing by the desk, took from his pocket two objects. One was the green snake lent to us by the priest; the other was a jewel in the form of a seven-pointed star.

"This is the amulet from Barton's collection," he said, "to which I referred, Father."

Father Ambrose changed his glasses and, sitting down, carefully examined the glittering jewel. Presently he looked up.

"The snake emblem, as I have told you," he said, "denotes a shepherd, *papaloi*, or—shall we say?—a lodge master. But this"—he touched it gingerly—"is the badge of a high adept, or grand master. Strange how the significance of 7 haunts the pagan mysteries. I cannot imagine where Sir Lionel obtained it."

Smith laughed.

"The same has been said of many pieces in Barton's collection! But may I take it that these tokens will pass?"

"I have little doubt of that but grave doubt of my wisdom in countenancing this thing. Both are emblems of Damballa, the serpent-god, and are anti-Christ like the swastika. However—I have promised, and I do my part. I have shown you the way to the spot where the donkeys are tethered, and when we have sampled a glass each of my rum cordial—a very special honour, I assure you—I fear you must set out."

We sampled his rum cordial in the lamplighted room, a book-lined oasis in a Haitian jungle, and anxiously he gave us final advice, unwittingly displaying as he did so a vast knowledge of this country in which he was absorbed. Finally, glancing at a clock upon his desk:

"It is time that you started," he said. "I should like to give you my blessing."

A queer dignity invested the stout priest as, laying down his vast calabash pipe on a tray, he stood up. Although neither Smith nor I were communicants of his church, we knelt as though prompted by one instinct whilst, his deep voice lending authority to the Latin, he blessed our journey. . . .

Five minutes later we had groped our way to the end of a narrow lane which bordered the bottom of the priest's garden, where scarcely visible lizards shot phantomesque from before our advancing feet. The lanterns of fireflies seemed to guide us. Two well-kept, patient donkeys were tethered there, saddled and ready, but unattended. As we tightened a strap here and there and presently mounted:

"This end of the business has been perfectly handled," said Smith. "Barton is dining with the American consul tonight as arranged, but amongst the servants there will almost certainly be one spy, and our absence will be reported."

We ambled out onto the road that led up to the mountain; others, mostly on foot, were making in the same direction. And as though our joining that mysterious procession had been the signal, from before us, in the high forests, from behind us in the valleys, from all around . . . the drums began.

"After dark," said Smith in a low voice, "Haiti reverts to its ancient gods."

But we had jogged onward and upward for many miles, talking in low tones, before we came to the beginning of the most perilous road which I remembered ever to have seen.

It skirted sheer precipices, and I doubt if two riders could have passed upon it. But this way the dark figures were going and none were coming back. I could see it ahead, a silver thread picked out by the moon, antlike humans moving along it. In a sort of rocky bay Smith reined up.

"We have three hours yet," he said. "I want to listen to the drums."

We stayed there listening to the drums for five, seven, ten minutes. It was a language strange to me. Messages and responses merged into one confused throbbing; that throbbing which had haunted my nights, kept me wakeful when I should have been sleeping. Figures afoot, figures mounted, passed by the little belt of shade in which we lingered—all bound for the secret meeting place on the crest of the mountain. Some of the pilgrims carried lanterns; some carried torches. Presently:

"I am in the news," said Smith in a low voice, "but I can gather no more. You see, I know what may be termed my 'signature tune.'"

Then, mounted on a mule, clearly outlined against the pearly moon, a figure rode slowly by. Apart from a sensation of lowered temperature, impossible to mistake the angular figure—impossible to mistake the profile.

It was Dr Fu Manchu. . . .

29 / *The Song of Damballa*

"SMITH," I whispered, "did you see? Did you see? It was Doctor Fu Manchu!"

"I saw."

"I could have shot him!"

"That would have been a tactical blunder. But apparently he did not see *us*. There is even a possibility that he does not know we are on this road. You noticed his retinue?"

"Six or eight thickset fellows seemed to be preceding and as many to be following him."

"His Burmese bodyguard."

"But what does this mean? That the voodoo ceremony is organised by Fu Manchu, that we are walking into a trap?"

"Somehow I don't think so, Kerrigan, although I admit I may be wrong. But the presence of Fu Manchu in person rather confirms the theory on which I am acting."

The eerie throbbing of the drums was now unbroken, a sort of evil pulse as of a secret world awakening. Figures, mostly on foot, singly and in groups, passed the shadowed bay in the rocks which shielded us. Sometimes, but rarely, a mounted man or woman went by.

"Surely, Smith," I said, "we should have kept him in view?"

"That would have been too dangerous. Moreover, it is reasonable to assume that he is bound for the same destination as ourselves. Great caution is indicated—we carry our lives in our hands, although I have not failed to take suitable steps to prevent the worst befalling. I may add that I don't like the look of the mountain path which now lies before us, but nevertheless we must push on."

We resumed our journey along a path cut from the face of a sheer precipice, a path which at no point was more than ten feet wide and at many less. No wall or parapet was present, and the donkeys, Smith's leading, after the way of their kind, resolutely refused to hug the rugged wall and picked their ambling way along the very rim of the road.

I found it to be quite impossible to look down into that moon-patched valley below. I concentrated on the path ahead where, emerging from shadow into silvery light, countless figures toiled onward and upward, their going marked by woven at a dizzy height into the mountainside.

Now there was a frosty nip in the air, and I was thankful for the advice of Father Ambrose, acting upon which we had wrapped ourselves warmly beneath our ancient drill jackets. Once—and my throat grew dry—a more speedy party passed us on the way: a group of three Haitians swinging along with lithe, almost silent tread. Having attempted to urge my donkey to the inner side of the path and succeeding only in torch or lantern. Clearly one could trace it—a jewelled thread inducing him to kick a number of stones into the yawning chasm below, I was compelled to allow them to pass on my left. They were tall, powerful fellows, and it occurred to me that a good thrust from any one of them would have precipitated me and the obstinate little brute which I rode into the depths beneath. Others there were on the path behind, but they did not seem to be overtaking us.

Then from that seemingly endless procession, from thousands of feet above, and from behind, where the tail of the pilgrimage straggled up from the valleys, arose a low chanting. It seemed to mingle with the throb of the drums, to be part of the black magic to which this night was consecrated.

"Do you hear it?" came Smith's voice.

"Yes—it's horrible."

"It is known, I believe, as the Song of Damballa. Of course it is purely African in character."

142

He spoke as one who criticises some custom depicted upon a movie screen or mentioned by a travelled member in the bar of a club. Knowing, and I knew it well, that we were surrounded by devil worshippers, by those who delighted in human sacrifice, among whom, if they suspected our purpose, our lives would be not worth a sou, I was amazed. Often enough I had been amazed before at the imperturbable self-possession, a concentration on the job in hand, a complete disregard of personal hazard which characterised this lean and implacable enemy of Dr Fu Manchu. And I confess that above all other perils I feared Dr Fu Manchu.

Discovery by the woman called Queen Mamaloi was a prospect bad enough, but recognition of the fact that the Chinese doctor was possibly directing this black saturnalia frankly appalled me. And now from far in the rear came a new sound.

There were cries, greetings; above the Song of Damballa, the throbbing of drums, I detected the clatter of a horse's hoofs.

"This may be difficult," said Smith, speaking over his shoulder. "Some senior official is apparently approaching—and it is just possible——"

"God help us!" I groaned.

"We can probably manage," Smith replied, "assuming that he is Haitian—although I confess I should prefer to have my back to the wall. You have no Chinese or Hindustani?"

"Not a word."

"Arabic, then? This has a powerful effect on these descendants of West Africans. It has come down to them as the language of their oppressors."

"Yes—I have a smattering of Arab."

"Good. If anyone addresses you, reply in Arabic. Say anything you can remember—don't stop to consider the meaning."

Now the outcry grew nearer. The horseman was forcing his way up the mountain path, passing the slow-moving pilgrims to the shrine of voodoo. I looked back. We had just negotiated a dizzy bend and I could see nothing of the approaching rider.

"HAVE YOUR GUN READY," said Smith and brought his donkey to a halt.

I did the same, although the iron-jawed little beast was strongly disinclined to pull up. The horseman was now not fifty yards behind.

"If he is looking for us," said Smith, "and we are recognised, don't hesitate."

Looking back, I could make out dimly that the pilgrims between ourselves and the perilous bend had halted their march and were standing back against the rocky wall to give passage to the horseman. A moment later he rounded the corner, riding a lean bay mare and obviously indifferent to the chasm which yawned beneath him. As he passed each of the standing figures he bent in his saddle and seemed to scrutinise features. A moment later he had reached us.

He partly reined up and bent, looking into my face. I sat in shadow, the moon behind me, but its light shone directly upon the features of the mounted man.

He was that fierce-eyed mulatto whom we had passed on our way to the house of Father Ambrose, who had stared so hard into the car!

He shouted something in a strange patois, and remembering Smith's injunction:

"*Imshi! Rûah! Bundukîyah!*" I replied sharply.

The mulatto seemed to hesitate; then, as the prancing bay almost lashed the flanks of my donkey:

"*Yâlla! Yâlla!*" cried Smith.

The mulatto spurred ahead.

"Move!" said Smith; "or others will overtake us."

And once again we proceeded on our way. . . .

We presently came to a welcome break or bay in that perilous mountain road, and here I saw that a number of the marching multitude had halted for a rest. An awesome prospect was spread at our feet. We were so high, the moon was so bright and shadows so dense, that I seemed to be looking down upon a relief map illuminated by searchlights. Eastward, at a great distance, shone a lake resembling a mirror, for in it were the inverted images of mountains which I assumed must lie beyond the Dominican border. As I reined up and gazed at this breath-taking prospect a hand was laid upon my saddle. Swiftly I glanced down at a man who stood there.

He was a pure Negro, and when he spoke he spoke in halting English.

"You come from Pétionville—yes?" he asked.

"*Kattar khêrak,*" I replied and extended my hand in a Fascist salute.

Smith edged up beside me.

"*El-hamdu li'llah!*" he muttered and repeated my gesture.

The Negro touched his forehead, stepped aside and was swallowed in shadow.

"So far," said Smith, speaking cautiously, "we are doing well, but it is fairly obvious that when we have mounted another two or three thousand feet we shall arrive at the real gateway to the holy of holies. There we must rely upon our amulets. Above all, Kerrigan, never speak a word of English and pray that we meet no one who speaks a word of Arabic!"

He was looking about him at dimly perceptible groups who had paused there to rest. Of the mounted mulatto there was no trace, nor—and of this above all things I was fearful—of Dr Fu Manchu. Many of the pedestrians were refreshing themselves, seated upon the ground. Newcomers arrived continuously. Chanting had stopped, but from near and far came the throbbing of the drums.

"A drink is perhaps indicated," said Smith, "and then for the next stage."

As we extracted flasks from our pockets I was watching that silver and ebony ribbon speckled with moving figures which led higher and higher towards the crest of the Magic Mountain. What awaited us there? Should I learn anything about Ardatha? What was the meaning of this monstrous congregation patiently toiling up the slope of Morne la Selle? That it was something of interest to Dr Fu Manchu we knew, but what was the mystery behind it all—and who was the Queen Mamaloi?

Smith was very reticent throughout the halt. I recognised the fact that he was afraid of being overheard speaking English, and I fully appreciated the danger. So, our flasks stowed away, we presently started again with scarcely a word exchanged, the padre's donkeys obediently ambling along at our command.

The chanting began again as we ascended the mountain— the drums had never ceased.

30 / The Seven-Pointed Star

"THIS," said Smith, "I assume to be the voodoo customhouse. Here we shall be called upon to produce our passports."

We were up, I suppose, between seven and eight thousand feet. We had traversed some of the most perilous mountain paths I had ever met with, but I had learned that the little donkeys, provided one did not attempt to interfere with them, particularly with their fondness for walking upon the extreme outer edge of the precipice, were sure-footed as goats.

For the past two or three miles the road had led through a

pass or gorge to which no moonlight penetrated. A mountain stream raged and splashed at the bottom and the path lay some little way above it. Darkness at first seemed impenetrable, but the procession wound on without interruption and our plodding steeds proceeded with unabated confidence. And so presently through that velvety darkness dotted with moving torches I, too, had begun to discern the details of the route.

Now it opened with dramatic suddenness upon what seemed to be an almost circular valley, hemmed in all around by mountain crests. Its slopes were densely wooded, but immediately facing the gorge there was a clearing flat as a sports stadium and fully half a mile across. Torches moved among the trees; there were drums very near to us now; and I saw hundreds of figures gathered before a long, low building which blazed with lights. Away on the right there was a sort of compound where horses, mules and donkeys were tethered. Towards these horse lines Smith led the way.

"Stick to Arabic," he snapped.

The place was staked out with lanterns and proved to be, in certain respects, an up-to-date parking ground. Furthermore, the man in charge, despite the religious character of the ceremony, was something of a profiteer: a burly Haitian wearing a check suit which was too small for him and a stock in which there was an enormous pearl pin. Momentarily I was translated to Epsom Downs on Derby Day. In the queer patois which I had not yet fully grasped I understood him to say as we dismounted and tethered our donkeys:

"A dollar for the two."

"Imshi, hâmmâr!" snarled Smith and, taking fifty cents from his pocket, handed it to the man.

"Not enough! Not enough!" he exclaimed.

"Etla bárra! Gehánnum!" I growled and gave the Fascist salute.

As before, this singular behaviour proved effective. He looked from face to face, pocketed the money, glanced at the donkeys and walked away.

"So far so good," muttered Smith. "Now let us take our bearings and make our plans. Here, you observe, is a perfect landing ground."

We walked slowly towards the verandah of the lighted house on the further side of the clearing, and it soon became apparent that the place was a sort of resthouse or caravanserai. All around in the extensive space before it pilgrims were squatting on the ground, devouring refreshments which they had brought with them. But, as I saw, the more prosperous were entering the building. Many already were seated upon the verandah, and I could see movement in a room beyond. The front of the house was masked in shadow, and Smith grasped my arm as we stepped into the dark belt.

"You see what this is, Kerrigan: a separation of the sheep from the goats. Judging from the sound of the drums, our real objective is beyond."

I stood there listening.

In some manner which I find myself unable to explain this continuous throbbing of drums had wrought a sort of change of the spirit. It had stirred up something Celtic and buried, provoked urges of which hitherto I had been unconscious. My desire for Ardatha had become a fever; my hatred of the Si-Fan, of Dr Fu Manchu, of all those who held her captive, had increased hour by hour until now it was a burning fiery torrent. This recognition, or rather, I suppose, the reassuming of control by the conscious over the subconscious, rather shocked me. Unperceived by my Christian self, I had been reverting to savagery!

"Yes"—I spoke with studied calmness—"as you say, here is the gateway. The Queen Mamaloi is somewhere beyond."

"Here is the gateway," Smith replied, "and here is our test. Remember, stick to Arabic."

Whereupon, still grasping my arm, he moved forward to the verandah of the lighted building.

As we mounted three wooden steps I was thinking of Ardatha. . . .

CROSSING THE VERANDAH, I found myself in a long, low room which in many respects resembled a canteen. One glance convinced me, in spite of the light complexions of some of those present, that Smith and I were the only people in the place of non-African blood. There were a number of chairs and tables spread about the unpolished floor, and I think nearly as many women as men were present.

Their behaviour was so strange that I wondered what they had been drinking—for at one end of the room there was a counter presided over by two coloured women. I saw that in addition to a quantity of solid fare, most of it unfamiliar and from my point of view unappetising, bottles of rum, gin and whiskey were in evidence. In some of the faces a sort of ecstasy began to dawn; and, watching, I realised the fact that they were responding to the drums.

Movements of shoulders and arms, shuffling of feet and already a muted chanting told me that at any moment all the great coloured throng might obey that deep tribal impulse

147

which is part of Africa and throw themselves wildly into the abandonment of a ritual dance.

Smith spoke in my ear.

"Don't seem to be curious," he whispered, "and remember—nothing but Arabic. Let us stand here for a while and smoke. I see that some of the men are smoking."

I lighted a cigarette whilst he began to load his briar. I cannot say if it was the drums, the overstrung human instrument represented by those about me or something else. But I was tensed to a pitch of excitement which I knew to be supernormal. I tried, as I lighted the cigarette, to drag myself down to facts, to watch Smith, calmly loading his pipe; to study those about me; to appreciate our perils and how we were to deal with them.

"Hang onto yourself, Kerrigan," said Smith in a low voice. "We are near the master drums. They have a queer effect—even upon Europeans."

"Why do you say that?"

"I have been watching your eyes." He replaced the pouch in his pocket and lighted his pipe, his penetrating glance fixed upon me over the bowl. "It's a kind of hypnotism, but you mustn't let it touch you."

His words acted like a cold douche. Yes, it was a fact. In common with the Negroes and Negresses about the place, I had been reacting to those satanic drums! I knew it now and, knowing, knew also that the insidious influence could never prevail upon me again.

"Thanks, Smith," I said. "I agree. It *was* getting me."

"I am particularly interested," he went on, "in the fact that there seems to be no one in the room whom we know. But the traffic at the bar has curious features."

"What are they?"

"Well, if you watch you will be able to check my own impressions. You will observe, I think, that certain customers go there, give an order and then almost immediately head for that door on the left and go out. The others either remain at the bar or carry their purchases back to their table. Just watch this pair, for example."

A man and a woman coming in from the verandah outside crossed straight to the counter. The girl was a full-blooded Negress and physically a beautiful creature; her male companion was light brown, his complexion pitted like that of a smallpox patient, his small yellow eyes darting from right to left suspiciously as he crossed the room. But, failing

148

other evidence, his hair, for he wore no hat, must have betrayed his African origin.

"Watch," said Smith.

I watched.

The pair walked to the counter; the man gave an order to one of the women. Glasses were filled and set before them. But as payment was made I detected a change of attitude on the part of the server. She glanced swiftly at the girl and then at her companion. In a businesslike way which momentarily made me think that we had intruded upon some harmless feast-day frolic she handed change to the man.

"Now," whispered Smith, "watch closely."

The drinks—I was unable to judge of their character—were quickly dispatched; the man squeezed the girl's hand and lolled upon the counter. The girl walked quickly along left, and I saw the second attendant open a door and close it again as the Negress made her departure.

"Exactly what does that mean?" I murmured.

"It means," said Smith, "that, still speaking Arabic, we go to the counter and order drinks. Do nothing further until I give the word, and leave the talking to me."

We crossed.

There was something hellish, something of a witches' Sabbath, in the behaviour of those around us. To a man, to a woman, now, they were swaying in time with the beating of the drums; eyes were rolling and in some cases teeth were gnashing. I did not know what to expect, but presently I found myself at the bar and with affected nonchalance leaned upon it.

One of the women attendants, who had been chatting in quite a natural way with the pock-marked man, broke off her conversation and approached us; she had feverishly bright eyes.

"*Giblī el . . . ismu êh,*" said Smith imperiously, indicating a bottle of Black and White whiskey.

The woman spoke rapidly in Haitian, then in English.

"You want some whiskey, Black and White?"

"*Aîwa, aîwa!*"

The woman poured out two liberal portions and set before us a bottle of some kind of mineral water. Smith put down a dollar bill and she gave him change. At first she had seemed somewhat suspicious, and the pock-marked man had looked at us with jaundiced eyes; now, however, she seemed to have accepted us. Someone else came up to the bar and her attention was diverted. The newcomer was a full-blooded Negro and a magnificent specimen. He nodded casually to the pock-marked man, who returned the salutation and then turned his back upon him. Smith touched my arm.

I watched intently. The newcomer ordered a packet of cigarettes; they were placed before him, and he set several coins on the counter. Smith bent to my ear:

"Look!" he breathed.

Held in the Negro's palm, as he had opened it to drop the coins, I had a momentary glimpse of a green object. . . . It was the coiled snake of Damballa!

The signal exchanged between the woman who had served him and the other at the further end of the counter must have been imperceptible to one not anticipating it. The Negro walked along, nodded to the second woman; the door was opened, and he went out.

"That's our way!" murmured Smith.

An evil spiritual excitement, a force that could be physically felt, was throbbing about the room. Out in front of the verandah drums began to beat softly, and starting as a whisper, but ever increasing in volume, came that hymn of Satan, the Song of Damballa:

> *Damballa goubamba*
> *Kinga do ké la*

As I looked men and women, singly and in pairs, sprang up and began to dance. They appeared to be entirely oblivious of their surroundings, to be, in the evil sense, possessed; one after another they threw themselves with utter abandonment into the rhythmical but incomprehensible dance. They moved out to the verandah, across it and out into the torch-speckled dusk of the clearing beyond. The atmosphere was foul with human exhalation. Treating us to a further and comprehensively suspicious glance, the pock-marked man also walked out.

"Now for it," muttered Smith. "Don't touch this stuff!"

Surreptitiously he emptied his glass onto the floor. I followed suit.

"When I call the woman show her the green snake. Leave the rest to me." He turned in her direction. *"Ta 'alla hîna!"* he rapped.

She started, stared for a moment and then drew near.

Opening my palm, I exhibited the green serpent.

"Ah!" she exclaimed and seemed taken aback.

Smith held the seven-pointed star before her eyes.

"Ahu hîna Damballa!" he muttered and concealed the jewel.

For a moment extraordinarily penetrating eyes had surveyed us, but at sight of the star the woman pressed her hands to her breasts and bowed her head. Smith confidently strode towards the left and I followed him. The other woman opened the door and stood in that same attitude of subjection as we walked out—to find ourselves in a lean-to porch, almost right up to which the mountain forest grew.

For here it seemed the pines climbed unbroken to the mountain ridge, and at first it was so dark that I found it bewildering. But as we stood there taking our bearings I presently noticed, in what little moonlight filtered through from above, that a track, a mere bridle path, led from the door onward and upward amongst the pines.

No living thing was in sight. From before that strange house of entertainment which we had left singing and drumming grew ever louder. Beyond, very far beyond, it seemed, deep in the forest . . . other drums were beating, deep-toned, mysterious drums . . . and I thought that they were calling to us.

"Clearly this is our way," said Smith in a low voice. "I am evidently a person of some consequence, as Father Ambrose assured us, and one presumes that initiates are supposed to know the path. Come on."

We set out. The track climbed up and up through the trees, and although I was keeping a tight hold upon myself, one obsession there was which I could not conquer. It seemed to be fostered by those distant drums. It was not fear of those who worshipped the serpent, bloodthirsty though their rites might be—indeed, according to some accounts, cannibalistic—nor tremors that we had been betrayed. It was a fear which constantly made me mistake some odd-shaped bush, some low-growing branch for the gaunt figure of Dr Fu Manchu. Amid all the other horrors of the night I found it impossible to forget the fact that the great and sinister Chinese doctor was somewhere near.

Large nocturnal insects flew into our faces; other unseen creatures rustled in the undergrowth. The sound of the deep-toned drums grew ever nearer, so that that of the saturnalia we had left behind was rarely audible at all. More and more stars gleamed into view until the darkness beneath the pines became a sort of twilight; we had glimpses of the disk of the moon. We were nearing a crest beyond which it was evident that there lay another plateau or perhaps a high valley. The going was very heavy; we had been steadily climbing for close upon an hour, and my condition was not too good. Suddenly Smith pulled up.

"Do you know, Kerrigan," he said, breathing rapidly, "except for the fact that we are nearing the place at which the drums are beating, I should have begun to doubt if we had taken the right route."

"Why?"

"Unless the pace of everyone using the path is more or less attuned to ours, how is it (a) that we have overtaken no one and (b) that no one has overtaken *us?*"

It was a curious point, the force of which struck me at once. Smith took out his flask, and I was not sorry to resort to mine.

"I am inclined to believe," I replied, "that all, or nearly all, the chosen few preceded us. In other words, we are late——"

"Ssh!" He checked me. "Do you hear it?"

And during a momentary diminuendo in the passionate throbbing of the drums I heard it: a faint but unmistakable disturbance of the pine needles which formed a carpet upon most of the path below. Someone followed in our footsteps.

"Just time to take cover," snapped Smith, "if we are quick!"

On the right of the path at this point a ravine yawned darkly; only the crests of the tallest trees rose above it. On the left the ground sloped gently upward; some kind of flowering shrub abounded, and here the pines were scanty. Smith scrambled up this slope and dived into its sheltering darkness. His voice reached me in a whisper:

"Down here, Kerrigan! There's a perfect view of the path, and we can't be seen. Also it may be dangerous to go further. There may be unsuspected chasms."

I groped my way until he seized my hand. He was lying prone near the corner of a flowering bush. Wearily I threw myself down beside him. The throbbing of the drums was producing an effect wholly dissimilar to that which it seemed to exercise upon the black devotees: a sort of stupefaction. It was bemusing me, drugging me; I found it difficult to think connectedly.

"I am glad we are not alone on the path," I said in a low voice. "Evidently it is the right one after all."

"Quiet!" said Smith. "Someone is very near."

As he spoke I realised the fact that from where we lay concealed, owing to the position of the moon and the falling away of the forest on the right of the path, a considerable expanse, perhaps twenty yards, was clearly visible. Illuminated by a bluish haze of light, the stirring of the pine cones continued as the sound grew nearer.

Who was approaching?

As to whom I expected, it would be difficult to speculate. But what I saw was this: The tall Negro who had preceded us from the resthouse and the Negress who had come later and separated from her pock-marked companion.

Clearly the girl had waited for the man, and we must have passed them at some point on the route. In response to that hereditary instinct which the drums stir up in the African heart, they had reverted to nature. The man's arm was around the girl's waist, her head rested upon his breast, as with a uniform step in time with the drums they paced upward through the pines. Utterly aloof from the world of today, the last shackle which bound them to the chariot of the white man was cast aside with the garments of civilisation. She had woven a chaplet of flowers into her hair, and watching them as they passed and were lost to view, I knew that although a woman missionary might have been shocked there was nothing bestial and nothing vile and nothing of shame in the strange reversion to primitive type.

The ancient gods had called them; and, simply, they had obeyed.

The rustling of the pine cones died away. I could hear no sound of other approaching footsteps, and the throb of the drums seemed to have increased again in volume.

"You see," said Smith in a low voice, "there is power in voodoo. One wonders what proportion of the inhabitants of Haiti have come under its spell. A great primitive force, Kerrigan, a force we must now assume to be directed by Doctor Fu Manchu."

"Presumably women are admitted to the higher mysteries."

"Certainly," Smith replied. "This I knew. Remember it is the Queen Mamaloi they go to meet, and I strongly suspect——"

He paused.

"What?"

"That there will be some further comb-out before we are admitted to the holy of holies."

"Since we are ignorant of the routine," I said, "this comb-out may mean our finish."

"I have been considering the point, Kerrigan." He stood up and walked down the path. "I have been considering it since the moment that we started. I think if we follow the black lovers, who will be unlikely to pay any attention to us, and observe what occurs, it may be to our advantage."

WE PASSED THE CREST and looked down into a tiny sheltered valley. Mountain trees fringed it in thinly, and set amid those on the opposite slope I saw a one-story building surrounded by a high stockade. Lanterns and torches competed with the moonlight pouring down upon the stockade, and in silhouette, an ebony god and goddess of voodoo, the pair ahead of us stood for a moment on the lip of the declivity outlined against a tropical sky. They began to descend.

Recollections of our distance from the caravanserai which was the first gate to the mysteries at this moment stampeded in my brain. Assuming that we succeeded in surviving whatever test might lie before us, how were we to return? Together Smith and I watched the receding figures until they were lost amongst the scattered trees which grew upon the lower slopes.

"We must not lose sight of them," he said rapidly. "Short of stripping, I am prepared to follow whatever routine they may adopt."

I laughed, perhaps not very mirthfully.

"Have you any idea, Smith," I asked, "how we are going to get back?"

"Whatever the purpose of this meeting may be and whether we escape or are discovered, I have arranged, Kerrigan, as you know, that in roughly one hour from now three planes, suitably armed, will land on the plateau from which we have come. I am convinced that no opposition will be met with. Barton will lead them here. In other words"—he glanced at the illuminated dial of his wrist watch—"if we can survive for two hours, we shall not be unsupported."

We began very slowly to descend in turn.

It seemed to me that under the moon there was nothing in the world but drums. I began to understand the symptoms of the rhythm-drunk people I had known—people who when they were not dancing or listening to swing music had swing echoes in their brains. This was the apogee, the culmination of that hypnosis which is created by *beats*. Although we approached the clearing there were dark patches in the path, and once as I stumbled Smith caught my arm.

"The drums," he said; "it's a kind of dope, you know."

"I know," I groaned.

"Try to deafen your ears to it; I mean, concentrate on the

idea. This is what gets them; their primitive intelligences can't battle against it. The music of the Pied Piper. Cover up, Kerrigan. I know it is making you stupid. Our real fight is ahead."

His cold, incisive words acted, as they had done so often before, as a swift sedative. Yes, it was the drums. They filled the night with their throbbing, and in some way that throbbing had got into my brain. I adopted a violent method of repelling this insidious intrusion.

I thought hard of Dr Fu Manchu; and when I had succeeded in conjuring up a vision of that Shakespearean brow, that satanically brilliant face, those catlike emerald eyes, I believe I returned to sanity and to a new fear—the fear of Dr Fu Manchu.

Smith, I am sure, understood the internal struggle which was going on, for he walked beside me in silence until:

"Look!" he rapped suddenly. "There is the second gate—the second test. Can we pass it?"

I looked down; we were quite near to the level space before the stockade which, at closer view, clearly surrounded a temple of sorts. The path which we were following had become a ravine. Long since, the Negro and Negress ahead had become lost to view, and now we proceeded cautiously.

Twenty or thirty paces brought us around a sudden bend and into full view of the stockade. A huddled group of perhaps a dozen pilgrims was gathered before a great gateway. A murmur of voices became audible above the throbbing of the drums.

Even in the bluish shadow of the gulley I could see Smith looking about him, and then:

"There is no other way," he muttered; "it's on or back."

Could we ever get back?

THE GROUP AHEAD before the gateway was explained by the presence of a pine log thrown like a barrier across the opening. Right and left of it, backed by seminaked Negroes holding torches aloft, were two men. One, he on the right, was a pure and obese Negro who continued to wear the uniform of Western slavery; the other, on the left, was the fierce-eyed mulatto who had stared into the car as we had driven to the house of Father Ambrose, who had passed us on the mountain path!

Smith recognised him as swiftly as I.

"It is known that we are here," he muttered. "That mulatto is posted to intercept us. But even if he sees us there is still hope."

"What hope?"

"He is certainly not familiar with our appearance, for he was deceived on the road; he *cannot* know that we carry the seven-pointed star. Glance over the gang now undergoing inspection. The gateway is in shadow, but you can see them in the torchlight. Some of them look whiter than you or I. They are from over the border. This thing goes very deep."

"Let us join the group waiting to be passed by the fat Negro."

"I disagree," said Smith. "If ever I saw a eunuch, he is one. Think of our Arabic! No, I prefer the mulatto."

"But, Smith, it's madness!"

"In an emergency, Kerrigan, madness is sometimes sanity."

I resigned myself. We entered the gateway and moved to the left of the barrier. Glancing back, I saw that a few stragglers, all Haitians, were coming down the slope. As we approached the mulatto I saw directly in front of us the black lovers. Six or seven others preceded them. Smith bent to my ear:

"You see, Kerrigan," he whispered, "it is unnecessary to strip!"

But I had seen, and the sight afforded me a momentary relief. Two figures at least, at right and left, were those of men dressed much as we were dressed. Others were there who had thrown off the yoke and gleamed black beneath the moon. But we were not alone.

"Watch closely," Smith whispered. "All turns on the man not identifying us. Next, stick to Arabic. Finally, if challenged, shoot him."

I watched those who had been allowed to pass the barrier. They had all exhibited some token which they held in their hands. An interrogatory seemed to follow; then, making an odd gesture to the forehead, they were allowed to pass.

"Note that salute," muttered Smith.

When the Negro and Negress approached the mulatto we were close behind them.

He concentrated his fierce gaze upon them, ignoring us. The man opened his hand; the girl touched an amulet which hung upon her breast. The mulatto spoke rapidly in the strange patois which I had been unable to learn, but Smith was listening intently. He pressed his lips almost against my ear.

"Stick to Arabic," he reiterated.

And as the Negro and Negress went through we followed.

Those fierce eyes were fixed upon me; they glittered fierily in the light of surrounding torches, and I confess that my heart sank. Silently I held out the serpent amulet. The mulatto glanced at it; then his evil gaze returned to my face, and suddenly he addressed me in English!

"What is your name and number?" he demanded. "From what place do you come?"

Thrown temporarily off my guard, I believe I was about to answer him in the same language when Smith kicked my ankle so hard that I stifled a cry. . . . But he had saved the situation.

"*Uskût!*" I hissed. "*Daraga âwala!*"

And as I spoke Smith threw his left arm about my shoulders and held out in his right palm the seven-pointed star.

"*Ahu hîna Damballa!*" he said menacingly.

The result smacked of magic. The mulatto fell into that curious pose adopted by the women at the resthouse, his hands pressed to his breast, his head bowed. Smith gave the salute which we had noted.

We were through.

As we walked across the enclosed space towards the temple of voodoo:

"I have taken special note of the fact," said Smith, "that owing to the position of the moon one side of the stockade casts a complete shadow for some ten feet out from its base. That is the spot to make for."

We gained the shadow belt unmolested. Drawing a deep breath, I looked about me. There were, as I have said, many torches and some lanterns. I saw now that they were distributed in a rough circle before the building, which on closer inspection proved to be a sort of shrine embedded in the trees. Before it was a platform, or dais, flanked by tall masts resembling totem poles. Double doors, massively carved and brightly painted, gave onto this platform. Right and left of these doors, which were closed, stood two motionless figures as if sculptured in ebony. But in the light of the full moon pouring down upon them I recognised the forest lovers!

Drums, although I could not see the drummers, continued their sinister throbbing. And now, all those summoned presumably being present, torches and lanterns were extinguished. The drum throbs died away. A great voice cried out in a tongue which I had never heard spoken. The double doors swung open.

A sort of rapturous sigh passed through the multitude. With complete unanimity they dropped to their knees and bowed their heads. A woman came out into the moonlight, and I knew that she was the Queen Mamaloi. . . .

HER HAIR WAS HIDDEN by a high jewelled head-dress; jewels all but covered slim bare arms; a girdle resembling that seen in ancient Egyptian pictures, glittering with gems, hung from her waist. There, radiant in silver light, from proud head to curving hips, to little sandalled feet, I saw an ivory statue—a statue of Isis. The deep-toned drums entirely ceased to beat. Every man and every woman who gathered before the temple fell prone. A long, queerly modu-lated phrase, a moaning sigh, passed like a breeze among the worshippers.

I was dumfounded, fascinated, swept for a moment into a mystic vortex which her presence had created. She stood no more than twenty paces away, wholly bathed in the radiance of the moon; and I looked, as if hypnotised, into the brilliant jade-green eyes of Queen Mamaloi, the witchwoman, high priestess of voodoo . . . Koreâni, Dr Fu Manchu's daughter!

Smith pulled me down just within that fraction of a second which otherwise might have shown me standing alone. Earlier I had knelt to a priest; I lay now prostrate before a sorceress!

His grasp on my arm warned me to be silent.

She spoke, in Haitian, in French and in some other lan-guage which I had never heard spoken before (save by that voice which had announced her coming). But the sound of it seemed to act upon her listeners like a maddening drug. They moaned, cried out inarticulately; they gesticulated as they rose to their knees. Smith drew very near.

"The Unknown Tongue," he whispered; "the secret lan-guage of voodoo."

Koreâni had a bell-like voice—this I remembered; a voice which, because of its production and unusual quality, was audible from a distance: in short, the voice of a trained elocutionist and of one who might have been a great actress. Her speech was accompanied by a subdued but passionate throbbing of unseen drums.

More and more, as she spoke, I appreciated the power of the spirit driving her. Here was a mastery comparable with that of Dr Fu Manchu. French, Haitian (of which I knew little enough), in turn were discarded, so that presently Koreâni spoke altogether in the Unknown Tongue—of which I knew nothing. Frenzy grew upon her audience until some among the throng might have been said to have become possessed. They groaned, gnashed their teeth, contorted their bodies. The substance of the address I found some difficulty in tracing, but the danger to the community represented by this woman's influence was all too apparent.

Suddenly, in obedience to some command from the Queen Mamaloi, all threw themselves upon their knees; faces buried in hands, they began to pray fervently. Koreâni, silent, statuesque, stood with uplifted arms.

"She has asked them to pray for a sign from Damballa the snake-god," whispered Smith. "I suspect that the real purpose of this ceremony is about to become evident."

But even he could not foresee the miracle which we were to witness. The drums became silent.

Thanks to the position which Smith had taken up, we stood, as I have mentioned, in deep shadow cast by the stockade. We should become visible only if the ring of torches were lighted again before the temple. Within this ring devotees were writhing on the ground in an ecstasy of supplication. Koreâni stood motionless, her brilliant eyes raised to the moon.

And magically those supplications were answered.

A harsh, guttural voice spoke. Smith's sudden grip on my arm made me wince. The opening words were unintelligible, but following them came a phrase in Haitian; finally, in French, the imperious voice declaimed:

"I, Damballa, have been called. I answer. I am here among you, but your blind eyes cannot see me. I come because there are traitors here, spies—those who work not for the glory of the African races but to gain for themselves. Tonight there shall be a great smelling-out. True men, stand fast. Spies—I shall find you! To me, my servants. Damballa speaks."

The jewel-laden ivory arms of Koreâni dropped to her sides; I saw her clenched hands. The Negro and Negress right and left of the painted doorway seemed to be stricken immobile. Stupefaction silenced every prayer. There was movement—then stillness, broken only by panting breaths. Although the speaker seemingly stood beside the high priestess, no one was there.

But the voice of Damballa was the voice of Dr Fu Manchu!

THREE FIGURES wearing hideous ritual masks and carrying torches came out from dense undergrowth on the left of the temple; three others appeared on the right. Finally, stalking into torchlight from the direction of the barricade, there came a seventh—a herculean man, masked, robed and carrying a glittering scimitar. The hush about us was electrical with suspense. Although I knew that he hurt me unconsciously, Smith's grip on my arm was as that of steel pincers.

"Touch and go, Kerrigan!" he hissed in my ear. "We are spotted! Don't fight: it's hopeless. We can only trust——"

"The smelling-out begins!" cried that harsh voice. "Sons and daughters of Damballa, you are safe. . . ."

This phrase was repeated in Haitian, then in that incomprehensible language, the Unknown Tongue. Urged to his task by the bodiless Voice, the giant sword-bearer began a sinister inspection. Frightened groups were huddled together within the stockade; I could hear chattering teeth. Other masks had appeared at the entrance. Retreat was cut off.

Every face was scrutinised. The Voice seemed to speak from immediately beside the sword-bearer. Koreâni stood motionless as that ivory statue which she resembled.

Alternately sibilant and guttural, that uncanny voice muttered—muttered—in what language I could not make out. Then came one short, sharp command. The scimitar shot out and touched a cowering Haitian. He shrieked so wildly that I thought the blow had been a mortal one. But his shriek was of fear. One of the masked torchmen sprang forward, grasped the selected man and hurled him into the open space before the temple. He fell and lay there quivering. A woman who had stood beside him moaned and collapsed. . . .

So the "smelling-out" began, and so it went on; until ten victims, women as well as men, stood, knelt or lay in the open space. All about me were whispered prayers—and they were not voodoo prayers. The children of Damballa who had called upon their black god now prayed to the God of the Christians to exorcise him!

Many devotees had fainted after the seekers had passed. But Koreâni, proud, motionless, stood silent, her brilliant eyes widely opened.

The sword-bearer drew near with his hideous company. "Remember," Smith whispered.

And now the muttering Voice began to speak in English. "I smell other enemies. . . . More light—more light!"

Torches were lifted before us.

"Ah—there!"

The scimitar flashed towards me. The voice of Dr Fu Manchu had spoken from the left side of the sword-bearer. And I succumbed to a mad impulse.

I side-stepped, hauled away and drove a straight right at the spot where the head of the speaker should have been.

Amazing to relate, it *was* there! I registered a glancing blow on an unmistakable human jaw . . . and I saw a *green hand* appear out of space!

A wild cry and a crushing weight which seemed to descend upon my skull . . .

33 / Dr Marriot Doughty

OF MY AWAKENING, or rather my first awakening, I retain one vivid memory—a memory etched upon my brain. My head ached with a violence greater than I had ever experienced; coherent thought was impossible. I lay in a bunk in a small white cabin, and because of a gentle swaying sensation and of the silence I thought that I must be afloat in an anchored ship. Every detail of my immediate surroundings was clearly discernible in moonlight which poured in at a long, low porthole directly above the bunk. I struggled to sit up. The effect upon my head was disastrous, but just before I fell back again into unconsciousness I had a glimpse of what lay beyond the porthole.

I looked down upon forest-clad mountain slopes, ravines and scattered dwellings; upon something resembling a coloured relief map—and a map that swept up and then receded at an incredible speed. Just ahead and not far beneath I saw a mighty building crowning a dizzy crest, a giant's castle, a fabulous structure towering up to the moon.

Almost as I saw it I found myself over it, and it was gone! But I knew that it was the Citadel, the impregnable fortress built by King Christophe, now deserted, shunned, save of the uneasy spirit of the Negro king. . . .

My second awakening afforded the discovery that the pain in my skull was almost gone and that a cool, wet bandage surrounded my forehead. I was in bed, wearing silk pyjamas which did not belong to me, in a scrupulously neat room—a room, as I determined after that first glance, in a hospital. No doubt that vision of the Citadel, of flying silently through space, had been delirium. I tried to reason out what had happened after I had struck, madly, at a Voice and had contacted flesh and bone. The rear guard for which Smith had arranged must have arrived ahead of time, so I reasoned.

I had just come to this conclusion when the door (it had neither handle nor keyhole) slid noiselessly open and a man came in who wore a long white linen coat; undoubtedly a doctor.

He paused for a moment, smiling with satisfaction to see me awake. He was an elderly man, wearing a pointed greyish beard; he had a fine brow and those penetrating eyes which mark the diagnostician. He was a Vandyke type, and for some reason I found his features familiar.

"Good morning, Mr Kerrigan," he said in a pleasant, light voice. "It would be superfluous to inquire if you feel better."

"Quite, Doctor. Except for a certain drumming in my skull, I never felt better in my life."

"Well, you know"—he seated himself on the side of the bed, taking out a clinical thermometer from its case—"even a thick skull like yours is calculated to buzz a bit when struck hard with the flat of a heavy sword."

He took my temperature and nodded.

"Normal," he announced as he went into an adjoining room which was evidently a bathroom.

I heard him rinsing the thermometer, and all the time I was thinking furiously: where had I seen the doctor before? In some way the elusive memory was bound up with another —something to do with student days and also with the Royal Navy. It was as he came out again that I tied up the links . . . Peter Marriot Doughty, who was reading medicine and who had the rooms above mine; he was now in the navy; I had seen him off before I left for Finland. His father, a celebrated Harley Street consultant, had once had tea with Doughty and myself. . . .

Probably my change of expression was marked.

"Yes, Mr Kerrigan—what is bothering you?"

"Am I addressing Doctor Marriot Doughty?"

"John Marriot Doughty, M.D., at your service."

Momentarily I closed my eyes, doubted my sanity. Clearly now I recalled the long obituary notices, remembered almost the exact words of my telegram of condolence to my friend. Dr Marriot Doughty, his father, had died in the spring of 1937—but this was Dr Marriot Doughty who stood before me!

When I opened my eyes John Marriot Doughty was smiling again.

"You remember me, Mr Kerrigan? I once had the pleasure of taking tea in your rooms with my son."

Words failed me; I merely stared.

"Have you recent news of Peter?"

I reconquered control of my tongue.

"He is with the destroyers operating off Narvik, Doctor. I had word from him last some four weeks ago."

The dead man who lived nodded.

"Good. Peter was always best in action. I broke a long family tradition, Mr Kerrigan, when I abandoned the sea for surgery. Peter has gone back. I think his mother would have

162

wished it so. And now I am going to get you on your feet. To lie there any longer, sir, would be pure malingering."

But nevertheless I lay there, watching him. My complaisant analysis of the situation had been grossly at fault. My heart was behaving erratically. The rear guard had *not* arrived. Where was Nayland Smith? Since Dr Marriot Doughty was indisputably dead, logically I must be dead also. Here was just such a passing-over as I had heard described at spiritualist meetings.

Undoubtedly I was dead; this was the Beyond.

Dr Marriot Doughty's gaze held a deep compassion, but it was the compassion which belongs to greater knowledge.

"Mr Kerrigan," he said, "my part is not to enlighten you regarding your new circumstances: my part is to set you on your feet again. There are toxic elements in your system based upon a faultily treated wound in your left shoulder and affecting the lung structure, but not gravely. You are a healthy, powerful man. This trouble will disperse: in fact, it shall be my business to disperse it. The blow on the occipital area has resulted in no hemorrhage: forget it. In short—I know what you are thinking, but you are not dead. You are very cogently alive."

I swung out of bed and stood up. A slight dizziness wore off almost immediately.

"Good," said Dr Marriot Doughty. "See that the bath is no more than tepid. Your own clothes are all here—at least those you were wearing. I believe you will find the cartridge belt missing and the pistol. When you are dressed I will come back and prescribe your breakfast."

He turned to go.

"Doctor!" He pulled up. "Where is Nayland Smith?"

"Mr Kerrigan, I would gladly answer your question—if I knew the answer. I shall return in about twenty minutes."

"One moment! How long——"

"Have you been unconscious? Roughly, four days. . . ."

AS MARRIOT DOUGHTY signalled to me to precede him I found myself in a long corridor in which were many white doors numbered like those in a hotel. An hour had elapsed.

"Some of the staff occupy this annex," he said. "It is new, and the apartments, as you have seen, are pleasant. My own quarters are in the main building near the research laboratories."

He spoke in the manner of one conducting a visitor over a power station. Nothing in my memories of those grim days is more grotesque than the easy conversational style of this physician who had been dead for three years. I could think of no suitable remark.

"Our headquarters at one time were in the South of France," he went on, "but there we were subject to too much interference. Here, in Haiti, we are ideally situated."

We came out into a large quadrangle, its tile paths bordered by palms. I saw that the place we had left resembled a row of bungalows joined together. Most of the windows were open, and there were vases of flowers to be seen on ledges, rows of books. A swim suit hung out of one. It might have been a holiday camp. On the other side of the quadrangle was an extensive range of buildings which I could only assume to be a modern factory, although I saw no smokestack. Several detached structures appeared further off; and in and out of the various buildings men, most of them Haitians and wearing blue overalls, moved in orderly industry. I heard the hum of machinery. Wherever I looked, beyond, forest-robed mountain slopes swept up to the bright morning sky. This was a valley entirely enclosed on all sides. I turned to my guide.

"Where am I? What place is this?"

He smiled.

"Officially it is the works of the San Damien Sisal Corporation. Geologically it is the crater of a huge volcano, fortunately extinct. The best sisal in the world is cultivated and treated here. Although the output is small, it is of the very highest quality. The enterprise had been in existence for a long time, but we acquired control less than six years ago."

"It appears to be most inaccessible."

"There is a small railway by which produce is sent out. The hemp is grown on the lower slopes behind you. Over a thousand workers are employed by the corporation."

So we chatted. There was nothing ominous, no trace of the sinister anywhere. The well-ordered path, flanked by palms, along which we were walking; the fresh mountain air; a cloudless sky; those waves of verdure embracing the valley: all these things spoke of a bountiful nature well and gratefully appreciated. But I looked askance at every figure moving about me, and I had conceived a horror of the proximity of Dr Marriot Doughty which I found it hard to conceal. I was in the company of a living-dead man—a zombie; were all these workers zombies also?

Before the door of a house which looked older and which was of a character different from the others my guide paused and pressed a bell.

"Here," he said, "I hand you over to Companion Horton with a clean bill of health." The door was opened by a

Haitian. "Tell the manager that Mr Bart Kerrigan is here."

As the man stood aside to allow me to enter Dr Marriot Doughty nodded cheerily and turned away. The profoundly commonplace character of everyone's behaviour, that reference to "the manager" and now the businesslike office in which I found myself began, insidiously, to frighten me. Companion Horton, a lean, slow-spoken American, rose from a workmanlike desk to greet me. Above his chair I noticed a large photograph of a hemp plantation.

"You are very welcome, Mr Kerrigan. Please sit down and smoke."

I sat down and accepted a cigarette which he proferred.

"Thanks—Mr Horton, I presume?"

"James Ridgwell Horton. That's my name, sir; and I was born in Boston June first 1853———"

"Eighteen fifty-three!"

"Sure thing. I don't look my age, but then none of us does here. I will admit that there was a time when the thought of going right on living did not appeal. But when I found out that all my faculties became not dulled but keener, when I realised that I could assimilate new ideas and examine them in the light of old experience, why, I changed my mind."

No doubt my expression made the remark unnecessary, but:

"I don't think," I said, trying to speak very calmly, "that I follow."

"No? Well, that's too bad. May I take it you know that this is the headquarters of the Order of the Si-Fan?"

I suppose I had known—for some time past; yet, bluntly stated, the fact made my heart wobble.

"Yes—I know."

"Just so; and you feel about it the way I felt twenty years ago. To you the Si-Fan is plain and simple a Black Hand gang; an underworld ramp; a bunch of professional crooks. I thought just that way. But if you will consider the methods by which any totalitarian state makes progress, you will find that the ancient order has merely perfected them. Because you have met some of the high officials—maybe one of the council —in shady quarters you have jumped to wrong conclusions."

But now this man's sophistries began to infuriate me.

"I regard the heads of such states as glorified gunmen, Mr Horton. Their methods—I grant the parallel—are the methods of any other criminal."

"But consider how different their ends are from ours."

"However noble you believe these to be, I cannot agree that the end justifies the means."

"Well, well—I am instructed to pass you over to someone who may adjust your standpoint, Mr Kerrigan." He stood up. "If you will please come this way."

He opened a door and invited me to follow. I thought he seemed to be a little crestfallen, as if my obstinacy saddened him. Certainly one less like a desperate criminal than James Ridgwell Horton it would have been difficult to find. And now, as I walked along an uncarpeted and dimly lighted corridor by his side, a ghastly explanation of his presence there occurred to me. . . . He was dead!

I was in the company of a zombie; a soulless intelligence; a robot controlled by a master wizard.

Before an arched opening a green light was burning. Even as Horton stopped a swift sensation as of momentary dropping of temperature warned me of the identity of him to *whom* I was being conducted. He touched a button, and a heavy panelled door slid noiselessly open. On its threshold stood Hassan, the white Nubian!

"Mr Kerrigan is expected," said Horton, and Hassan stood aside.

I went in, and the heavy door closed behind me. But the appearance of Hassan had gone far to revive my waning courage. Did it mean that Ardatha was here?

The place was a lobby, lighted by a square silk lantern and pervaded by a curious perfume; another door was beyond.

"Wait, please."

Hassan opened the further door, stepped in and immediately came out again, indicating with a movement of one huge, muscular hand that I should enter. Clenching my teeth, I went into a small library. There were volumes on the shelves of a character which I had never come across before. The only illumination was provided by a globular lamp on a square black pedestal set on a large desk. Upon this desk lay a number of books and papers and other objects which I had no leisure to observe.

For seated behind the desk in a grotesquely carved ebony chair was Dr Fu Manchu. . . .

34 / The Zombies

HE WORE A WHITE LINEN COAT similar to that worn by Marriot Doughty; on his head was a black skullcap. He glanced at me as I entered—and I avoided his glance: it was a protective instinct.

"Be seated, Mr Kerrigan. You have not failed to note contusion and a slight abrasion in the neighbourhood of my left maxillary muscle. Had your very forceful blow struck me on the bone structure, I fear that the damage might have been more serious."

As I sat down facing him I ventured to look. His left jaw was bruised and cut. Perhaps his quiet, deliberate speech was responsible (he spoke, in a sense, perfect English but gave each syllable an equal value which made familiar words sound strange) or perhaps sudden hot resentment—resentment of all he stood for—inspired me, but:

"A long-cherished ambition is realised," I said. "At least I have hit you once."

He toyed with a jade snuffbox which lay upon the desk; his disconcerting eyes grew filmed. That sensitive hand, with its long, tended fingernails, fascinated me.

"I bear no malice, Mr Kerrigan. Animal courage is not one of the higher human qualities, but it is a quality, nevertheless, and I respect it—I can use courage. You have it. I welcome you. I absorb gladly all that is useful in the animal kingdom. Suitably directed, such a specialised army can defeat great but ignorant hosts."

His voice, as always, was acting upon me like a drug. There was something of the inevitable, superhuman, a quality akin to those hidden but known forces of nature, in his mere presence.

"You have met some of the companions whom you believe to be dead. No doubt you have studied the tradition of the zombie—a tradition which persists in Haiti. Persistent traditions always rest on fact. It was exactly sixty years ago today that I devoted myself to a close examination of this subject. I had heard, as no doubt you have heard, of dead men working under the orders of witch doctors; these automata were known as zombies. There are examples in Haiti at the present moment, and I do not refer to my own experiments."

During the weeks that had elapsed since I had faced Dr Fu Manchu in that underground laboratory beside the Thames a marked change had taken place in him: then I had thought him dying; now he was restored to his supernormal self.

"These hapless creatures are not—as superficial observers have supposed—a kind of vampire, a corpse reanimated by sorcery; they are the products of a form of slow poisoning which induces catalepsy. When buried they are not in fact dead. The voodoo man disinters them and bends them to his purpose. They have no conscious identity; they remain slaves of his will."

Opening the jade box, he raised a pinch of snuff to his nostrils.

"After researches which led me from Haiti to Central Africa, to the Sudan and finally to Egypt, I discovered the nature of the drugs used and the manner of their administration. The process was known to the priests of Thebes. I was quick to realise that its possession placed a power in my hands which should secure for me mastery of every other secret of nature!"

His voice rose. His brilliant green eyes, fully opened, revealed momentarily the mad fanaticism which inspired him. I had a glimpse of that terrifying genius which more than once had shaken governments.

"I determined, Mr Kerrigan, to establish a corner in brains. For the purpose of carrying out those numerous experiments in physics, botany, zoology, biology, which I had projected, I would secure a staff of researchers from the best intellects in those sciences." He tapped the jade snuffbox with a long, varnished fingernail. "I sought my staff all over the world, employing the resources of the Si-Fan to aid me. I was not invariably successful; nevertheless I secured a notable collection of first-class brains. My conquest of that age-old mystery, the *elixir vitae*, enabled me to arrest senility in suitable cases—as, for example, in my own."

He stood up and, stepping to a door recessed between bookcases, pressed a button. The door slid open.

"Since you are to remain with us—as an active participant in our work to create a sane world, if you choose (but since, in any event, you will remain)—I shall give you an opportunity of judging of our labours before any decision is demanded of you."

A man came in, a young man who had an untidy mop of dark brown hair and very steadfast hazel eyes. He was a powerful fellow, wore blue overalls and had the hands of a toiler; but when he spoke I knew that he was a man of culture.

"Companion Allington," said Dr Fu Manchu, "this is Mr Bart Kerrigan. As you are of about one age I thought he might appreciate your company as guide. You may show him anything that he wishes to see."

"Delighted, Mr Kerrigan, and much obliged to you, sir."

As I followed my new acquaintance along a short passage and out into a tree-shaded courtyard I thought that he had used just the words and just the tone of one speaking to his commanding officer.

"DO YOU MEAN that you are Squadron Leader Allington?"

"Well, I used to be," said Allington, grinning cheerfully. "Only regret I'm out of the service because I'm missing the gorgeous show in France."

"You held the Royal Air Force altitude record."

"Yes—for a time. Then I tried to be too clever on a non-stop flight and crashed in the Timor Sea. Remember?"

"Well—I remember you were missing. Were you——"

I hesitated, looking almost furtively into those smiling eyes.

"Killed? Oh no! I'm not one of the *conscripts;* I'm a volunteer!"

He laughed gaily, grasping my arm and leading me in the direction of a long, low building on the right. But his reference to "the conscripts" had turned me cold.

"Do you mean that you voluntarily joined the——"

"The Si-Fan? Yes, rather. So will you when the time comes. I was picked up by a steamer which happened to belong to them, you see. You have a lot to learn yet, Kerrigan. Whatever your job may be, this is the most wonderful service in the world."

He selected a key from a number attached to a chain and opened the door of what I assumed to be one of a range of garages. If there had never been a Fuehrer or a Duce—one who had persuaded an entire nation to believe in his godlike mission—I should have been unable to trust my senses, to credit my reason; but what such men could do certainly Dr Fu Manchu could improve upon.

"Here we are," said Allington, wheeling the wide doors apart. "You've got to see my taxis first whether you want to or not!"

His buoyant enthusiasm, his typical Air Force manner, at that time and in those circumstances, I bracket in my memories with the informative remarks of Dr Marriot Doughty as he had conducted me to my interview with Fu Manchu.

I found myself to be in a place resembling a long garage. Some twenty machines were there in line. At first sight they looked like small monoplanes; further inspection led to confusion. Squadron Leader Allington laughed.

"Screams, aren't they?" he cried. "No undercarriage, no propeller! And"—he tapped my shoulder knowingly—"how do you suppose we get 'em into the air?"

It was a poser. There was no airfield outside; no runway. "Look!"

He moved a lever. That section of roof immediately above

169

the machine which I had been inspecting swung open. I saw the sky.

"Straight up, Kerrigan! Even a hawk needs a take-off, but these birds rise straight from their heels."

"How?"

"One of our conscripts, Professor Swain—whose name you may have heard—discovered a meteoric substance in Poland (his native land) which was antigravitational——"

"Whatever do you mean?"

"I mean that these planes are fitted with an insulated disk of *swainsten* (named after its discoverer) which, when exposed or partially exposed to the earth's influence, sends the bus flying upward towards some unknown planet for which *swainsten* has so keen an affinity that it overcomes gravity and atmosphere to get there! Uncontrolled, one would reach the stratosphere!"

"But——"

"The *swainsten* disk is operated from the controls. The pilot can climb at terrific speed or hover. It's simply miraculous. I have learned since I came here that I didn't know the first thing about flying! You begin to feel the fascination of having access to knowledge which others are groping to find. The whole show is like that. These things take the air as silently as owls. One could start from a bowling green and alight on a billiard table. Once afloat, propulsion is obtained from Ericksen waves——"

"But the Ericksen wave——"

"Disintegrates? I agree—if so directed. But as fitted to the Bats (that is our own name for these small planes) it enables the pilot to 'tune in' to a suitable wave length, as one does with a radio set, and to pick up from it all the power he needs to develop anything up to three hundred miles an hour. There are larger models, of course, which can do more. I had the pleasure of bringing you here in one from the jamboree at Morne la Selle."

It was dawning upon my mind that I was acquiring knowledge which I should never live to use; part, at least, of the mystery of Dr Fu Manchu's secret journeys was explained.

"The whole outfit is silent as a radio set; in fact, it is broadly operated on the same principle except that the energy is converted. I would give you a trial spin, but I have no instructions. Some other time . . ."

When he had partially exhausted his enthusiasm for this, his pet subject (I gathered that he was chief pilot), I asked him a question which had been in my mind throughout:

"Aren't there—urges to return to your former friends?"

His mouth twisted into a wry expression.

"At first—yes; lots. I believe there have been cases where unwilling workers have been allowed to go. We have Professor Richner here——"

"But Professor Richner——"

"Is dead, you mean? My dear Kerrigan, every soul on the headquarters staff (I refer to the officers) is legally dead! *I* am legally dead; we are all dead. But in those rare cases I have mentioned Companion Richner has prescribed, and one of the doctor's medical staff has dealt with the case. A painless injection and the patient returns to the world with a blind spot in his memory. He can tell his friends nothing; he remembers nothing. Do you see?"

I saw. Ardatha had had such a "painless injection."

"When, as it were, normally one goes on leave—well, it is merely necessary to avoid old haunts and, if caught up, to stick to the new identity; profess ignorance and say, 'Sorry, you must be mistaken.'"

"But then you elect to stay under these conditions and there are no pulls to your old life?"

We were walking along a path which evidently led back to the main quadrangle, and Allington grabbed my arm in his impulsive way.

"In my own case, as no doubt it would be in yours, the pull was a girl. I was crazy about her. All the same I consented to see Richner and I submitted to the injection he prescribed."

"What occurred?"

"Well—it was a good deal like recovering from a tropical fever! I saw Joan—she is one of the many Joans—in correct perspective. I realised, for the first time, that she had most irritating mannerisms and that although her figure was good her complexion was dreadful! It became clear to me, Kerrigan, that there are millions of pretty women in the world and that a companion of the Si-Fan has a wide field of choice."

I was silent for a while. My feelings about Squadron Leader Allington underwent a swift change.

I understood . . . and that first moment of understanding was a shattering moment. It became evident to me why Marriot Doughty, Horton and Allington—men, in their normal lives, honourable, above reproach—now embraced the ideals of the Si-Fan wholeheartedly, unquestionably. They were truly zombies; slaves of a master physician. Better death than the "painless injection"!

Perhaps Nayland Smith was already dead—perhaps I was alone in this head office of hell!

35 / Ardatha Remembers

ALLINGTON LEFT ME in my new quarters; the number on my door was 13, and I disliked the omen. I had seen so many things which transcended what hitherto I had regarded as natural laws that I was bewildered. There was a well-stocked buffet in the small sitting room, and I was about to take a drink when I paused, glass in hand.

The power of the Si-Fan was appalling; I was afraid to think about it. Men of genius laboured in the workshops, in the laboratories; men, some of them, whose names figured in every work of reference. "The conscripts," as Allington termed them, had been poisoned, buried for dead and then secretly exhumed. Their lives had been prolonged by means of some process known only to Dr Fu Manchu. Allington had introduced me to Professor Richner. At the time of his death in 1923 he had been seventy-two. He looked like an old man but not like one nearing ninety!

Four days—I had been here for four days. . . .

I set the glass down. Even as I did so I know that I flattered myself, for Dr Fu Manchu would not go to so much trouble about a mere journalist. . . . A corner in brains? I had seen but a small part of what this meant, but already I was appalled. The fate not only of the United States but of the world hung in the balance. . . . I turned swiftly. Someone had opened my door.

Dr Marriot Doughty came in.

"You're very jumpy, Kerrigan," he said professionally. "I was anxious to see how you had taken your first tour of headquarters. If you are going to have a whiskey and soda, may I join you? It's an allowance, you know, and not deducted from pay!"

Reassured, I served out two drinks.

"You know," said the physician, "I have got to get your blood stream clean. Yours is one of those cases that put me on my mettle. You consulted Partridge in London, you told me. Between ourselves, Partridge is an old fool. I'll have you fit inside a month."

"What does it matter!"

"Oh! Feeling like that about it? Well, well—I passed through that phase myself. When I 'died' it was Partridge who signed my death certificate. I was *conscious* all the time, Kerrigan!"

"Good God!"

"They did me well and consigned me to the family vault in a Roman Catholic cemetery; we are a Catholic family, as you know. I knew that I was a case of catalepsy; I knew that Partridge had failed to make the proper tests. I wondered how long the agony would last——"

"How long *did* it last?"

"I was exhumed the same night! I believe the watchman had been drugged. The fellows who hauled me out were Asiatics; they belong to a special guild and do no other work. My coffin was replaced and the tomb resealed. A smart job. They hoisted me over a wall into a waiting car, and I was rushed to a house in Cadogan Square. A very competent Japanese surgeon gave me an injection—and I was a living man again!"

"But," I said breathlessly, "after that—what happened?"

John Marriot Doughty finished his whiskey and soda and stood up.

"No time to tell you now. I have been sent to take you to a second interview with the doctor."

"Why? . . . Does this mean that I have to make a decision —at once?"

"My dear Kerrigan, only the doctor knows that."

Once more I walked along a tiled, palm-bordered path across the big quadrangle; once more Marriot Doughty rang a bell. This time, for it was a different door, Hassan the Nubian opened. I was conducted straight to the room of Dr Fu Manchu.

He sat behind the big desk and through half-closed eyes watched me.

"Be seated, Mr Kerrigan."

I was fighting for self-mastery. Some great ordeal pended; I knew that its outcome meant compromise—or extinction.

"You have had an opportunity to glance over some of the work being done here. I would not hurry you. Clearly you apprehend that my design is to force a decision. Mr Kerrigan, you must correct your perspective; you are not of sufficient value to the Si-Fan to justify your extravagant egoism. I could bind you to me now if I wished; I could kill you by merely depressing a switch. Search your memory."

That harsh guttural voice was mastering me as always it had mastered me.

"What do you wish me to remember?"

"Two things. The first, that I have never broken my word; the second, that I promised to restore Ardatha to complete freedom."

And as he spoke a sort of violet haze seemed to obstruct

173

my vision—a haze which resembled in color Ardatha's eyes. I saw the pit yawning before me, a trap set for my feet. I knew that when I chose the path—death or service to Dr Fu Manchu—I should make no free choice.

He pressed a button. A door opened silently.

Ardatha came in.

"THE PART PLAYED by Ardatha in my organisation," said Dr Fu Manchu, "is an important one. She is the successor to some of the most beautiful women who have decorated the world. I employ beauty, Mr Kerrigan, as a swordsman employs a rapier. Now—she has gone the way of her predecessors. I accept the fact because you have twice succeeded in transmuting the base metal of feminine caprice into the gold of love."

Ardatha stood motionless, watching me. In the subdued light of Fu Manchu's study she looked like a lovely phantom; her eyes seemed to hold some message which I could not read. Dr Fu Manchu opened his jade snuffbox.

"I said"—he spoke softly—"that I would restore her. There is, as you know, a blind spot in her memory, which I shall presently correct." He raised a pinch of snuff; Ardatha did not move. "You have had an opportunity of meeting members of my staff, of glancing over some of the results which we have achieved. There has been, for the second time within ten years, an attempt, and an attempt from the same quarter, to disturb my authority. Ardatha was one of the enemy's prizes. I recovered her."

He took up a sycamore box from the desk and opened it.

"This attempt shall be the last."

His long nails scratched unpleasantly on the surface. He took out a small telescopic rod attached to a metal base and set it on the desk before him. From a projecting arm at the top of the rod an object which resembled a large black diamond hung suspended upon what seemed to be two strands of silk.

"A form of lignite—known to commerce as jet; a remarkably fine specimen from an ancient British barrow of the Bronze Age."

Fu Manchu turned the fragment of mineral between his long fingers until the suspending strands were knotted. His gaze became fixed upon me.

"You have my word," he said softly, "that I design no harm to Ardatha. I merely propose to correct that blind spot in her memory to which I have referred."

He turned to Ardatha, who stood less than two paces from

the ebony chair in which he was seated.

"Come forward." She obeyed, moving like an automaton. "Bend down and watch closely."

He released the piece of cut jet, and it began to spin.

"Tell me what you see. . . . Speak."

"A spot of bright light," Ardatha whispered. "It grows larger . . . it is a gleaming mirror. . . . A picture is forming in it."

"Describe the picture."

"It is of myself. I am going into a hut on a riverbank; I am seeking for something . . . Ah! a man is hiding there! He stands between me and the door——"

"Who is the man?"

"It is too misty to see."

Ardatha was describing our second meeting! It had taken place in an eel fisher's hut on a Norfolk river.

"Go on."

"I talk with him." There was a subtle change in the tone of her voice which hastened my heartbeats. "I trick him . . . I escape."

"Do you wish to escape?"

"No—I wish to stay."

"Follow this man and tell me his name."

And as I watched Ardatha bending over the spinning lignite, the light of the globular lamp striking sparks from her hair, she described every one of our meetings, in London, in Venice, in Paris. The jet became stationary, but she went on without pause, her voice that of one speaking in a trance. At last:

"Name this man," Dr Fu Manchu said softly.

"It is Bart—Bart Kerrigan!"

"Do you love him?"

An instant's pause, and then:

"Yes," she whispered.

But she remained there, bending forward, even when Fu Manchu raised his eyes—brilliant green in concentration—and addressed me.

"A device which we owe to the Arabs. It stimulates the subconscious mind." He clapped his hands sharply. "Return, Ardatha. Is this the man you desire?"

Ardatha stood upright, sighed and looked about her as one suddenly awakened; then, as her gaze rested on me, she grew so suddenly pale that I thought she was about to collapse. But as I watched her hungrily a wave of crimson swept to her pale cheeks and a glory came into her eyes which was heaven.

"Bart!" she sobbed. "Oh, my darling—where have you been?"

Momentarily that sinister figure in the ebony chair seemed to have ceased to exist for her. She ran to me with a joyous cry and threw herself into my arms. . . .

36 / The Vortland Lamp

"YOU OBSERVE," said Dr Fu Manchu, "that residence here is not without its attractions."

Ardatha he had sent away in charge of Hassan, whom he had summoned. As I last glimpsed her those beautiful eyes were radiant. His sibilant tones brought me down to realities. Love can raise some natures to great heights. I faced him more fearlessly than I had supposed ever to be possible.

"I owe you my gratitude . . . but what do you ask in return?"

He began to toy with the jade snuffbox.

"I am not a huckster, Mr Kerrigan. It lies in my power to do with you as I please. Let us suppose that I give you leave to go."

"It would not be real freedom. Ardatha is bound to you by a tie she cannot break—and live."

"So? In what I may, perhaps, term your second romance she confided this to you? Here, I perceive, is some deep affinity. You must certainly marry. The progeny of such a union could not fail to be interesting."

His voice remained low, sibilant. Was he mocking me?

"That member of my staff responsible," he went on, "treated Ardatha psychologically. The injection to which she submitted was harmless; the antidote a mild stimulant. Localised amnesia I induced by hypnosis; I have removed it. There is no finer example of physical fitness in the world than that afforded by Ardatha."

An emotional wave swept me. Ardatha was *not* doomed to the living death! Then came the aftermath—a vision of those long months of slavery, horror, fear, which she had endured.

"Your methods are those of hell!" I blazed. "Yes—I have met members of your 'staff'—men who once were good men, honest men. Now they are zombies, automata, their sense of proportion destroyed——"

"A simple operation, Mr Kerrigan. The drug used—a discovery of my own—is known as 973."

But I went on, fists clenched, speaking at the top of my voice:

"They live in a dreamworld, labouring day and night to achieve some damnable ambition of yours!"

Dr Fu Manchu stood up—and I prepared for the worst.

"Must my ambitions necessarily be damnable?" he asked in that low, even tone. "In order that any radical change be brought about it is inevitable that thousands shall suffer. Where is the ethical difference between poisoning an enemy in his sleep and bombing his house by night? You have not angered me. I admire your spirit—although it is so correctly English; as correct as the attitude of your Foreign Office which compelled you to alter your account of certain facts in my previous encounter with Sir Denis Nayland Smith——"

This touched me professionally: it was true.

"In order that his identity might be hidden they demanded that you should describe the funeral of 'Rudolph Adlon.' Actually he was at his usual post at the time. Nevertheless you have not only disturbed a molar which has served me for a period of years longer than you might credit but also defied me in my own fortress. Come—I have plans for you."

He pressed a bell; a door opened, and one of those short thickset Burmans of whom I had had experience in the past entered. He wore a sort of blue uniform; his yellow face was expressionless.

"Follow," Fu Manchu commanded in English.

The Burman saluted and stood aside. Dr Fu Manchu, with an imperious gesture of the hand to me, walked along that passage where earlier I had set out with Allington. Fu Manchu led, however, in a different direction, walking quite silently in thick-soled slippers. I discovered that he was fully an inch taller than myself, but the difference might have been due to the padded slippers; his catlike tread was deceptively swift.

Opening a door set in the white wall of a large building which possessed no windows:

"Here you change your shoes," he said.

I saw a row of what looked like galoshes ranged along a shelf, but on inspection they proved to have unusually thick soles. I unlaced and discarded my shoes, and as the Burman knelt to assist me I was transported in spirit to an Eastern mosque. . . .

A metal door being opened, I found myself in a vast laboratory. The floor was covered with some substance which might have been rubber; the walls and ceiling were apparently opaque glass. Numerous pieces of mechanism, some in motion, were set about the place, and suspended from the centre of the ceiling was a copper globe some twelve feet in diameter. On one wall was a huge switchboard. There were glass-topped benches supporting chemical appliances of a kind I had never seen—vessels of all sorts containing brightly coloured fluids.

There was a perceptible, although not an audible, throbbing. Some powerful plant was working. But there was no one on duty.

"My private laboratory, Mr Kerrigan. As your knowledge of science is slight I will not burden you with details concerning the Ferris globe—which, nevertheless, has revolutionised all earlier systems of lighting. Sir John Ferris is with us. This is a Stendl radio transmitter—no larger than a typewriter. A receiver, as you are aware, could be contained in this snuffbox and operates without electrical power."

He tapped the jade snuffbox which he carried. I glanced at him, striving to retain the fighting spirit, but my challenge faltered before those glittering green eyes.

"My purpose in bringing you here," he continued, in the manner of a professor addressing a class, "was to relieve your mind regarding certain recent occurrences. Follow."

I obeyed—and the Burmese bodyguard was a pace behind me.

"This—is the Vortland infra-azure lamp."

And standing on a long, narrow, glass-topped table I saw just such a lamp as that which I had seen in the Thames-side workshop!

"Johann Vortland died before he completed the lamp—a martyr to science. Sir William Crooks was pursuing almost parallel inquiries. I acquired all his material and began a series of experiments which I carried out uninterruptedly for three years. You may recall that I was at work on this subject in London. Many other martyrs (I narrowly escaped canonisation myself) went the way of the inventor. Vortland, the physicist, had triumphed; I, the chemist, failed. The lamp did its appointed work, but he who used it either died or suffered serious injury. You may remember some characteristic specimens I had collected and the unusual appearance of the late Doctor Osler."

An added sibilance on the last four words chilled me uncomfortably.

"Hassan, the Nubian who came to me with Ardatha, in many respects advanced my inquiries. Exposure to the lamp had no deleterious effects. He was born blind. But complete *leucodermia* supervened. From coal black he became snow white. The texture and glands of the skin remained normal. There was no organic reaction. From this point I began to make headway."

My blood seemed to be turning cold. This monster, this satanic genius, spoke of human suffering as a bacteriologist speaks of germs.

"If," he continued, "during any of my visits to the Regal Athenian in New York a trained observer had been present, he could not well have failed to notice a small lucent object, no larger than a grain of mustard seed, moving at a uniform height above the floor."

As he spoke he was enveloping his gaunt body in just such a green garment as that which he had worn in the room beside the Thames. Gloves and a mask were added. He presented a terrifying appearance. Muffled, his strident tones came through the mask.

"I will now ignite the infra-azure lamp."

He bent and touched a switch. Again that strange amethyst light appeared.

"You will observe that above the lamp there is a smaller lamp, and above that a third, smaller still. I shall now ignite the smaller lamp."

He did so . . . and the larger one disappeared!

"Finally, the third——"

The entire apparatus vanished!

"Look closely," the imperious voice directed. "The top of the third lamp remains faintly visible—you see it?"

"Yes—I see it."

"The reflector is adjusted in a particular manner: the lamp can be attached to the headdress—in this way."

Raising the lamp, he fitted it to the top of the mask . . . and disappeared!

My heart leapt madly. This man was not a scientist; he was a wizard.

"I have not become transparent," his voice said out of space; "the effect is on the vision of the beholder. Movement is constrained, of course. I was clumsy when I came to recover Peko in Colon. Observe."

A green-gloved hand appeared—and disappeared.

This it was that Barton had seen in Colon—that I had seen on Morne la Selle!

"One must remain wholly within focus. By the use of this lamp I obtained a view of Christophe's chart during that meeting in New York—and took appropriate steps. . . ."

I FOUND MYSELF in half-light surrounded by glass cases the fronts of which were flush with the wall. These cases had interior illumination as in an aquarium.

"A good collection," said Dr Fu Manchu, "was destroyed in France some years ago; but in certain respects this is better."

He paused before one of the glass windows. The case had a thick floor of moist sand, and over it ran some kind of spiny weed. Silent, he stood there looking in. The Burman remained a pace away. I looked also—and presently I saw one of the inhabitants. It was a monstrous centipede, a thing incredibly swift in its movements, and its colour was brilliant red.

"Owing to a number of mysterious deaths along a certain caravan route in Burma," the harsh voice explained, "I personally visited the neighbourhood. It was then that Police Commissioner Nayland Smith (now Sir Denis) first crossed my path. The incidence was particularly marked in the *zayats*, or resthouses, along this route. It was near one of them that I found my first specimen. These were the creatures responsible."

He moved on.

I knew, as I followed that high-shouldered figure and his yellow guard followed *me*, that I was in the company of a scientist greater than any whose fame fills whole pages of encyclopedias. He had the intellect of a Shakespeare and the soul of Satan. When he paused again I grew physically sick. He scratched with his long nails upon the front of a case littered with birds' feathers and fragments of limbs and claws.

From a sort of clay nest there sprang out the most gigantic black spider I had ever seen; indeed, I had not supposed such a spider to exist. Its hairy legs were as thick as a man's finger; its body was as large as an orange. I could see the *eyes* of this horror—watching me.

"The soldier spider, found in Sumatra. He instantly attacks any intruder, and his bite is fatal in thirty-five seconds. There is a female in the nest. I have succeeded in isolating the neurotoxin which distinguishes this insect's vemon; it is new to science."

He turned from the glass cases and walked to a low wall which surrounded a pit in the centre of the place. In obedience to a guttural command the Burman switched on a group of suspended lights. I became aware of a miasmatic smell, and I looked down into a miniature swamp. The interior walls were smoothly polished. I saw unfamiliar aquatic plants and a surface of green slime.

"Particularly note the fernlike grass growing on the margins. Some of this was introduced among the roses which decorated Colonel Kennard Wood's apartment at the Prado in New York. *Hoemadipsa zeylanica* has an affinity for this grass, from which it is not readily distinguishable. Before feeding, this creature resembles a fragment of string or a bristle from a brush. These examples actually come from a swampy area south of Port-au-Prince and are much larger, more active and voracious than any I have examined."

He gave an abrupt order. From a sort of cupboard the

Burman took out the body of a newly slain kid and attached it to the hook of a tackle fitted over the pit. He lowered the kid to a point some six feet above the scum and marginal plants, when it began to spin slowly.

"*Hoemadipsa* works in the dark," muttered Dr Fu Manchu. All the lights went out. "Listen!"

Scarcely had he hissed the word when I heard again that evil thing—the Snapping Fingers!

"Now watch and you will see them."

Lights sprang up and I saw a strange, a revolting sight. One has seen caterpillars arch their bodies in moving forward; now I saw a number of pale, slender things, some two inches in length, arching their threadlike bodies all over the suspended carcass. But in this case the movement served a different purpose. One by one they sprang back to the long feathery grass, each spring creating a sound almost exactly like that of snapping fingers!

"They shun light. Even when feeding they drop off if light disturbs the feast. The largest land leech known to me, Mr Kerrigan. When sated they can, nevertheless, compress themselves in such a way that they can pass through very narrow apertures—such as between the slats of a shutter. . . ."

He proceeded to details so nauseating that once more I became fighting mad and turned on him, fists clenched. I met a glance from fully opened green eyes which checked me like a blow.

"Anticipating a further display of Celtic berserker, I ordered a guard to attend me. One more attempted assault, and I shall order him to throw you into the pit and to extinguish the lights."

37 / *The Subterranean Harbour*

I LOOKED ALONG a stone passage, or tunnel, which was patchily illuminated: I mean that the effect was of a badly lighted arcade. An insidious acceptance of fatality, of the hopelessness of this fight, was beginning to prevail. Smith had told me many things about the power behind Dr Fu Manchu, of the resources of the Si-Fan, but I had not properly appreciated his words. Here, in this veritable town concealed behind the sisal factory, I grasped some part of their significance.

"You may wonder—indeed, you *are* wondering—why I take you so closely into my confidence," said Dr Fu Manchu. "This will be made clear later. No doubt you have appreciated the fact that my daughter, known as Koreâni, a second time, under certain influence, has presumed to challenge me. Her part as the Queen Mamaloi she has successfully played for nearly two years and has enslaved the voodoo elements of the Republic. She has, naturally, access to the higher secrets of the creed and therefore control of its devotees. Follow."

But I had followed no more than three paces when I paused.

The luminous patches which I have mentioned were due to the presence of a series of crystal coffins (I cannot otherwise describe them), each having a shaded light direct upon it. In these, bolt upright, their glassy eyes staring dreadfully before them, I saw men and women—some of whom I remembered to have seen "smelt out" by the sword-bearer at the voodoo temple!

"Follow," Fu Manchu rasped.

I had been standing, astounded, before the figure of the handsome Negro who had passed Smith and myself on the mountain road. Unashamed, in statuesque nakedness he glared out at me from his glass sarcophagus.

"They are all—dead."

"On the contrary, Mr Kerrigan, they are all alive."

Before one sarcophagus containing the rigid form of a mulatto, a young man with a fine head and intellectual brow, Dr Fu Manchu raised his clawlike hands and shook them frenziedly before the glass. He poured out a torrent of vituperation in the Haitian dialect, his voice rising shrilly, demoniacally, as once I had heard it raised before. These outbursts from one normally more imperturbable than any man I had known inclined me to believe that Smith was right. Smith had maintained for many years that in the case of the Chinese doctor genius had overstepped the narrow borderland —that Fu Manchu was insane.

He laughed and turned away. It was an appalling exhibition.

"Do not suppose, Mr Kerrigan," he said, "that I waste my words. They can see—they can hear."

"What!" I exclaimed.

"They cannot move an eyelid. That mongrel and the man Lou Cabot, who was conveniently stabbed by his mistress in Colon, were prime movers in the conspiracy against me. The woman you know as Koreâni—my daughter—seduced him from his vows; he was a man who would sell his soul for a woman. It was she who conceived the idea that by seizing your charming friend Ardatha the offensive of Sir Denis Nayland Smith might be checked. I suffered her intrigues against me right up to the meeting at Morne la Selle. And there I gathered to me all the pitiful conspirators. Here is the chief criminal."

And in the last of the glass coffins, or the last one illuminated, I saw Koreâni!

She stood exactly as I remembered her standing before the door of the voodoo temple, her arms beside her, her hands clenched; those brilliant eyes, which were so strangely like the eyes of Fu Manchu, staring straight before her: an ivory goddess. Beginning almost in a whisper, Fu Manchu addressed her. He spoke in Chinese, and as he spoke his voice rose stage by stage until again it reached that pitch of wild frenzy; his long fingers twitched, closing upon the air as if he would have strangled this perfect outcome of his union with an unknown mother. Then he turned away. . . .

In obedience to a short command the Burman pressed a button in the wall at the end of the vaultlike corridor. A door opened and I saw an elevator.

"Follow!"

I followed Dr Fu Manchu; the yellow man entered last, closed the gates, and the elevator began to descend. This proximity to Fu Manchu was almost unendurable. He spoke again, softly, unemotionally:

"The entrance discovered and used by Christophe, the black king, is unknown. According to an ancient chart in the possession of your inquisitive friend Sir Lionel Barton, it was masked by the erection of a chapel on a hillside some miles away. My inquiries there did not enable me to find it, but as a precautionary measure I destroyed the chapel." The lift continued to drop. "My own entrance—a volcanic fissure in the ravine below the prow of the Citadel—was discovered by accident. This fissure I have effectually blocked, and the shaft by which we are now descending strikes it at a point a hundred and fifty feet east of the original entrance. From thence a sort of path exists down the wall of the cavern itself. It is a tedious journey. I avoided it when I had this lift installed by Mr Hopkinson, one of Vickers' senior engineers, who is with us. It is the second deepest in the world."

When, after an awe-inspiring descent, the elevator stopped, the door opened and I stepped out a new amazement claimed me.

I was in a stone-faced corridor brightly lighted; many doors were visible right and left. There were thousands of such corridors in the office buildings of New York.

"We are now," came the cold voice of Dr Fu Manchu, "only thirty feet above sea level, and you are one of that privileged few who have ever entered the interior of a volcano."

IN THE COMPANY of Mr Hopkinson, late of Vickers, a

prosaic Manchester man whose presence enhanced the fantastic character of my surroundings, I set out. We walked down a flight of steps; he opened a door and I found myself to be in broad daylight!

I stood on a long, wide quay where coloured gangs were at work unpacking crates and loading the contents, which I thought were machine parts, onto trucks. The still water was of a strange black colour, and ten or twelve small vessels were dotted about its surface. I supposed myself to be in a small landlocked harbour, for from where I stood I could see right to the other side, formed by a sheer wall of towering black rock.

The fact dawned upon me that whether I looked to right or left it was the same and that when I looked upward I could see no sky, only a sort of mist out of which glowed the light of a brazen sun, or so one might at first have assumed. A moment's consideration convinced me of my error. The sun should not be directly above; nor, looking harder, *was* this the sun!

I turned in bewilderment to my guide. He was lighting a cigar and smiling with quiet amusement.

"In heaven's name, where am I, and where does the light come from?"

"You are in the interior of a volcano, Mr Kerrigan. The light comes from a Ferris globe. The doctor may have shown you the one in the laboratory."

"Yes, he did. But this is not artificial light—this is sunlight."

Hopkinson nodded, staring at the glowing end of his cigar thoughtfully for a moment.

"I suppose in a way it is," he conceded. "Speaking unscientifically, the Ferris globe absorbs energy from the sun and redistributes it as required. It's a revolutionary system, of course, and in use nowhere in the world but here. Yes"—he saw me staring upward—"it's very deceptive. You see at one point the roof is higher than the dome of St Paul's Cathedral; and now"—he grasped my arm and turned me about, pointing—"do you see a red buoy floating out there, roughly halfway across?"

I looked and, out on the surface of this vast subterranean lake, presently picked up the object to which he referred.

"That marks the deepest spot. We haven't been able to plumb it yet."

"What!"

"It's true, Mr Kerrigan. That's put there for navigational purposes. The sea off this coast is very deep, you know. So what occurred in some past age was this: the sea broke in—

184

we use the opening it made as our water gate—and, quite simply, put out the volcano."

"But such a thing——"

"Would make a lot of steam? I agree that it would. It was the steam that made this huge cavern, and that buoy marks the very centre of what used to be the crater."

I said nothing; I could think of nothing to say.

"The potentialities of such a base as this it would be difficult to exaggerate. The use that has been made of it under the driving genius of the doctor surprises even those who work on the spot. In addition to the private lift by which no doubt you came down I completed here, less than two years ago, the deepest hoist in the world, or the deepest known to me. There is no difficulty about shipping stuff to the works and no questions are asked. It's brought down here in sections if necessary. As you see, labour is cheap."

I looked about at the coloured gangs working, and:

"Surely, where so many men are employed, secrecy is impossible?"

"Not at all, Mr Kerrigan—just a question of organisation. You won't find happier coolies anywhere, as you can see for yourself. Once these fellows are brought below ground they *stay* below."

"What do you mean? Like pit ponies?"

"That is, until we are done with them. Then they are shipped across to Tortuga, with plenty of money and a blank spot in the memory."

I wanted to say to him, I wanted to shout at him: "You, too, have a blank spot in your memory! You, too, are living in a delusion! Your fine intellect is enslaved to a madman who one day will destroy the world, unless some miracle intervenes!" But, looking at his comfortably stout person as he puffed away at his cigar, the merry twinkle in his eyes, I remained silent; for words would have been of no avail.

"Only the heads of departments come up and down," he added. "Those who load the hoist at the top have no idea where it goes to. Oh, organisation can accomplish miracles, Mr Kerrigan."

"I agree with you," I replied and spoke with sincerity.

"The working staff of the sisal corporation have nothing to do with the Si-Fan, you see; they are just ordinary labourers who have no idea that there is a belowground. If one becomes inquisitive—well, we bring him down here and let him see for himself! And now my instructions are to introduce you to Doctor Heron."

"Is he——"

"What Allington calls a conscript?" laughed Hopkinson. "Yes, as a matter of fact, he is. He used to be chief technician to the German navy. His success attracted the doctor's attention. I can assure you that in the twelve years that he has been employed here and elsewhere he has evolved something which nullifies the power of every navy in the world."

We walked along the busy dock, bathed in synthetic sunshine, beside the unknown depths of what must have been one of the largest volcanoes in the world. I talked to a talented and worthy engineer whose brains had been commandeered by Dr Fu Manchu. In Europe battles greater than any known in history were being waged, whilst here in this community of accumulated genius a superman quietly planned, in his own words, "to tip the scale."

What exactly did he mean and in what direction did he propose to tip it?

We entered a small neat office where an elderly German, whose high bald forehead was almost as striking as that of Fu Manchu himself, stood up to greet us. He wore gold-rimmed spectacles; a short, bristling grey moustache lent him some resemblance to pictures I had seen of the former Kaiser. Unlike Hopkinson, who most grotesquely, as I thought, wore a Harris tweed suit and displayed a thick gold watch chain across his ample waistcoat, Dr Heron wore blue overalls.

"Companion Heron—this is Mr Bart Kerrigan."

"I am pleased here to see you, Mr Kerrigan. Always I am pleased when an opportunity comes my playthings to show off. So rare are opportunities, and always the artists for recognition craves. Eh? Is it not so?"

"I'm coming too," said Hopkinson; "it's a long time since I was on board a Shark."

Here, in this strange world, England and Germany were not at war.

"Always I am pleased to show you, Companion Hopkinson," the German replied, "although I know the subject to be beyond your understanding quite."

He winked at me with heavy Teutonic humour, then led the way down a stair at the back of his office. I found myself on an iron platform which projected out to the open conning tower of one of those odd craft which I had sighted on the surface of the lake. From the moment that I climbed down the ladder to the interior I plunged into the heart of a dream, for what I saw and what I heard did not seem sanely to add up. I had expected heavy petrol fumes, but of these there was no trace.

"But of course not!" said Dr Heron. "Why, if you please? Because we use no petrol."

"Then what is the motive power?"

"Ah!" he sighed and shook his head. "A lot I may brag, Mr Kerrigan, a national characteristic this may be; but always we come back to the genius of Sven Ericksen. Power is generated in the Ericksen room, which takes the place of the engine room in any other submersible craft. I will show you and shall also explain, for at least the credit to me is for this adaptation to underwater vessels."

We went along a tiny alleyway—there was no more than room for Hopkinson to pass—and into a room which certainly could not have accommodated more than two men. There were fixed revolving chairs or stools before a glittering switchboard upon which were levers, dials, lamps and indicators of a more complicated character than anything I had ever seen.

"A protective headdress is worn," Dr Heron explained, "by the Ericksen operators; otherwise exposure to the waves created would shorten life speedily. Now here is the main control. If I am ordered by the officer in the turret to proceed, this lever I depress. It creates before the bows of my ship a new chemical condition."

"Call it steam," suggested Hopkinson.

"Very well. Instantaneously it reduces a large number of cubic feet of water to vapour."

"I should expect a tremendous explosion," I said.

"You get one—you get one!" said Dr Heron. "But what do I do with this tremendous explosion? I use it as the tremendous explosion is used in the Diesel engine. Through the Heron tube"—he turned to Hopkinson—"these at least my own invention are—I transfer that power from the bows to the stern. Here it becomes motive, and because as it is created I withdraw it, what happens?"

I shook my head blankly.

"I have before me a continuously renewing partial vacuum. I have behind me a driving power that even without the vacuum would give me great velocity. By means of these two together I have an underwater speed, Mr Kerrigan, which no submarine engineer has ever to dream of dared."

I suppose I bore a puzzled expression, for:

"Sounds like mumbo jumbo," said Hopkinson. "But of one thing I can assure you—these things really *go!*"

"But what power do you use to empty your tanks?"

"Ballast tanks? No ballast tanks I carry."

"No ballast tanks?"

"I am weighted so that I sink like a thousand tons of lead. I sink deep, deep, many fathoms deep. But three *swainsten* dials, one forward, one amidships, one aft, I operate from here—see."

He indicated sections of switchboard which seemed to be insulated from the others.

"This forward, to lift my bows—gently or suddenly, as I move the indicator. This aft, my stern the same. This the centre control, and I rise, up, up, on an even keel."

"Where are the torpedo tubes?"

Hopkinson laughed gruffly.

"The doctor's ships come out of *Alice in Wonderland*," he said; "they carry no torpedoes."

"No torpedoes? Then of what use are they in war?"

Again the German shook his head enviously.

"Again it is Ericksen. I have no periscope, but I have a complete view of sea for miles around which reaches me from a float or several floats and is thrown upon the control screen in the conning tower. It is possible that the doctor has shown you the improved television which we have?"

"He has not demonstrated it to me," I replied, "but some time ago in London I came in contact with it."

"Good, good—the same thing, or an adaptation of my own. These floats or buoys, of which I shall presently show you several models, are operated from the firing turret. They remain in contact by means of a cable operating over a drum of a material so light and yet so strong—a preparation of the doctor's—that half a mile of such cable weighs only twelve pounds; yet the float can be towed back upon it."

"But what are the objects of these floats?"

"They are motor driven and radio steered. Each carries an Ericksen projector."

"Ericksen again," murmured Hopkinson.

"True—too true. The range of such a projector is limited. Someday, no doubt, it will be increased—the doctor is carrying out experiments—but at present it is limited. When the float is within range of its target the operator—we carry no gunnery officers—directs the wave——"

He paused, drew a deep breath and extended his palms.

"There is no substance, Mr Kerrigan, no form of armour plating, however thick, which is not destroyed by it as if through a paper bag one pushes one's finger. From here, our base, we control every movement the United States could make. A fleet of one hundred Sharks—we have more than one hundred—could destroy the whole shipping of the Caribbean in a week."

188

"What is your speed?" I asked.

"It increases as I dive. At twenty fathoms it is forty knots."

"What!"

"On the surface, as you see me now, it is only fifteen. But I have no occasion on the surface to remain. My motive power, my armament, I draw from the elements through which I pass. I require only material provisions for my crew, and I carry six."

38 / "I Give You One Hour"

"ALTHOUGH YOU BELONG to a wiser and more imaginative race," said Dr Fu Manchu, "as I have already observed, you are curiously English in your outlook. The German hordes overrun Europe. But other governments of the world, including the government of the United States, continue to treat with them as with equals. I use the methods of those German hordes, but more subtly and more effectively. Quality rather than quantity distinguishes the master. Yet because I hold no diplomatic portfolio I, Fu Manchu, am a criminal."

He drew himself up to his great height, a grotesque figure in that prosaic office deep in the heart of an extinct volcano. I anticipated an outburst. But as he stood those glistening eyes grew filmed, introspective. He dropped down again into the chair from which he had risen and reflectively took a pinch of snuff.

"Yes, you possess a good but not a first-rate intelligence," he went on musingly, his voice now low; "you have trained powers of observation. You possess that Celtic fire which, transmuted, sometimes produces genius. You are a man who honours his word; I recognise one when I meet him, since I honour my own. I could take other steps, but I trust my judgment. The world is in the balance; I hold in my hand that decimal of a gramme which shall determine which way the scale tips. I am going to send you as my nuncio to Sir Denis Nayland Smith and the American authorities. Neither he nor Washington has communicated with me."

Only one thought entered my mind at that moment: Smith had escaped—Smith was free! Thank God for this knowledge! Smith was free!

"You will say that my services are at the disposal of the Allied governments and of the government of the United States. You will tell him what you know of my facilities, and you will make it your business to bring him back with you entrusted by his own government, by that of the United States, or by both, with plenipotentiary powers to negotiate—not with a criminal but with one who holds the destiny of the world in his hands. I have said that I am prepared to accept your word; but Sir Denis, being bound by no such obligation, might forcibly detain you. Therefore I shall take steps to limit the time of your absence; you will have seventy-two hours in which to return. It is a painless operation; I shall operate personally. You may decline this commission if you wish. It is now six o'clock. I give you one hour. Report to me here at seven. . . ."

Faced by this ghastly prospect, every hissing syllable of Fu Manchu's ultimatum repeating itself over and over again in my brain, I wandered along the busy quays of that subterranean dockyard. No one paid the slightest attention to my presence. I walked straight ahead—aimlessly—hopelessly—thinking. For me it was the end; I should never see Ardatha again, for that Nayland Smith should compromise with Dr Fu Manchu was a thing unthinkable. Yet, whatever became of me, heaven be thanked! Smith was free; the fight went on!

And now, as I wandered along past groups of workers, some of whom glanced at me but none with any evidence of curiosity, an explanation presented itself: in my shabby drill suit, my skin reduced by the hot sun to a dusky brown, I was indistinguishable from many of the labourers; they mistook me for one of the belowground staff!

This theory to explain their indifference to the presence of a stranger was strengthened a moment later. At the head of some steps against which a boat was tied up a man dressed almost as I was dressed sat splicing a length of rope. There was no one within twenty yards of the spot, and for this reason I particularly noted him. His bowed shoulders were turned to me as he bent over his task. I had almost passed him when he spoke:

"Don't stop—don't look back. Walk right ahead."

The speaker was Nayland Smith!

39 / Christophe's Path

"SMITH!" I gasped, "this is a miracle!"

"No. Sound organisation and top marks go to Barton. This way, and mind you don't stumble."

A coil of rope slung over his shoulder, Smith had slouched along in my wake until, leaving dockside activity behind, I had found myself on the further shore pursuing a path overhung by frowning rocks. Then suddenly he had caught up and thrust me into a narrow cavity. . . .

One backward glance I threw across the waters of the inky lake, glittering in synthetic sunshine. I could see gangs at work on the quays. One of the Sharks was submerging; it disappeared with the speed of a moor hen. Ring after ring of gleaming black water spread out from the spot where it had been.

Then, as I stumbled along behind Smith in impenetrable darkness, he turned, grasped my hand and pulled me up and around a bend into a small cave. Several electric lamps were set on the rocky floor, casting their light upon a group of armed and uniformed men. It was a party of United States marines!

They had their carbines at the ready, and:

"Made a capture, sir?" growled the petty officer who was evidently in charge.

"Yes!" snapped Smith. "The one I went for: Mr Kerrigan."

A sort of gruff murmur greeted this announcement.

"And now," Smith continued rapidly, "we have to work fast. Stand easy, you fellows. Come over here, Kerrigan— thank God you *are* here!—and tell me all you can in the fewest possible words."

Madly excited as I was, frantically keyed up by this unforeseen solution of a problem which had threatened my faith, my principles, my soul, I strove hard to comply. I told him of the infra-azure lamp, described the Snapping Fingers; I named some of those brilliant men who laboured here to bring the world under the domination of Dr Fu Manchu.

"He has agents everywhere, Smith!" I cried.

"I know that."

"Six of his submarines could destroy a battle fleet. His planes, armed with Ericksen projectors, can manœuvre like hawks. Whatever happens to Europe and the rest of the world, it is certain that at the present moment he holds the fate of the United States navy in his hands."

"At this stage of history that *means* the rest of the world," said Smith gravely. He turned. "Stand by here, Sergeant," he directed. "Post your men one in touch with another along the passage. When a search party comes—and it can't fail to be long now—all fall back to the ladder, haul it up and leave no sign."

"All clear, sir."

In single file we walked up a narrow passage in which there were many bends, and at each of the bends a man dropped out until at the point where the passage seemed to end in a great, jagged, natural chamber in the rock I saw a rope ladder hanging from a ledge high above.

"This was Christophe's road to the great cavern," said Smith. "Just above this point, as we explored, it seemed that we had come to the end. You see, there have been earth tremors during the past century, and in places the way is blocked." He raised his head. "All ready above there?" he hailed.

"All ready, sir," came a distant reply.

"We brought climbing tackle and fortunately the kind of men who know how to use it. Hang onto the ladder there. Up you go, Kerrigan."

There were two more marines on duty at the head of the ladder. As one helped me to scramble up:

"Welcome, Mr Kerrigan!" he said. "I guess you are lucky to be alive!"

"I think so too!"

I was in a much wider passage, which, however, was obviously natural; and when Smith had joined me and had given directions to the men we began to climb up a steep ascent, he carrying an electric lamp.

"Smith," I said, "at all costs we must rescue Ardatha!"

"Leave Ardatha to me," he replied shortly. "Her safety is assured. We have a long way to go, Kerrigan, and so we must step out."

We stepped out, along that mounting, winding rock corridor, the floor of which was icy smooth in places where in some earth agony of long ago streams of lava had flowed down or, perhaps, steam had spurted up from the great cavern below which had been the crater. The air was foul as that inside a pyramid; colonies of bats clung to the roof in places and sometimes came sweeping down to the light.

Smith rapped out a staccato, abbreviated report as we climbed:

"In distraction caused by your striking at Voice—cursed you at the time, but seems to have come out for the best—I dived down into shadow. Invisible Fu Manchu had not had time to indicate me to smeller-out with big sword. Blow had staggered him, and, for reasons understood now, he became partially visible for a moment. Effect on those poor devils —glimpse of ghostly green figure—something I can't describe. One long wail went up and all fell flat on their faces."

At a bend in the passage we passed another armed marine, who saluted.

"All clear. Stand by," said Smith.

"But what did you do?"

192

"About you could do nothing. Two masked thugs picked you up as you fell; carried you into the temple. Sticking to shadow of stockade, got back to the gate. Two masks on duty there, but I flashed the master amulet in the moonlight. Never questioned me; just saluted. I made along the path through trees to the resthouse and big clearing at which it had been arranged for three planes to alight. Got through unchallenged. Saw a sight I shall never forget. Minor ceremony being performed, with drums, feathered witch doctor and number of voodoo priestesses, dancing until 'they fell in convulsions. Everyone dancing; drums beating; scores of panting bodies on the ground; shrieks, half-animal cries . . .

"The resthouse was deserted. I stood there watching the orgy. Often glanced at my watch; wondered if you were dead or alive, counting the minutes, seconds. Then, on the dot of appointed time, came drone of the engines. The scene changed magically. As the fighters circled overhead and then glided down to that perfect landing ground every soul scattered to cover! Most of those who had seemed to be insensible staggered to their feet—joined in the rout; others dragged away. Drums ceased; the witch doctor alone continued frenzied dancing. He did not seem to come to his senses until the first plane grounded right beside him."

"Whatever happened?"

"Nothing. Entire crowd took to the woods. Barton was in second plane. We posted guards and set out helter-skelter for the stockade. Kerrigan—there wasn't a soul in the place!"

At this point in our upward climb we passed another marine.

"Impossible to give you any idea activity of next few days. Haitian police like a pack of wolves. Suspects rounded up; hundreds of people questioned. But voodoo is a very powerful force, Kerrigan. Air reconnaissance showed no suspicious movements. Naval units inspected every mile of shore. Marines landed at likely spots. Inquiries extended from coast to cost, beyond Dominican border. Had reasoned that secret base must be masked by some big industrial enterprise. San Damien Sisal Corporation seemed to fill bill. Called personally upon Mr Horton, the manager. Except for certain strangeness of manner, which I was disposed to ascribe to drug habit——"

"The man is a zombie," I interrupted; "he is nearly ninety years old!"

"Ah! This I did not know; his manner quite disarming. Most courteous; good enough to conduct me over the hemp refinery. Even offered to drive me out to largest plantation. This offer I declined. In short, Kerrigan—defeated."

I pulled up. The atmosphere of the tunnel was telling upon me, for I had passed through an exacting time.

"Have we much further to go, Smith? Or is this passage unending?"

"No; ends on other side of a ravine immediately facing ruined chapel."

"Not *in* the chapel?"

"No. Fu Manchu made a slip. Having inspected *original* chart, he learned that Barton had tricked him; site of opening faked. Had very little time, though, to search for it. Therefore blew up chapel."

"With what result?"

"None at all. One thing he had not seen—most important thing of all."

"Why had he not seen it, since he had seen the chart?"

"Because it was written on the *back!* It read, roughly, 'The altar faces the entrance, which is on opposite hillside, marked by granite cross set among trees'!"

"Astounding bit of luck!"

"Plus Barton's genius for secrecy. Went to work like galley slaves. Had to work under cover. Posted hidden sentries all around area. Providence with us. Explosion had left altar practically intact; gave us our bearings . . . granite cross long since vanished. Took Barton two days to find tiny cave, no more than crevice in rock—but only way down to great cavern known to Christophe!"

"The other entrance, that from the sisal works, was discovered by accident some years ago. . . ."

I saw a peep of daylight, and a voice hailed us. It was a loud, unmistakable voice—the voice of Sir Lionel Barton!

"All's well, Barton!" cried Smith. "I have a surprise for you."

Two armed men were guarding the entrance, which indeed was no more than eighteen inches wide and which opened onto a ledge some ten feet below the crest of a jagged and jungle-choked ravine.

As I stepped out behind Smith:

"My God!" cried Barton. *"Kerrigan! . . .* Heaven be praised!"

He shook my hand so hard that my fingers became limp, and then, pointing west:

"Look at that," he said. "We have just time to get back to camp. There's a hell of a storm brewing."

And as we set out I looked into the west and saw that the sky was becoming veiled by a sort of purple haze.

The "camp" was an army tent with a smaller one set up

behind it near a grove of trees. I observed a quantity of kit, a number of rifles; and here another marine was on duty. Barton was so happy to see me that he kept throwing his arm around my shoulders and giving me bearlike hugs.

I suppose the boom of his great voice reached her from afar, for as we approached, the flap of the smaller tent opened . . . and Ardatha ran out!

40 / *The San Damien Sisal Corporation*

WHEN I HAD in some measure recovered from a shock of joy which I confess left me trembling, when I had fully appreciated the fact that this was the real Ardatha, the Ardatha who had so mysteriously disappeared in Paris, and not her shadow whom I had met again in London, I had time for wonder and time for questions.

"But how did it happen?" I asked breathlessly. "Even now I find it hard to believe."

"It happened, Bart dear, because even the genius of the doctor nods—sometimes. You remember that he gave me over to the charge of Hassan. Hassan has served my family ever since I can remember, except that he was black then and not white. He came with me when I joined . . . the Si-Fan. But when I left to come to you in Paris—you remember——"

"Remember? I remember every hour we spent together, every minute."

"Well"—there was a haunting inflection in the way she pronounced the word—"he becomes like all the others, except for one thing: he can never refuse to obey any order which *I* may give him."

"I think I understand."

"The work which I have done in the past for . . . them has been away from their headquarters, you see. Those here in Haiti, where I have been only once before, who do not know me, know Hassan. I ordered him to come with me to the gate, and no one stopped us. I ordered him to get into one of the staff cars, of which there are always five or six waiting there, and to sit beside me like a groom. He obeyed. I drove away. The doctor had made a mistake. You see, I was myself again, and I *knew!* I meant to go to the consul at Cap Haitien, but on the way——"

"On the way," snapped a familiar voice, and I saw that Smith had joined us—"pardon my interruption—Ardatha met myself and a party of marines going to join Barton."

"And, oh! how glad I was to see you—how glad!"

"As a result of this meeting," Smith added, "certain steps were taken in regard to the activities of the San Damien Sisal Corporation. But Ardatha I rarely let out of my sight again."

So utterly happy was I in our reunion that ominous claps of thunder, a growing darkness, that present danger to the United States which I knew to lurk in the Caribbean, were forgotten. Smith brought me sharply to my senses.

"At last," he said, "we have the game in our hands, if we play our cards carefully. The great brains which support Doctor Fu Manchu, the machinery which his genius and that of his dupes has brought into being—all are here. I have failed before, but this time I do not mean to fail. In the next twenty-four hours either we win our long battle or hand what is left of the civilised world over to Doctor Fu Manchu."

Darkness increased; thunder growled ominously over the mountains. . . .

"THERE'S THE SIGNAL, Barton! Since you are determined—good luck! But you're in for a rough passage."

Smith, Barton and I stood on a jetty at Cap Haitien. The night was completely black, except when bursts of tropical lightning created an eerie, blinding illumination. A signal had been arranged, and a moment before we had seen a rocket burst against the inky curtain of the storm. A naval cutter was dancing deliriously at our feet.

"I worked out the bearings and I'm going to check them with the officer in charge," said Barton. "If Christophe's chart is wrong in this respect, why, then we fail! Cheerio!"

He went to the head of the ladder, waited until the cutter rose within two feet of the jetty and jumped. In more respects than one Sir Lionel Barton was a remarkable man. I saw him scrambling forward to the bows. As the cutter pulled out:

"Barton has earned his reputation," said Nayland Smith. "He fears neither men nor gods. If I know anything about him, he will stop at least one of Doctor Fu Manchu's ratholes tonight."

An old freighter of three thousand tons, sunk well below her loadline with a cargo of concrete blocks, was lying off there in the storm, escorted by a United States destroyer. In the interval which had elapsed since I had been swallowed up by the organisation of the Si-Fan Smith and Barton had worked furiously. The freighter was destined to be scuttled at the spot indicated in the ancient chart as the submarine entrance to Christophe's Cavern. Inquiries from local fishermen had revealed that a shelf of rock, or submerged ridge, jutted out there. This ledge must be the lintel of Fu Manchu's underwater gate.

An American skipper who knew the Haitian coast was in command, and the destroyer was standing by to take off the officers and crew. It would be necessary practically to pile up the ship on the gaunt rocks below which the opening lay— on such a night as this, with a heavy sea running, a feat of seamanship merely to think about which turned me cold.

I stood there beside Smith, watching. The thunder was so shattering when it came that it seemed to rock the quay; the lightning so vivid in its tropical brilliance as to be blinding. In those awesome flashes I could see both ships lying close offshore; I could see the cutter breasting a white-capped swell as she made for the freighter, riding lumpishly, overladen as she was. How clearly I remember that night, that occasion, for it was the prelude to what I believed and prayed would be the end of Dr Fu Manchu and all his works.

We waited there through blaze after blaze of lightning until we saw the cutter brought alongside the freighter. By this time a tremendous sea was running, and I trembled for Barton, a heavy man and by no means a young one. I had visions of a jumping ladder, of the smaller craft shattered like an eggshell.

Then, during a moment of utter blackness, thunder booming hellishly among the mountains, a second rocket split the night.

"Thank God!" whispered Smith; he stood close beside me. "He's mad, but he bears a charmed life. He's on board."

It was the agreed signal.

"Now—to our own job."

Through that satanic night we set out for the San Damien works; it was a wild drive, a ride of the Valkyries. Sometimes, as we climbed, white-hot flashes revealed forest valleys below the mountain road which we traversed; sometimes, in complete darkness which followed, the mountain seemed to shiver; our headlights resembled flickering candles. Our lives and more than our lives were in the hands of the driver. But as he had been allotted to us by the American authorities as the one man for the job, I resigned myself.

"I have it in my bones," said Nayland Smith during a momentary lull, "that tonight we shall finally defeat Doctor Fu Manchu. The very elements seem to be enraged."

But I was silent. I had, in a sense, come closer to Dr Fu Manchu than Nayland Smith had ever had an opportunity to do. Something of the almost supernatural dread with which the Chinese scientist had inspired me was gone. He was not an evil spirit; he was a physical phenomenon, and his strength resided in the fact that he had perfected a method for enslaving the genius of the world and bending it to his will. At last I understood that Dr Fu Manchu was something which human ingenuity might hope to outwit. But his armament was formidable.

Of that drive up to the lip of the valley which once had been the crater of a great volcano I retain strange memories. But memorable above all was that moment when, coming around a hairpin bend on the edge of a sheer precipice, the black curtain of the storm was rent by dazzling light, and there, away beyond a forest-choked valley, an eerie but a wonderful spectacle, I saw, for the second time, the mighty bulk of the Citadel, upstanding stark, an ogre's castle, against the blaze.

Indeed, a jagged dagger of lightning seemed to strike directly down upon its towering battlements. Almost I expected to see them crumble. Darkness fell, and there came a crash of thunder so deafening that it might well have echoed the collapse of Christophe's vast fortress into the depths. . . .

At long last we turned inland, from the road skirting the precipice, and plunged into a sort of cutting. I heaved a sigh of relief.

"There are *two* sides to this road," said Smith. "I confess I prefer it."

We were now, in fact, very near to our destination; but since I had never seen the outside of the place but only the extensive buildings which surrounded the quadrangle, I was surprised by its modest character. A wide sanded drive opened to the right of the road, and across it was a board on which might be read: "The San Damien Sisal Corporation." The drive was bordered by tropical shrubbery and palm trees; some fifty yards along I saw a bungalow which presumably served the purpose of a gate lodge. Smith checked the driver; we pulled up just beyond.

"There are three possibilities," he said. "One, that we shall find the place deserted except for legitimate employees of the corporation, against whom it would be difficult to bring a case. In this event the presence of the zoological exhibits and of the experimental laboratory might plausibly be accounted for; hemp cultivation, after all, is conducted today on scientific lines. The glass coffins you describe might be less easy to explain."

"And the second possibility?"

"The second possibility is—some trap may have been laid for us. I doubt, assuming that the doctor and his associates have gone belowground, if it would be possible under any circumstances to obtain access from this point. However, you see, my instructions have been well carried out."

In a dazzling blaze of lightning he looked around.

"I warrant you can find no evidence of the fact, Kerrigan, that a considerable party of Federal agents, supported by two companies of Haitian infantry with machine guns, is covering the area."

"There is certainly no sign of their presence, but why did they not challenge the car?"

"They have orders to challenge nothing going in but anything or anybody coming out. Now let us have a report."

He flashed a pocket torch, in—out, in—out.

From a darker gulley in the bank of the road just above the sanded drive two men appeared; one was in the uniform of the Haitian army; his companion wore mufti. As they came up Smith acknowledged the officer's salute and, turning to the other:

"Anything to report, Finlay?" he asked.

"Not a thing, chief—except that Major Lemage, here, has got his men under cover, and my boys all know their jobs. What's the programme?"

"Are there any lights showing?"

"Sure. There's one right in the gate office. Night porter, I guess."

"Anywhere else?"

"Haven't seen any."

"Then we will stick to our original plan. Come on, Kerrigan."

As we walked past the car and up the sanded drive Finlay dropped back, following at some ten paces, and:

"What was the *third* possibility you had in mind, Smith?" I asked.

"That Doctor Fu Manchu evidently regards himself as a potential world power. He may still be here. He may attempt to brazen the thing out. Your absence will have puzzled him; but there are numbers of burrows in all volcanic rocks such as those which compose the cavern, so it seems highly unlikely that he will be able to find out what occurred. But the absence of Ardatha and Hassan is susceptible of only one construction: a major mistake—and Fu Manchu rarely makes major mistakes. However, we must move with care. You say

199

that the lift is at the end of a sort of tunnel in which are the glass coffins?"

"Yes; a cellar built, I believe, in the foundations of the laboratory."

"Which you can identify?"

"I think so."

The bungalow when we reached it was so like a thousand and one inquiry offices at entrances to works that again, as had occurred many times before, the idea seemed fabulous that anything sinister lurked behind a façade so commonplace. Lightning blazed and cast ebony shadows of palm trunks bordering the drive, shadows like solid bars, across to the spot where we stood. There was a brass plate on the door, inscribed: "The San Damien Sisal Corporation." A light shone from a window.

Smith pressed the bell—and a sort of tingling excitement possessed me as I stood there waiting to see who would open the door. We had not long to wait.

A Haitian, his shirt sleeves rolled up above his elbows, a lanky fellow smoking a corncob pipe, looked at us with sleepy eyes.

In the office I saw a cane armchair from which he had evidently just risen, a newspaper on the floor beside it. There was a large keyboard resembling that of a hotel hall porter's. At the moment that I observed this the man's expression changed.

"What do you want?" he asked sharply. "You do not belong here."

"I want to see the manager," snapped Smith. "It is urgent."

"The manager is in bed."

"Someone must be on duty."

"That is so—I am on duty."

"Then go and wake the manager, and be sharp about it. I represent the Haitian government, and I must see Mr Horton at once. Go and rouse him."

Smith's authoritative manner was effective.

"I have to stay here," the man replied, "but I can call him."

He went inside and took up a telephone which I could not see, but I heard him speaking rapidly in Haitian. Then came a tinkle as he replaced the receiver. He returned.

"Someone is coming to take you to the manager," he reported.

Apparently regarding the incident as closed, he went in and shut the door.

I stared at Smith.

"One of the corporation staff," he said in a low voice. "I doubt if he knows anything. However—wait and see."

We had not waited long before a coloured boy appeared from somewhere.

"You two gentlemen want to see Mr Horton?"

"We do," said Smith.

"Come this way."

As we moved off behind the boy I glanced back over my shoulder and saw Finlay raise his hand and turn, then flash a light into the darkness behind him. We were being closely covered.

The boy led along the back of those quarters in which for a time I had occupied an apartment. I saw no lights anywhere. Just beyond, and fronting on the big quadrangle, was a detached bungalow. Some of the windows were lighted and a door was open. The coloured boy rapped upon the door, and James Ridgwell Horton came out, holding reading glasses in his hand and having a book under his arm. The storm seemed to be moving into the east, but dense cloud banks obscured the moon and the night was vibrant with electric energy. He peered at us in a bewildered way.

"You want to see me?"

At which moment the reflection of distant lightning showed us up clearly.

"We do," said Smith.

"Why, Mr Kerrigan! Sir Denis Nayland Smith!" Horton exclaimed and fell back a step. "Mr Kerrigan!"

"May we come in?" asked Smith quietly.

"Certainly. This is . . . most unexpected."

We went into a room furnished with tropical simplicity; the night was appallingly hot, and Horton had evidently been lying in a rest chair reading. In the rack was an iced drink from which two straws protruded. I noticed with curiosity that illumination was by an ordinary standard lamp. Horton stared rather helplessly from face to face.

"Does this mean——" he began.

"It means," said Smith rapidly, "as the presence of Kerrigan must indicate, that the game's up. Do exactly as I tell you and you will come to no great harm. Try to trick me, and the worst will happen."

Horton made an effort to recover himself.

"In the first place, sir, I cannot imagine——"

"Imagination is unnecessary. Facts speak for themselves. I am here on behalf of the government of the United States."

"Oh!" murmured Horton.

"I am accompanied by a number of Federal officers. The

entire premises are surrounded by armed troops. This, for your information."

"Yes, I see," murmured Horton, and I saw him clench his hands. "In spite of this, and I speak purely in your own interest, I fear that steps will be taken against you of a character which you may not anticipate. I strongly urge you——"

"It is my business to take risks," snapped Smith. "You may regard yourself as under arrest, Mr Horton. And now be good enough to lead the way to Doctor Fu Manchu."

A moment Horton hesitated, then stretched his hand out to a telephone.

"No, no!" said Smith and grasped his arm. "I wish to *see* him—not to find him gone."

"I cannot answer for the consequences. I fear they will be grave—for you."

"Be good enough to lead the way."

I was now riding a high tide of excitement; and when, walking dejectedly between us, Horton crossed the quadrangle in the direction of that large building without windows which I remembered so well, which I should never forget, I confess that I tingled with apprehension. There was no one in sight anywhere; but, glancing back again, I saw that a number of armed men had entered from the drive and were spreading out right and left so as to command every building in the quadrangle. Two, who carried sub-machine guns, were covering our movements.

Before the door of that lobby in which I had changed into rubber shoes Horton paused.

"If you will wait for a moment," he said, "I will inquire if the doctor is here."

"No, no!" rapped Smith. "We are coming with you."

Horton selected a key from a number on a chain and opened the door. We went into the lobby—and there were the rows of rubber shoes.

"You must change into these," he said mechanically.

I nodded to Smith, and we all went through that strange ritual; then:

"Open this other door," said Smith.

The men armed with sub-machine guns were already inside.

"I have no key of this door. I can only ring for admittance."

"Ring," said Smith. "I have warned you."

Horton pressed a button beside the massive metal door, and my excitement grew so tense that my teeth were clenched. For perhaps five seconds we waited. Smith turned to the G-men.

"When this door opens, see that it stays open," he ordered. "Pull those rubber things over your shoes. I don't know what it's for—but do it."

The door opened. I became aware of that throbbing sound which I had noted before . . . and there before me, wearing his white surgical jacket, was Dr Marriot Doughty!

"Kerrigan!" he exclaimed. "Kerrigan!"

His naturally sallow face grew deathly white. The short Vandyke beard seemed to bristle.

"My name is Nayland Smith," said my friend. "I am here to see Doctor Fu Manchu. Stand aside if you please."

Entering, out of darkness broken only by gleams of lightning, into that vast and strange laboratory was very startling: one came from night into day. Whereas when I had seen it before the place had been but dimly illuminated, now the Ferris globe shone as though it were molten and the effect was as that of daylight. Standing behind one of the glass-topped benches at the other end of the laboratory—a bench upon which some experiment seemed to be in progress—and still wearing a long white jacket and black skullcap, as I remembered him, was Dr Fu Manchu!

"There's your man!" said Smith aside.

"Hands up!" rasped one of our bodyguard; both raised their machine guns; we all moved forward.

At the moment that we did so I saw one of those long slender hands touch a switch, so that to the peculiar throbbing which I have already mentioned was added a new kind of vibration. Otherwise no perceptible change took place. Standing there, tall, square shouldered, challengingly, Dr Fu Manchu watched us.

"At last," cried Smith on a note of sudden excitement, "at last I hold the winning card!"

Dr Fu Manchu continued to watch but did not speak.

"The entire works are surrounded," Smith went on; "every exit covered, high and low, except the air. . . . And you have missed your chance there."

The green eyes became contemplative; in that unnatural daylight I could see every change of expression upon the evilly majestic face. Fu Manchu nodded his great head thoughtfully.

"You have acted with your accustomed promptness and efficiency," he replied, but his voice, though even, was pitched on a harsh strident note. "Exactly what steps you have seen fit to take it is not my purpose to inquire. But I was expecting you, and you are welcome."

There was something chilling in those words, "I was expecting you," something which increased the effect, which the presence of this man always had upon me. If he spoke the truth—why had he remained?

"Indeed," said Smith, and I noted a change in his tone.

Although I never took my eyes from Dr Fu Manchu, I was aware of the fact that other men were crowding in from the lobby.

"Order those men not to cross the red line on the floor behind you," Fu Manchu said harshly.

And at the very moment that he spoke I knew the worst. I turned and cried shrilly:

"Stand where you are there, for your lives! Don't cross the line. Smith"—I clutched his arm—"do you understand what this means?"

"Yes," he said quietly. The fire had gone from his grey eyes. "I understand."

"An Ericksen screen," that guttural voice continued, and now I detected a note of mockery, "has been thrown across the room some fifteen feet in front of me, and another behind you at the point marked by the red line on the floor. You are prisoners, gentlemen, in a cell from which no human power can rescue you unless *I* choose to do so."

"We'll see about that," growled Finlay, who had evidently just come into the lobby. "I don't like the looks of you and I'm taking no chances."

Followed three sharp, ear-splitting explosions. . . . But Dr Fu Manchu never stirred.

"Merciful heaven!" said Finlay hoarsely. "God help us! What *is* he—a man or a spirit?"

"Both, my friend," the guttural voice assured him; "as you are."

The effect of this seemingly supernatural demonstration upon the two men beside me was amazing. Plainly I saw them blanch, and for the first time they lowered their guns, peering into each other's eyes. Then one turned to me, and:

"What is it, mister?" he asked. "What is it? You seem to know."

"Yes, I know, but I can't possibly explain."

"In your absence, Sir Denis," Dr Fu Manchu went on, "which I regretted, I chose Mr Kerrigan as your deputy and gave him an opportunity of glancing over some of my resources. His unaccountable disappearance threatened to derange my plans. But his return in your company suggests to me that he may have acquainted you with these particulars."

"He has," Smith replied tonelessly.

"In that case you are aware that as the result of many years of labour I am at last in a position to dictate to any and every government in the world. The hordes now overrunning Europe could not deter me for a week from any objective I might decide to seize. Their vaunted air force, or, if you prefer it, that of the Allies, I could destroy as readily as I could destroy a wasps' nest. The methods pursued by the Nazis are a clumsy imitation of my own. I, too, have my Fifth Column, and it is composed exclusively of men who understand their business. Those, for I am not infallible, who seek to betray me are disposed of."

He took up the jade snuffbox and delicately raised a pinch of snuff to his nostrils. He was not looking at us now but seemed to be thinking aloud.

"There is a peril threatening the United States which, although it might be defeated, would nevertheless create a maximum of disorder and shake the national unity. I charge you, Sir Denis, to dismiss from your mind your picture of myself as a common criminal. I am no more a criminal than was Napoleon, no more a criminal that Caesar."

His voice was rising, quivering, and now his eyes were widely open. He was an imposing but an evil figure.

"Transmit the order to the agents and to the troops who have entered these premises to return to their posts outside until further instructions reach them. Washington has sent you here, and I wish you to put before Washington a proposal which I have drawn up, which I shall place in your hands whenever you ask me to do so. Knowing something of your prejudices, of your misconceptions, of your ignorance, I give you time to adjust your outlook. I can grant you one hour, Sir Denis. Word has reached me of a shipwreck which threatens to block my sea gate. I shall go down to investigate the matter. When I return, no doubt you will have made up your mind. I leave Companion Doughty in your company. As it would be unwise to remove the Ericksen screen at present, you would be well advised to remain nearer to the centre of the laboratory. Proximity to the screen is dangerous."

41 / An Electrical Disturbance

"BARTON HAS DONE IT!"

Smith spoke in a hoarse whisper. The two men of our bodyguard sat on a long bench, mopping their perspiring foreheads and glancing about them with profound apprehension. Dr Marriot Doughty was seated on the other side of the room, and Finlay alone remained in the lobby beyond the red line. Smith had ordered the others to withdraw. The heat in the windowless laboratory was indescribable, and that "consciousness of cerebral pressure" created by Ericksen waves was all that I could endure.

"Yes—Barton has succeeded, but we are trapped."

Although no reflection of lightning penetrated, apparently the great storm had not passed but had gathered again overhead. A crash of thunder came which rattled the glass instruments in their racks; the sound of it boomed and rolled and echoed weirdly about us and about. Marriot Doughty stood up and approached.

"If you will permit me to prescribe," he said, "there are several masks of a kind we wear during Ericksen experiments. I can reach them without leaving the free zone."

He crossed to a tall cabinet, opened a drawer and took out a number of headpieces resembling those used by radio operators.

"Can we trust him?" whispered Smith.

"Yes. He is thinking primarily of himself, I believe."

Marriot Doughty distributed the headpieces.

"There are six," he said, "but I fear that the gentleman in the lobby will have to go without one. The lobby, however, is partially insulated."

We adjusted the things, and that unendurable sense of inward pressure was immediately relieved.

"Anything like an hour's exposure," the physician explained, "might result in cerebral hemorrhage."

Smith turned to him. With the headpiece framing his lean features he suddenly reminded me of Horus, the hawk god.

"Doctor Doughty," he said, "knowing nothing of the circumstances, I am not entitled to question your principles, but may I ask some questions?"

"Certainly—and I shall be prepared to answer them."

"Is there any means of disconnecting the Ericksen apparatus?"

"From our point of view, none. The controls are out of reach."

"Is there any exit from this room other than that beyond the lobby or that at the other end used by Fu Manchu?"

"None."

Smith nodded grimly and attempted to pull at the lobe of his ear, but a part of the headpiece foiled him. Marriot Doughty seemed to hesitate, and then:

"There is one feature of our present situation," he said, "which contains elements of great danger."

"What is that?" asked Smith.

"Expressed simply, it is a certain affinity which exists between Ericksen waves and lightning. You cannot have failed to notice that the electric storm, which had passed to the east, is now concentrated directly above us. One of the doctor's own precepts—which he would seem to have overlooked——"

The sentence was never finished.

A veil of blinding light—I cannot otherwise describe it—descended between me and the farther end of the laboratory . . . the rubber-covered floor heaved like the deck of a ship . . . fragments of masonry fell all about! The Ferris globe crashed from the roof into a cavity which suddenly yawned in the centre of the long room. The whole of one glass wall fell in!

Somewhere a loud voice was shouting:

"This way! This way! All the floor's going!"

I remember joining in a panic rush. Who ran beside me I cannot say—nor where we ran. The earth heaved beneath my feet; the night was torn by spears of lightning which seemed to strike down directly upon us. Through a hell beyond my powers to depict I ran—and ran—and ran . . .

"THAT'S BETTER, MR KERRIGAN!"

I stared up into the speaker's face, a sun-browned, bearded face, not comprehending; then, aware of an unpleasant nausea, I looked about me. I was in bed; the speaker was a doctor. A dreadful suspicion came—and I sat up.

"Where am I?"

"You are in my house in Cap Haitien. My name is Doctor Ralph——"

"You are not——"

"I am a United States citizen, Mr Kerrigan," he said cheerily; "but there is no English physician here, so Mr Finlay ran you into me."

I dropped back with a long sigh of relief.

"Smith——"

"Sir Denis Nayland Smith is here. His recovery was a quicker business than yours."

"His recovery?" I sat up again. "What happened to us? Was I struck by something?"

"No, no—fumes. The earth tremor which partially destroyed the San Damien sisal works released fumes to which you both succumbed. What you were doing there last night with so large a body of men is none of my business. But, you see"—he tapped me on the chest—"there has been passive congestion in the left lung, and you were more seriously affected than the others. However"—he stood up—"you will be all right now, and I know you would wish to see your friend."

Dr Ralph went out, and a moment later Nayland Smith came in.

"Thank God we're alive, Kerrigan!" he said. "We lose the triumph, but we were the instruments of retribution!"

"Smith! What happened? What hellish thing happened?" He began to walk up and down the small room.

"So far as I can make out—I have been over there all this morning—lightning struck the laboratory and was conducted (possibly down the lift cable) into the great cavern! At any rate, a new gorge has appeared, a gorge of extraordinary depth. It has swallowed up part of the sisal works and the whole of one plantation: in fact, the side of a mountain has moved!"

"Good God!"

"The first blast split the laboratory in half. That was when Doughty went."

"Then he——"

"Fell into the pit which yawned not five feet from where *you* were standing! I hauled you back, and we all ran out through the gap in the wall. We were halfway across the quadrangle when the second blast—which seemed to come from underground—threw us off our feet. The *fumes* were appalling, but we all managed to struggle on for another hundred yards or so. . . . I don't remember much more."

"Good God!" I said again. "Can you picture what happened belowground?"

"Yes," he snapped, "I can . . . and Fu Manchu was belowground!"

"What news of Barton?"

"Did the job. But they had to put out to sea and make for Port-au-Prince. All's well with Barton; and I think, Kerrigan, my long fight is won. Now—I am going to send your nurse to see you."

Before I could utter any word of protest he went out but left the door open.

Ardatha came in. . . .